NO ONE KILLS A DRAGON

BOOK TWO

ADAM ORION NORTH

No One Kills A Dragon: Book Two
© 2022 Adam Orion North

Cover art by Alessia Valastro

EPUB	ISBN	978-1-957324-03-6
Paperback	ISBN	978-1-957324-05-0
Hardback	ISBN	978-1-957324-04-3

Dedication

This book is dedicated to anyone that read the first one and liked it. If you did not enjoy the first book in this series, and still purchased the second... Thank you?

Acknowledgments

I would like to thank my proofreaders. (And let everyone know who to blame if something is wrong.)

Thank you, Caleb. (He is an actual rocket scientist.)

Thank you, Daniel. (He prefers anonymity to praise.)

Thank you, Alynda. (She is a grade school teacher that has in fact slapped me with a ruler.)

Prologue

His steps echoed on water and stone as he strode from the Temple of the Deep. It had been a productive night. His disciples were growing. Every pledge increased their power, and every voice, their reach. The world could still have salvation.

He knew it would not be he himself who championed the light. He would do all he could to prepare, but it would be another to right the world. The forces set against him were too great. He could not hope to conquer that darkness alone.

Eleron lowered himself into the shallow boat and allowed his acolytes to row him out of the secluded cave. As they followed the coast toward the sprawling docks of Harbridge, he stared away into the ocean. In all his years, he had never found anything to compete with the beauty of moonlight on black waves. The ocean was part of him, and he could almost feel the moon's caress.

With an effort of will, he pulled himself away. He could not afford to lose himself, not now. He had too much to do. For too long, the world had withered in darkness under a shadow of threatening malice. And now, finally, someone had come that could stand against that ancient creature. A champion had come to bring the world salvation.

Though Eleron's power came with many restrictions, he believed he had found a way. He had brought the people knowledge of the Deep. These esoteric secrets would give them a weapon against something that for too long had wrought destruction with impunity. Still, he knew that the Followers of the Deep would not be sufficient alone. They would need to be there for the one who was to come. They would need to support and aid their champion of the light. And, as had so often been required of heroes facing great evil, they would need to sacrifice.

Eleron prayed to the Deep that the loss would be bearable. It pained him how tragic it was that some must die so others might be free. He hated how the good must suffer in the opposition of evil. Most of all, he raged at the fact he could not simply pay the price himself.

When they arrived at the docks, he climbed from the modest craft. There was still so much to do. He would need…

Something broke his wards. Eleron knew what it must be. With a gesture, he sent his acolytes away. They could only die if they remained with him, and every voice was needed. He would stand alone. He would not however, stand defenseless. Eleron drew on the ocean, pulling in power and life. He had known he would not be the one to stop this creature, but he would never surrender. He too would demand a price. He would show this dark thing what it was to suffer. He would herald the light to come. And so, Eleron stood alone.

He felt the darkness of its approach. He reached out into the water and fed to it his will. An enormous hand of shaped water rose from the ocean beside him. The hand picked up a nearby fishing boat and ripped it from its moorings. With a tremendous force backed by the weight of the ocean, Eleron threw the boat.

The boat was swept aside in a spray of shattered wood and twisted iron. Eleron was prepared for the flames that answered. He angled the watery hand between himself and the oncoming storm. Steam filled the air as the hand pulled water from the ocean in his defense. He needed another attack.

Eleron reached out into the steam and focused it in a torrent of scalding water. He showed his teeth in defiance as he returned the fire's heat. And then, the fires took him. Eleron's screams of defiance pierced the night. However, defiance could not stop the flames.

One

"I hate prison!" He rattled the cell door.

"You are not supposed to like it, Belac." The orc's voice was infuriatingly calm.

"Die in a fire!" Belac kicked the bars of his cell.

In an amused tone, Vairug asked, "How is any of this my fault?"

With no reason readily apparent, Belac answered, "Pick a reason!"

After a moment of silence, Vairug said, "Because, I'm so handsome."

"What?" Belac looked in the orc's direction even though there were multiple walls of stone between them.

Vairug patiently explained his joke. "You told me to pick a reason."

Belac narrowed his eyes at the wall. *Orcs are not handsome.* It was hard to be handsome with gray skin and tusks.

When the elf did not respond, Vairug continued, "So, I chose…"

"I get it, Vairug!" Belac scanned his cell, searching for some way to escape. Steel bars caged him within the shadows of his stone prison with nothing but a wooden bucket. He did not think the wooden bucket would be of any help, so he kicked it into the back of the cell. The bucket broke in half against the stone wall. Now, he did not even have a bucket. Belac growled.

When the two of them had been brought to their cells, one of the guards had carried a lantern. The light had filtered through the bars and moved along the dirty off-white stone walls. The guards had put Belac in the cell on the far left and Vairug in the one on the far right, leaving two empty cells between them. Then, the guards had taken the light with them, leaving the cells in a grim grayness. The only light now was the dim glow spilling down the corridor to their cells.

Belac gazed over to the open corridor. *Only one single way toward freedom and light.* He disliked how familiar the situation was. "We need to escape."

"Is there a privy on your side?" Vairug asked.

"I am not crawling through the privy, Vairug!" Despite his words, if there had been a privy, Belac would have crawled through it.

Disgruntled, Vairug said, "Then, unless you turn into a gorilla-wolf-monster and rip out the bars, I do not think we are getting free any time soon."

Belac narrowed his eyes at the wall. Then he turned his back to it and sat down on the cold stone floor. He leaned back against the wall in frustrated surrender. The wall moved. It was almost imperceptible, but the wall moved.

The elf jumped to his feet and turned to study the wall. Belac grinned. He did not know much about stone, but he was fairly sure that walls made from it were not supposed to move. He began placing his hands on the wall in different locations and applying pressure. It did not take him long to determine where the wall was weakest. Low and center, he could just barely see the wall move when he pressed.

Belac brushed a lock of stray hair out of his face, tucking it behind his pointed ears. "Sing something."

"What?" Vairug asked.

"I don't care. Just do it." Belac told the orc.

"Do, What?" Vairug was obviously confused.

Oh. Belac stepped over to the bars of his cell. "I need you to sing something."

"What?" Vairug asked again.

Belac growled and then raised his voice. "I need you to sing something!"

"I heard you," Vairug said. "What do you want me to sing?"

Oh. Belac shook his head. "It doesn't matter. I just need the noise."

"Why?" Vairug asked. "What are you doing over there?"

Belac looked at the wall. "Ah… Maybe killing us."

"I would prefer it if you did not," Vairug said flatly.

Belac frowned. "Just sing something, Vairug."

The orc began to sing. It was awful. Belac did not know if Vairug was one of the worst singers he had ever heard, or if it was simply impossible to make Orcish sound pleasing. Whatever the reason, the singing was sure to obscure any noise Belac made. He got down on the floor and laid on his back with his knees bent and his feet on the wall. He pushed as hard as he could, but all that happened was that he slid away from the wall. The elf scooted closer and began to stomp on the wall with both feet. Little by little, the wall moved more and more.

When his boots punched through the wall, Belac twisted to his side and curled up in a ball. He did not know how much of the wall was going to fall on him, but he covered his head and hoped for the best. It took him a moment to realize he was not dead, and that he had not been buried under an avalanche of stone.

Belac rolled onto his back and returned to kicking the wall, expanding the hole. Still worried that the wall might fall on him, he was careful where he kicked. He only kicked around the edges of the hole, and he stopped as soon as it was large enough for him to fit through.

Belac sat up and began moving the loose stones out of his way. "I made it through the wall!"

Vairug stopped singing. "What?"

"I said, I made it through the wall." Belac wriggled through the hole he had made.

"Then, why are you still here?" Vairug asked.

Belac stood and brushed his hands against his thighs. His black trousers were too filthy to clean his hands, but he was able to remove the grit. "I am in one of the other cells."

Sounding disappointed, Vairug asked, "Does it have a privy?"

Stupid orc. Belac opened the door to the cell and stepped out. He walked over to Vairug's cell and looked at him through the bars. The orc still wore his dark boots and trousers with the sleeveless white tunic; however, they were dirty and torn. The guards had taken his metal hand. Belac remembered how contemptibly they had cut the leather straps and tossed the prosthetic aside. They had not even let the orc keep his scarlet sash.

"I am not crawling through the privy, Vairug," Belac said through the bars.

Vairug looked up in surprise. "It was unlocked?"

"Why would they lock an empty cell?" Belac asked.

Vairug shrugged and then nodded his head. "Get me out of here."

Belac held up his empty hands. "What do you want me to do? Chew through the bars?"

Vairug looked the elf dead in the eyes. "Yes."

Belac frowned. "Try to find a weak spot in the wall. I will see if I can find something that will help."

The elf went to the corridor, but then stopped. No one had ever taught him how to sneak. He wanted to move quietly, but he did not know how to go about doing it. He thought about hunching over and walking on his tip toes, but that seemed silly to him. Finally, he decided to simply walk slowly and be careful where he stepped.

The corridor was relatively long, though there was only a single door along the way. Belac tested the door, but it was locked. He ran his fingers across the keyhole and wondered what was inside. The sound of laughter pulled his attention away. He continued down the corridor until it opened up to a larger room lit by lamplight. A stone stairway led up on the other side, promising freedom. An empty cot covered with a beige blanket had been pushed into the corner on the right side of the room, looking forgotten. On the other side of the room, two guards sat at a square table, drinking and playing dice. If it were not for their brown tabards with a red X across the chest, Belac would not have been sure they were guards. On the wall behind them, hung a set of keys.

Belac did not see how he could get the keys without alarming the guards. He also did not think he could have made it to the stairs and escaped alone. Even if he could have, he would not have abandoned the orc. *I need to go check on Vairug. I could really use his help.* He backed away as quietly as he could and retreated down the corridor. He paid special attention to the door as he passed it, worried someone might walk through at any moment.

When he returned to Vairug's cell, the orc was rubbing his shoulder.

Vairug heard the elf approach. "This wall is not moving, Belac."

Belac frowned. *What would Rolan do?* The elf thought for a moment. *He would probably just kill everybody.* Belac did not want to kill anyone, but he did have an idea. "Wait here," he told the orc.

Vairug gave the elf an irritated look.

Belac ignored him and returned to the open cell. He picked up a stone in each hand and then walked back through the corridor. *I am going to get myself killed.* He considered going back to his cell and waiting like he knew he was supposed to. He shook his head. They might eventually let him out, but he did not think they would do the same for Vairug. *Sometimes, risk is all there is.*

Belac tossed one of the stones toward the empty cot. The stone struck the hard floor and rolled under the edge of the hanging blanket. Both of the guards leapt up from their chairs and reached for the truncheons at their waists. They looked from the cot, to each other, and then back to the cot.

Belac stood absolutely still, hiding around the corner. When Rolan had used this trick, it had been used on ogres. *Humans are smarter than ogres. Not by much, but still…* They might not eat him, but he had witnessed what an angry human could do with one of those clubs.

"What was that, then?" one of the guards asked.

The other shook his head and drew his truncheon. The first drew his truncheon as well, and then they walked over to the cot. Belac almost laughed. *Yeah, not by much.* One of the guards gripped the coarse blanket covering the cot and flipped it back, his truncheon ready to strike.

Belac surged across the room toward the closer of the two guard and slammed his stone into the side of the man's head. The man fell to his knees, but Belac lost his grip on the stone. Unarmed, the elf jumped onto the back of the other guard. Belac tried to remember how Rolan had strangled the nude woman back at the magic castle. The guard, however, was not as cooperative as the mindless woman had been. He twisted around and crashed backward on to the edge of the cot. Belac took the force of the fall on the back of his shoulder but managed to hold on. The guard swung his truncheon up and hit Belac in the head. The blow hurt, but still the elf held on. The guard hit him again, though there was little strength behind it this time. The guard dropped his truncheon and went limp in Belac's arms. Belac continued to hold on to the guard until he was certain the man was unconscious. *Humans can be sneaky.*

Belac let go of the guard and stood, breathing hard. He remembered the other guard and turned, anticipating an attack. The guard was on his knees, sitting on his heels, staring at the wall confused. Cautiously, Belac stepped around him and ran over to grab the keys from the peg on the wall. He then returned to the unconscious guard and gripped the man's ankles.

Belac hurriedly began to drag the guard back to the cells, but the man was heavy. Just past the locked door, the guard started to thrash around as he regained consciousness. Belac released the guard's ankles and jumped on him. He tried to get his arms around the guard's neck but caught an elbow to the face. He fell from the guard and banged his head on the stone floor.

Belac forgot where he was. He looked up at the rough walls and ceiling. *Funny how even when the walls are white, they can still look gray.* A kick to his side focused his attention. He rolled away from the pain, but the guard kicked him again. Belac was ready for the next kick. He took the blow in his midsection and wrapped his arms around the guard's foot. The guard pulled away and fell back as his boot came off.

Belac scrambled to his feet and clubbed the guard in the face with his own boot. The guard rolled to the side and then climbed to his feet using the wall for support. Belac threw the boot at the back of the guard's head. The heel of the boot connected with the base of the guard's skull, and he stumbled into the wall. Belac jumped onto the guard's back, wrapping his arms around the man's neck.

The guard refused to go down. He staggered through the corridor as he tried to sling the elf off his back. Similarly committed, Belac refused to let go. Together, they crashed into the bars of the cells. The guard slammed Belac into the bars while the elf fought to secure his hold.

"Put your right hand inside your left elbow," Vairug instructed.

"I know how to strangle someone, Vairug!" Belac shouted.

"Then, stop playing with the man, and do it," Vairug countered.

Belac did as the orc instructed. The guard went limp, and Belac rode him to the floor. The elf maintained the hold longer this time. Partly to ensure the guard remained unconscious, but largely out of spite. Belac was not happy with the man.

Two

"You lost the keys?" Vairug complained.

Belac called back, "Shut up, Vairug. Or I will leave you in that cage." He scanned the dim corridor, searching for the lost keys.

"No, you won't," Vairug said confidently.

"Yes, I will!" Belac snatched the keys off the floor and returned to the cells.

"No. I do not think you will," Vairug insisted.

Belac locked the cell with an unconscious guard inside it, and then stepped over to the orc's. "Oh? Why do you think that?" he asked, looking at the orc through the bars of his cell.

Vairug stood a little taller and grinned. "Because, I know a secret."

Belac tilted his head to the side. "And what's that?"

Vairug looked at the door to his cell significantly.

Belac narrowed his eyes at the orc, but he unlocked the cell.

Vairug stepped out of the cell and nodded his thanks.

"Well?" Belac asked.

"Well, what?" Vairug asked in turn.

Belac narrowed his eyes at the orc. "What's the secret?"

"Belac." Vairug shook his head. "It is a secret."

"Die in a fire," Belac said smiling.

Vairug started down the corridor. "Let's leave this place."

Belac walked with him. "We still need to lock up the other guard before we go."

"There were two of them?" Vairug sounded surprised.

Belac was too offended to be proud. "Yes, there were two of them!"

When they passed the locked door, Belac considered stopping to open it, but decided they should see to the other guard first. *I hope he is still there!* The elf began to walk faster. If the guard had recovered his senses, he may already have gone for help. An alarm could be sounded at any moment.

Belac quickly discovered his concerns were unwarranted. The guard still sat on his heels, staring aimlessly. The elf let out a sigh of relief.

"What did you do to him?" Vairug asked.

Belac shrugged. "I hit him with a rock."

Vairug gestured to the guard. "I think you may have broke him."

"He might get better," Belac said defensively.

Vairug looked at the elf sideways. "You want him to get better?"

Belac kneeled in front of the guard. "I don't want to kill anyone we don't need to."

"I agree," Vairug said. "But we need to kill everyone that would seek to imprison us."

"You sound like Rolan." Belac unbuckled the guard's belt and set it aside.

Vairug grinned. "Then, my throat must be dry."

Belac ignored the orc's attempt at humor, and continued to focus on the task at hand. The guard offered no resistance, yet it was a chore to remove his tabard. When Belac finally got it off, he slid the tabard over his head and donned it himself. He picked up the discarded belt and buckled it around his own waist.

Belac nodded to the guard. "Help me get him into a cell."

Vairug reached down and hauled the guard up. Belac got under one of the man's arms and then Vairug released him. The guard offered no resistance as Belac directed their shambling through the corridor. Belac laid the man down in Vairug's cell and then locked him inside.

Vairug said, "I do not think he is going anywhere."

"He could get better," Belac insisted.

When they left the cells behind, the guard Belac had strangled was still unconscious. The elf tried not to think about it. *They could both be fine.* He went to the mysterious door, intent on finally unlocking it.

"We do not have time for this, Belac." Vairug sounded as if he knew he would be ignored.

"There could be anything in there," Belac argued, selecting a key. "It could be a super secret escape tunnel for all we know."

"In the prison?" Vairug asked skeptically.

Belac nodded. "Humans are sneaky." The key did not fit. He kicked the door. The keys were too large for the lock.

Belac turned to the orc. "Okay, you win. We can just forget the door." He started down the corridor. "But only because you asked."

Vairug grunted at him.

"Just remember this the next time I want something," Belac told him.

Vairug did not even bother grunting.

A woman walked down the stairs ahead of them. She wore a simple, chocolatey brown dress and carried a tray of food. Her dark hair shimmered in the lamplight and shadows played across her pale skin. The woman turned toward the guard's table, giving no indication she had noticed Belac and Vairug.

The elf froze. He did not know what to do. There was nowhere in the corridor to hide. They could try running back to the cells, but she might hear them. Also, one of the guards could regain their senses at any moment. She would be sure to hear that. *Maybe she will just leave.*

"Hello?" the woman called out.

Belac groaned.

The woman walked over to the corridor and was silhouetted by the room's lamplight. It was too late for them to run. Belac may have passed for a guard in the darkness, but there was no mistaking Vairug. The woman's hands covered her mouth in a moment of fright. *I have to stop her now.*

Belac rushed at the woman. She spun around and fled. He tackled her before she reached the stairs, and together they rolled across the floor. She twisted out of his grip and began to slap at him in a fury of blows. He tried to fend her off, but the woman was relentless.

"A little help here!" Belac called to the orc.

"You just killed two guards," Vairug said. "Now you're having trouble with a woman?" He walked over to the table and picked up an apple.

Belac looked over at the orc. "I did not kill them!" *They could still get better.*

Vairug stared back at the elf and said nothing. He took a bite out of his apple.

The woman kicked Belac between the legs. It was a glancing blow, but it hurt. He suddenly had far less patience for the woman. He grabbed her wrists and shook her.

"Listen, Woman!" Belac growled.

She went ridged in affront.

Without letting go of her wrist, Belac pointed a finger at her. "You need to calm down!"

"I will not!" she said.

Belac laughed angrily, trying to control his temper. "Woman…"

She attempted to pull free. "Let me go!"

Belac almost fell over as he struggled with her. "Stop it!"

She stopped and glared at him. "I will scream!" she threatened.

"And if you do, I will feed you to the orc!" Belac told her.

The woman looked at Vairug. He took another bite out of his apple. She looked back to Belac, eyes wide. The elf would have felt sorry for her if he had not still been in pain.

"What do you want?" She was scared.

Belac had to think about that. He had mostly just wanted her to stop hitting him. They could not take her with them, and they could not let her go. He looked around the room for something he could tie her up with. *Maybe if we could shred that blanket…*

"We can put her in the last cell," Vairug suggested.

That's right! We can just lock her in my cell. "Of course, we are going to put her in the cell," Belac told the orc. He then addressed the frightened woman, saying, "We are going to lock you up next to the guards. We're not going to hurt you, but you need to stop fighting us."

"She was fighting you," Vairug corrected him.

Belac narrowed his eyes at the orc.

"And you won't hurt me?" The woman drew his attention back.

Belac released her and stood. "That is what I said." He held his hand out toward the cells in what he felt was a polite invitation given the circumstances.

The woman stood and straitened her dress. She walked into the corridor sideways, keeping her captors in view. Vairug took the lantern from the table, and they followed her back to the cells. The guards were both unconscious.

The woman halted at the sight of the men. "What did you do to them?" Her frightened tone was accusing.

Vairug grunted. "He thinks they will get better."

Belac narrowed his eyes at the orc, and then said to the woman, "That is your cell there."

She stepped into the cell, closing the door behind herself as if the bars were there to keep the other two out. Belac locked the cell, but then had an idea. *This is genius!* He wriggled out of the guard's tabard and pushed it through the bars.

"Take your dress off and put this on." Belac pointed at the tabard.

The woman backed farther into the cell. "You said you wouldn't hurt me."

"I am not going to hurt you," Belac told her. "I just need your dress."

She crossed her arms. "I will not!"

"You can cover up with the tabard." Belac turned around. "Look. We won't even watch." He motioned for the orc to turn around.

Vairug gave him an exasperated look but turned away.

"No!" The woman was defiant.

Belac looked over his shoulder at her. "You can take the dress off, or he can take the dress off." He pointed at the orc. "What's it going to be?"

She stared bloody murder at him and then made an impatient shooing motion. "Well, turn around!"

He turned around and listened as she changed. The rustling of cloth was quick and angry.

"Here." She held her dress out between the bars.

Belac took the dress and smiled. "The tabard looks nice on you."

It was dark in the cell, but Belac could have sworn he saw her blush.

Three

Belac stepped away from the orc. "Are you ready to go, Sarah?"

Vairug looked like he might kill him. "This is not going to work."

Belac smiled. "Sure, it will." *This is genius!*

Vairug held out his arms. "No one is going to believe this, Belac."

Belac had taken the pillow from the cot and removed its cover. He had set the cover aside and then twisted the pillow in the middle, making two large lumps. He had then stuffed that into Vairug's tunic and wrapped him with the beige blanket. While it hid the orc's face, it only came down to his knees, and it looked nothing like a dress. It was a thoroughly unconvincing disguise.

"People see what they expect to see," Belac told him. "Besides, everyone is going to be looking at me." He twirled, and the hem of his dress lifted up.

"We look ridiculous," Vairug complained.

Belac covered his own head with the folded pillowcase and tied it under his chin, hiding his elven ears. "All we have to do is make it out of the prison. Then we can drop the act."

"Fine," Vairug conceded. "But do not call me 'Sarah."

They left the lantern behind and crawled up the stairs. The plan was to leave the same way they had been brought in. They knew it might be necessary to make a detour along the way, but at least they had a fair idea of where they were going. *And if Vairug knocks down a wall, we are not going through it!*

Hiding in the stairwell, Belac peeked into the room above. The first thing he noticed was the guard sitting at the large desk to the right. Belac did not know if the guard was a sergeant, a commander, or a secretary, but he was sure the man could raise an alarm. The guard was reading through papers Belac assumed were reports of some kind. There was a door next to the desk and two more on the far side of the room. However, it was the heavy door on the left that interested the elf. *That is our way out.*

One of the doors on the far side opened, and a guard walked into the room. The guard left the door open and went to speak with the man behind the desk. Belac did not give them any attention. He was too preoccupied staring through the open door. On the other side were rows and rows of cots, many of them with lumps that could only be sleeping guards. The doors had been closed when Vairug and he passed by on the way in. Belac had preferred it that way.

The guard walked back into the room filled with sleeping men and closed the door behind himself. Belac let out a sigh of relief. He looked to the guard behind the desk. The man had already returned to reading his papers. *If we are going to do this, it has to be now.*

Belac motioned for Vairug to follow him, and then he walked up the stairs. His heart raced, but he tried to walk as casually as he could. Too slow and they would look like they were sneaking, too fast and they would draw attention. Their pace needed to be natural. *Nothing to see here but two human serving women.*

They made it through the double doors and into an empty courtyard. Belac's fear transformed into elation. *This is going to work!* If they could make it through the checkpoint on the left, they would be free. Even if they were discovered, they might still be able to escape by simply running. Belac did not think it would be easy to run in a dress, but he was willing to try. It was more important that Vairug get free anyway. The humans were less likely to kill an elf. *And I can just blame him for what happened to the guards.*

Vairug started walking toward the gate on the right. "We need to go this way."

"No!" Belac hissed. "We came in through there." He gestured to the check point on the left.

Vairug continued walking the other way.

Belac considered letting the orc go get himself killed. Then he groaned and hurried to catch up with him. "This is the wrong way!"

Vairug ignored him.

"We need to go back," Belac pressed. "We are almost free." *You big, stupid orc!*

Vairug said nothing. He looked like a dog following a scent.

They passed through the gate into a stable yard. A cobblestone path followed the outer wall on the left and the stables hugged the base of the castle on the right. While the stables were rather plain, the castle was something special. An imposing fortress of grandeur and might, its hard utilitarian design was softened by the chalky off-white stone of its construction. It was a place of beauty; but one prepared to weather the storm.

"Hey, You!" a man called.

Belac pretended he did not know the man was talking to them. He walked faster, pulling Vairug with him. It was too late to turn back now.

"Wait a moment!" the man called.

Belac maintained their pace. They were committed now. Their only hope was that the man would not think that troubling two women was worth the effort of chasing them down.

"I said wait!" The man was getting angry.

Another stablehand moved into the path ahead, ready to stop them. The man held out a hand. His face grew more confused as they approached. Belac closed his eyes hard, trying to contrive some way out. They were trapped. He opened his eyes and kept walking, not knowing what else to do. Vairug walked straight up to the man blocking their way. Realization donned on the man's face right before Vairug punched it.

"Tommy, fetch the guard!" the other man called out.

Belac ran for the doors ahead. He did not know what was on the other side, but he knew they could not stay where they were. If they survived the army of vengeful guards, he would spend the rest of his life in prison.

A stablehand slammed into the elf, tackling him. Belac landed on his back with the man's shoulder in his gut. Belac drove his elbow into the back of the man's head and neck until the man went limp, and then he shoved the man off of him and stood. He looked down at the man and then kicked him in the head.

Another stablehand came into view. Belac took a swing at him without thinking. The man blocked the attack like someone who knew how to fight. Belac got tangled in the hem of his dress and fell face first onto the stones.

The man laughed. "Crazy woman thinks she can fight."

Belac rolled over and kicked out low. His heel connected with the man's ankle with a sickening pop. The man collapsed to the ground, his face twisted in paralyzing pain.

Belac stood. His head bobbed as he shouted at the man. "Who's the crazy woman now?!" *Wait. That does not make any sense.*

Vairug grabbed his arm. Guards were coming. Their boots sounded like a stampede on the cobblestones. Belac tossed his hair back out of his face and ran for the doors. He opened one and then followed Vairug inside. There was a heavy timber that could be used to bar the door, but there was more than one door and they did not have time to bar them all.

They were in an empty room with one hallway exiting to the right. Belac did not like the idea of going farther into the castle, but they did not have a choice. They ran down the hallway, passing closed doors on their left. There was no time to explore. They needed to get as far away from the guards as they could if they were to have any chance at escape.

The doors to the stable yard slammed open behind them. The guards were gaining fast. *I wonder if I can convince them that I really am a woman, and that Vairug abducted me.*

The hallway led to an open room with a long table in the center. Around the table sat hard looking men in chainmail. Belac and Vairug came to a halt. There was nowhere else for them to run. The men at the table stood, displaying a black anchor emblazoned across each of their tabards. Some of them drew swords. These men were not city guards.

Belac stepped away from the orc and pointed at him. "Do you know who this is?"

No one answered.

Belac continued, "This is Lord Vairdoe of Enevic, the only man to face the dragon Danorin and survive!"

Vairug stood taller, thrusting out his pillow stuffed chest.

Belac groaned.

Four

"Explain to me how this is not your fault!" Belac stood behind the bars wearing nothing but a faded blue bed sheet tied over one shoulder.

Vairug glared at him from behind the bars of his cell on the other side of the room. The orc too wore nothing but a faded blue bed sheet, though his was tired around his waist like a skirt. "I told you they were not going to believe us!" he shouted at the elf.

Another voice joined their own. "Apologies, Lord Vairdoe." The voice was rough but well trained. "But you are here precisely because they do believe you."

There were five cells arranged in an octagonal pattern, the exit flanked by two bare walls. The only light was what crept in from under the iron bound door. Their new prison was larger and had a considerably more substantial feel. The bars were thicker, the walls were thicker, and judging from the descent, the floor and ceiling were thicker as well.

Belac's gaze traveled across the other cells, but he could not see the man who had spoken. "And who are you?"

A disheveled man stepped up to the bars of the center cell. He was bearded and thin in a way that promised the misery of Belac's future. *At least elves don't have to grow all that ugly fur on their face.* Belac's face itched just looking at the man.

"I am Lord Ecard von Leaos of Enevic, General of the Ninth," the man said proudly.

That might be a problem. "I thought everyone from Enevic was dead," Belac replied.

The man's voice turned solemn. "So did I."

A lord would have a family. The man must have lost everyone he ever knew.

Ecard continued, trying to push past his despondency. "Until I learned of you, Lord Vairdoe. We may be the last, but at least we are not alone."

Belac did not give the orc a chance to respond. "How do you know about Lord Vairdoe?" *Especially if you really are a prisoner.*

"I am interrogated often," Ecard explained, "and soldiers are gossips."

Vairug asked, "And do you know me?"

Belac would have thrown something at the orc if there had been anything to throw. *How would he know you? You are not really a lord! Stupid orc.*

Ecard's answer was unsure. "I believe we may have met once at a banquet. It was long ago. Please, do not take offence, but I was young, and I had little time for local lords."

Belac could not tell if the man was lying or not. *Lords are good at that.* Obviously, the man had never met Lord Vairdoe. There was no Lord Vairdoe. However, even if Ecard was lying, he could be doing so simply to be polite. Most humans actually thought it was kind to lie to each other.

Belac decided to probe the man's story. "How long have you been here?"

Ecard accepted the question as genuine. "I am afraid this is my only measure." He gestured to his unruly beard.

Vairug asked a better question. "How did you survive Enevic?"

"I was not there," Ecard confessed. His voice was filled with sorrow and regret.

Belac believed him. Lords were liars and humans were sneaky, but that pain was real. It was something so profound and honest, it made the elf ashamed of his own lies. *"Everything you do."*

Vairug seemed unmoved. "And why were you not there?"

Belac thought the question harsh.

Ecard held his hands out to the walls of his cell. The gesture was one of both demonstration and submission. "I was captured; my men slaughtered." He gripped the bars of his cell and rested his forehead against them. "We were ambushed on the border." He ground his forehead into the bars and then looked up in the orc's direction. "They want Enevic, Lord Vairdoe. They wanted it before the dragon came." His voice lost its strength. "And now I fear they will have it."

"That's why they captured Vairu… Lord Vairdoe," Belac inferred.

"Indeed, it must be so," Ecard agreed.

Belac looked over at the fallen lord. The man might still be useful, but Belac would need to find some way to motivate him. "That just means they are going to be extra angry when we escape and take you with us."

Ecard's smile was patronizing. "You think you can escape?"

Sure," Belac said confidently. "We are great at breaking out of prisons."

Ecard seemed surprised by his own laughter. "Do you break out of prisons often?"

Belac nodded. "We just broke out of one earlier today."

"My apologies, but I fear you are mistaken. I believe you were being held in a jail. Though to be fair, you were to be moved here anyway."

"What is the difference?" Belac agreed with the orc's thoughts on prisons. *If I can't get out, it's a prison.*

Ecard explained, "I believe that a jail is meant to be temporary. They tend to have less security as a result. I fear you may find escaping a prison to be a bit more challenging."

Belac narrowed his eyes at the man. *Stupid Dwarven language.* "It does not matter. That was not the first prison we broke out of."

Vairug interjected, "He just told you it was not a prison."

Belac turned his glare on the orc. "Was your door locked?"

Vairug smiled. "Then, this is a prison," he quoted himself.

Ecard began to recite an ancient poem. "Locked doors do not a prison make. Only the mind must freedom forsake. When boundary…"

"Pretty words," Belac interrupted. *Prison is bad enough without having to listen to your awful poetry.* "But whatever you want to call it, we are breaking out of here." *Hopefully before you start spouting poetry again.*

"That sounds wonderful, my elven friend," Ecard said sadly. "But I fear that is not the case."

"Belac," the elf supplied.

"What's that?" Ecard asked him.

"That is my name," Belac told him.

Smiling mischievously, Vairug added, "The Dragon Slayer."

Ecard was taken aback. "You have slain a dragon?"

Belac frowned at the orc. "I am new at it."

The door groaned and light spilled into the cells, forcing Ecard to shield his eyes. The light emphasized how filthy the man was. His feet were bare, and his once noble attire tattered and torn. The clothes hung loosely from his withered form in wretched testimony.

Two men entered the room. The light behind them was too bright for Belac to see their chest, but he knew they would bear a red X across them.

One of the guards bent at the knees and leaned forward. "Hey, Lordy, Lordy." He spoke as if speaking to a dog. "Are you ready to have some fun?"

Ecard instinctually cringed. Something deep inside the man shifted. He got to his hands and knees, placing his head on the stone floor. Belac could hear him whine.

"Aw," the guard said in mock sympathy. "Does Lordy want to stay in his cage?" Laughing, he stood up straight.

Ecard did not answer.

The guard swept his gaze across the other cells in the room before returning his attention to the man whimpering on the floor. "Does Lordy like his new friends? Do you want to stay with your new friends?"

Belac could not comprehend what he was witnessing. The change in Ecard was simply too extreme to seem real.

The guard walked over and put his foot between the bars of Ecard's cell. The guard wiggled his foot a little and whistled. "Come on, Lordy. Show your friends who's a good lord."

On his hands and knees, Ecard crawled over to the bars of his cell and began to lick the guard's boot. Laughter came from the other guard standing by the doorway.

Satisfied his boot was sufficiently clean, the first guard pulled his foot back. "That's a good lord." He unlocked the cell and dropped a leather collar on the floor. "Put it on." His voice had turned serious.

Ecard picked up the collar and held it in his hand.

He stared down at the thing for a moment in hopeless indecision. Everything that the man was warred inside himself as he railed against what he knew he was about to do. It was not about saving face. It was pure dread at where they were going to take him and what would be done there. The scene terrified Belac. The elf knew his turn would come.

Ecard sat back on his heels and buckled on the collar. He returned to his hands and knees, looking down at floor.

The guard laughed. "Now look at that," the guard said. He looked down, once more speaking to a dog. "Come on, Lordy. Come on." The guard clapped his hands. "Lordy gets to go for a walk."

There were few things that could be as vile as a human. It was their empathy. They knew what it was to hurt. They understood degradation. It was easy to see how such a thing could be abused. However, Belac did not understand why some of them enjoyed it so much.

The guard attached a leash to the collar. Ecard's eyes never left the floor as he was led from the room on his hands and knees. The guards shut the door, leaving behind an oppressive silence.

"We need to get out of here, Vairug," Belac said seriously.

"Yes," Vairug agreed. "But how?" He did not seem as troubled as the elf.

"I don't care." Belac pointed at the closed door. "But they are not turning me into that."

Vairug shook his head. "They cannot."

"You think he was faking?" It did not look like the man was faking to Belac.

"No," Vairug said. "He is broken."

Belac felt the panic creeping into his own voice. "They did that! And we are next! They are going to starve us. They are going to torture us. They are…"

Vairug interrupted him forcefully. "There is pain in life, Belac. It can only show you who you are."

Belac focused on the orc. "You think the man was weak?"

"I think the man chose to be." Vairug stared into the elf's eyes as if there were no bars between them. "What will you choose, Belac?"

Not that. Belac realized that they had been put in the cells with Ecard to show them what would happen to them if they did not submit. *Maybe the truth is something different. Maybe that is what will happen to us if we do submit.*

Belac met the orc's stare. "They want to scare us into giving them something they can't take."

Vairug nodded, determination hardening his face. "I say we give them something else."

Five

"I told them," Ecard sobbed.

The guards had dragged the man into the cell by his feet, his limp form leaving behind a trail of blood as flesh scraped over stone. The man's ruined shirt hung in tatters around his waist, and his back was covered in blood and grit. In the dim of the prison, Belac had not known if the man was still alive.

When Ecard had regained consciousness, he sobbed; at first uncontrollably, and then in quiet shame. Belac could not look at him. He did not want to look at him. However, he could not block out the sound of the man's sobs, or the smell of his blood.

"I told them!" Ecard cried again. "I'm sorry. I told them."

Belac gripped the bars of his cell. "You told them what?"

Ecard continued to sob, repeating, "I'm sorry. I'm sorry. I'm sorry."

Belac could not take much more of it. "Burn your eyes, Ecard! You told them what?"

Ecard tried unsuccessfully to hold back his tears. "Everything! I told them everything."

Belac looked to the orc. "What could he have told them?"

It was dark, but Vairug may have shrugged.

Belac turned back to the man on the floor. "You are going to have to do better than that, Ecard."

"I'm sorry. I'm sorry. I'm sorry," the man sobbed.

"I don't care if you're sorry, Ecard!" Belac shouted. "I just want to know what you told them."

"Everything!" the man wailed. "I told them you were the Dragon Slayer. I told them he was Lord Vairdoe. I told them you were going to escape."

Belac laughed in relief. "Ecard," the elf shook his head, "they already know who we are. We told them. Remember?"

Ecard looked up at the elf. "But I…"

Belac continued, "And everyone that is in prison wants to escape prison. That's how you know it's a prison."

Ecard quit sobbing as he listened to the elf intently.

"Besides," Belac said, "we just escaped from one of their prisons. They have to know we are going to try again."

Vairug corrected him. "That was jail."

Belac pointed at the orc threateningly.

Vairug held up his hand and wrist.

There was desperation in Ecard's voice. "So, I have not betrayed you?"

Belac shook his head. "Nope."

"Yes, he did," Vairug denounced.

Belac turned his attention back to the orc. "He did not tell them anything they did not already know, Vairug."

"He would have," contended Vairug.

Belac tried to think of an argument, but he knew the orc was right. "At least now we know not to tell him anything."

Belac knew that what he had said would hurt Ecard's feelings. *It will also cover any holes in our story.* While the Harbridgers were keeping Vairug in prison because they thought he was Lord Vairdoe, it would be worse if they learned the truth. They would kill him. There would be no reason to keep a one handed orc alive.

Vairug nodded grudgingly.

Belac did not think the orc understood, but at least he did not argue. "Now, we just need to figure out how we are going to get out of here."

Vairug pointed his wrist toward the center cell. "And how are we going to do that with him listening?"

Once again, Belac wanted to argue but could not think of anything to say. *Maybe we can use him.* If they made fake plans while Ecard was listening, he would then convince the guards when he was interrogated. There might be a way to get the guards to do something in response to a fake plan that would help them escape. *The real plan would have to be complicated.* Belac began to contemplate how he might trick the guards.

The sound of cloth tearing interrupted his musings. Belac tried to locate the sound. He thought it was coming from the center cell, but he could not see anything. *Ecard is not there.* The man must have moved to the back of his cell.

"Ecard?" Belac called.

The tearing of cloth continued.

Belac looked over to the orc's cell.

Vairug held up his hand and shook his head in confusion.

Rustling in Ecard's cell drew their attention. The man limped resolutely to the bars of his cell holding a rope fashioned from his torn bedsheet. He tied one end to the top of the bars. The other was looped around his neck.

"What are you doing, Ecard?" Belac asked though the answer was obvious.

Ecard turned away from them, facing the back of his cell. "I'm sorry," he said in true contrition, and then leaned forward.

Belac watched in horror as the man strangled himself. There was nothing he could do. *That stupid human just insists on ruining my plans!*

Ecard was bathed in light as the door groaned open. The man began to twitch against the rope. Belac turned to see if the guards would help. He was sure they would save him if they could. *If they wanted him dead, he would be dead.*

"Cut him down!" Belac shouted into the light.

Someone far too short to be a guard ran into the room and drew a knife. Metal scraped against metal, and Ecard fell to the floor. The man twitched some more, and then began to breathe heavily.

"Rolan?" Belac thought he might be imagining the dwarf.

With his darkly stained wooden springer held in his off hand, Rolan sheathed his knife and then walked over to Belac's cell. The dwarf looked him up and down through the bars.

After a moment, Rolan grinned. "You are going to need shoes," he said.

"Ha!" Belac laughed. *I don't have to be a prison dog!*

Rolan unlocked the elf's cell and then tossed him the keys. "Go get Vairug out."

The dwarf moved to stand next to the exit with his springer held low and ready, his splotchy gray outfit blending in with the shadowed stone. *Anyone that comes down that corridor is going to die before they know they are in a fight.* Belac did not care in the least that the dwarf had no sense of fair play. No one could work in a place like that and not know what they were supporting. Belac opened Vairug's cell, hoping Rolan would get the opportunity to kill some of the guards while he did.

"Let's leave this place," Vairug said stepping out of his cell.

Belac nodded toward the center cell. "We still need to get him out."

Vairug frowned at him. "The man is wrong."

"Why? Because he smells funny?" Belac remembered the last person the orc called 'wrong.' "He has been locked in a prison, Vairug."

Belac hurried to Ecard's cell and unlocked it. The man had not moved from where he fell to the floor. Belac nudged the man with his foot. Ecard shied away and curled into a ball.

"Get up, Ecard," Belac ordered him.

When the man did not comply, Belac grabbed one of Ecard's scrawny arms and yanked him to a sitting position. The man did not resist, but nor did he respond. With his other hand, Belac slapped him.

"Get on your feet and walk out of this cell, or stay here and know that you deserve everything that comes next," Belac said without pity. There was no time for pity.

The elf had lost his patience. He was about to push Ecard away and leave him there to suffer and die. However, in the instant before he did, the man looked up at him. While what Belac saw was not resolve, it was at least a willingness to try. He released Ecard's arm and stood. He did not help the man stand. If Ecard lacked the will to leave the prison cell, Belac would abandon him. *I will not die for a man too weak to live.*

Six

The corridor was short. It led from their cells to a hexagonal room with three closed doors and two other corridors. In the center of the room stood an immense glass lamp that trickled smoke up into a channel in the domed ceiling. The off-white stone structure of the prison matched the aesthetics of the castle perfectly. *This has to be the nicest prison I have ever been in.*

Strewn across the floor lie four dead guards. It appeared as if Rolan had shot them all. *That would explain why we did not hear any screaming.* Belac took dark pleasure in the fact that he recognized one of them. That man being dead seemed to make the world a better place.

Belac nodded toward the dead guard. "Does that make you as happy as it does me?"

Ecard grinned despite his obvious pain. "More, I would imagine."

Belac hefted the man, repositioning Ecard to make it easier to support him. Rolan marched off to the left. Belac was glad the dwarf knew where he was going, but he could not help but wonder what was to the right. *Who else might be trapped in this nightmare?*

Belac raised his voice. "What's that way?"

Rolan did not look back. "What's, what way?"

Belac pointed. "That way!"

"You are going to need to be more specific," Rolan said without looking.

Belac would have hopped up and down if he had not been supporting someone. "You know what I mean, Rolan! It's the only other way to go!"

Rolan glanced toward the other corridor but did not stop walking. "I don't know, but it does not matter."

"How can you know it does not matter, if you don't even know what's down there?" Belac argued, following the dwarf out of the room.

"Because the exit is this way," Rolan told him.

"But there could be more prisoners," Belac pressed. "Maybe they could help."

"It does not matter." Rolan looked back at the elf and the man he all but carried. "We cannot take anyone else with us."

"But maybe they could help," Belac tried one last time.

"We don't need help. What we need, is to hurry," Rolan said, ending the debate.

Belac still wanted to go check, but there was no way he was going to go running off by himself wearing nothing but a bedsheet. *Even if I had a magic suit of armor that made me fly, I would still not go back there alone.* Belac thought about how much fun such a suit might be. *I take it back. I would totally be willing to go back there alone if someone would give me a magic suit of armor that let me fly.* Belac considered some more. *I would be willing to do it for a magic carpet and some clean trousers.* He would have been willing to forgo the trousers.

The corridor ended at a junction that led left and right. Rolan turned right without hesitation.

Vairug stopped. "We need to go this way."

"No, we don't," Rolan disagreed.

Vairug did not move. He appeared to be struggling with something. "It's my hand, Rolan."

Rolan stopped and looked back at the orc. "I can make you a new one. There is no way we can find it in all of this." He gestured negligently.

Vairug gave the dwarf a look that was almost pleading. "I can feel it, Rolan."

"That is probably not good." Rolan sounded as if he were understating.

Vairug looked down the other corridor. "It is not far."

Rolan's gaze traveled over Belac and Ecard, then he said, "We will have to be quick about it. There are people waiting on us."

Belac asked, "Do we have to return this way?"

Rolan nodded.

Belac lowered Ecard to the floor. He was willing to take the man with them when they escaped. He was even willing to help him walk. However, he was not willing to carry him deeper into the prison and risk getting himself or his friends killed. *He can just rest here. Maybe he will get some of his strength back.*

"Stay here and we will get you on the way back," Belac told him.

Rolan stepped past them. "If someone else shows up, just

close your eyes and keep looking like you are dead."

Belac stood and wiped his hands on his bedsheet. He followed after Rolan and Vairug, not wanting to be left behind. He was worried Ecard might die or disappear while they were gone, but there was only so much he could do for the man. *I am not going to just stay there and die with him.*

The first stretch of the corridor was clear. However, after a sharp turn to the left, they ran into more guards. Luckily, the guards were not prepared for escaped prisoners. Had they been, they still would not have been prepared for Rolan. *Who could possibly be prepared for that crazy little dwarf?*

There were two guards facing each other, speaking quietly. Rolan stepped around Vairug quickly and shot the one on the right. The man's head snapped to the side as the steel dart passed through. The other guard stepped back in confusion. Before the man could process what was happening, Rolan had another bolt loaded and the springer aimed. The guard searched for threats in the corridor, but he looked the wrong way. Rolan's bolt took the man in the back of the head.

The sound of the two guards falling to the floor drew the attention of another in a nearby room. The man walked out into the corridor and was promptly shot in the head. Belac marveled at how fast Rolan could reload. The dwarf's hands moved with a practiced ease, seeming to operate without his direct attention. *He does not even look at the thing when he loads it.*

Rolan stepped into the doorway of the room the guard had exited. His springer thracked twice more in rapid succession. There was a cry of alarm from inside and then another shot.

Rolan stepped back into the corridor, another bolt already loaded into his springer. A guard entered the corridor from a room on the other side and swung a truncheon at the dwarf. Rolan leaned away and low, the truncheon sweeping past where his head had been. He then pulled a knife free and leaned back in, burying the blade in the man's thigh. The guard fell to his opposite knee, stopping the fall with his open hand. The springer thracked and a bolt pinged off the stone ceiling after passing through the underside of the man's jaw and out the top of his head.

Rolan reloaded the springer while sidestepping next to the wall. Another guard stepped into the corridor and Rolan shot him in the face. The sound of Rolan reloading was followed by an anticipatory silence.

Belac and Vairug looked at each other and then back to the dwarf. *Anyone who says dwarves do not know how to make arrows right is just wrong.*

Rolan crept to the door, knelt down, and peeked into the room, scanning for threats. After determining the room was safe, he continued down the corridor.

"Wait," Vairug said. "I think it is in there." He pointed a truncheon at the room the dwarf had just cleared.

Rolan halted where he was, his springer held ready. Vairug hurried into the room, Belac following close behind. It was a small office dominated by an ornate desk. Vairug walked around the desk and went straight to a small table in the back corner. He tossed the truncheon aside and picked up his metal hand with the remains of its leather harness dangling from it. He tucked the hand under his left arm and grabbed his silvery cogged mace. Evidently, the guards had considered them a matched set. Vairug was grinning broadly when he turned around.

The sight of the orc's tusks jutting out of his happy grin almost made Belac laugh. He smiled with the orc, unable to do anything less. *Now, we just have to escape.* He turned around to leave but stopped. A scabbarded sword hung on the wall next to the door. The two-handed longsword had a black leather wrapped hilt with a black anchor enameled on the center of its polished steel cross-guard. A long black leather scabbard with steel accents concealed the blade, but the sword appeared to be a fine weapon.

Belac reached up and grabbed the sword off the wall. *I would not care if it were made out of rust and horse leather.* The elf needed a weapon, and he knew how to use a sword.

There were shouts from the corridor followed by Rolan's commanding voice. "We need to move!"

The springer thracked as Belac stepped from the office. He almost tripped over the dead man on the floor. Belac noticed that the man's tabard bore the black anchor.

"I have it," Vairug announced.

Belac and Vairug hurried back down the corridor. Rolan turned and chased after them, pausing only to retrieve his knife from one of the dead guards. When they reached the corner, the dwarf turned around and used it for cover as he sent another bolt flying.

"Run ahead and get your friend moving," Rolan instructed as he reloaded. "Just follow the hallway, I will catch up." He dug into one of his pouches and pulled out a small brass orb. He struck it on the wall and smoke began to spray out. The dwarf reached around the corner and threw the orb. "I said go!"

Belac hiked up his bedsheet and ran as fast as he could without tripping over the folds. When he saw Ecard, he thought the man might be dead. Ecard lie on his side motionless, giving no indication he was aware of Belac's return.

"Time to go, Ecard," Belac said, lifting the man up from under his arm.

Ecard came awake with a start. "What?" The man did not seem to know where he was.

"We have to go," Belac told him.

The man did not resist, but he was of little help, confused as he was. "Where?"

"Away from all the people coming to kill us, Ecard." Belac began to drag the man down the corridor.

Vairug's feet pattered on the stone as he joined the elf. "We need to move faster, Belac."

He wants me to leave Ecard behind. "How much faster?" Belac asked.

Vairug glanced back the way they had come. "There are many guards coming, Belac."

Belac looked back as well. Rolan was running down the corridor toward them. Belac thought Rolan ran well for a dwarf.

"We need to move faster," Rolan said joining them.

He is not even breathing hard.

"That is what I told him," Vairug said.

Rolan took the orc's metal hand. "Carry him."

Vairug growled but bent down and hoisted Ecard over his shoulder.

Rolan handed the metal hand to the elf. "Get moving."

Seven

They moved quickly, all things considered. Still, Belac could hear the guards charging through the corridor behind them. He did not understand how Rolan thought they were going to escape. The guards would catch them soon.

"I thought you stopped them with your gas ball thingy," Belac said.

Rolan shook his head. "That was just smoke. It is not going to slow them down much now that they know it won't hurt them."

"Then how are we supposed to get away?" Belac was trying not to panic but the guards were getting louder.

"Next door on the right," Rolan told him.

Belac did not trust how easy the answer had come to the dwarf. "Unless it's a magic door that leads to an enchanted forest, I don't think that is going to be good enough, Rolan."

Vairug ran past the door.

Belac stopped and called after him, "Vairug!"

The orc looked back, and then almost dropped Ecard changing course. Vairug was tired. Much like anyone in prison, life had not been going their way of late.

Belac stepped through the doorway and did not find himself in an enchanted forest. It was a loosely packed storage room that appeared to be used primarily to house lamp oil. Ecard's head bounced off the doorframe as Vairug rushed into the room. The man was either unconscious or too exhausted to complain.

Rolan shot a bolt down the corridor and then joined them inside. "Back of the room." He waved them on.

That seemed like a tactical mistake to Belac, but he trusted in the dwarf's expertise. *It's not like I have a lot of options right now, anyway.* Navigating around the crates as quickly as he could, the elf hurried further into the cluttered room. At the back of the room, large crates had been pulled away from the wall to expose a crudely chiseled passage. *Someone dug a hole into the prison!*

Belac took one look at the hole in the stone wall and stopped. "No. No. Nope. Nu uh. No more caves, Rolan."

"It's just a tunnel. Now move!" Rolan said impatiently.

Vairug did not stop for the elf. He collided with Belac and pushed him toward the hole. Belac stumbled into the stone tunnel. Behind him, he heard guards knocking over crates in their pursuit.

Even with the tunnel, Belac did not see how they were going to escape. *I bet the guards know how to use a tunnel every bit as well as we do.* The cramped tunnel would be easier to defend, but that would only buy them so much time. The guards were sure to overwhelm them before they could escape.

Rolan's voice called from the entrance to the tunnel. "Keep moving!"

Belac looked back over his shoulder as he fled. "I didn't plan on stopping!"

An explosion threw Belac to the ground. Lying on his back, the elf tried to remember where he was. He looked at all the stone. *Am I in prison again?*

"Iaezadon," Belac mumbled. He could not hear his own voice. He wondered what device his torturers were using to create the loud ringing noise that was boring into his brain.

"Your plan to not stop is not going very well." Rolan helped the elf sit up.

Belac could barely hear him. The dwarf was not making any sense. Belac shook his head and almost toppled over.

"Easy there." Rolan put his hand on the elf's shoulder to steady him. "Follow my finger." He moved his finger back and forth in front of the elf's face.

Belac tried to swat the dwarf's hand away and missed. "Lamawits!" he said unintelligibly. Belac did not even know what he was trying to say.

"You two, keep moving down the tunnel. There are people expecting you. Don't kill them." Rolan was still not making any sense.

"Crasadal," Belac muttered.

Rolan put a small vial up to the elf's lips. "Here, drink this." He poured some of it into the elf's mouth.

Belac tried to spit it out. "Galawadal!"

Rolan grabbed the elf's jaw forcefully and wrenched his head against the dwarf's chest. "We do not have time for this." He poured the rest of the vial between the elf's lips and then covered his mouth with a callused hand.

Belac fought as the dwarf forced him to choak down the

bitter liquid. When Rolan was satisfied the elf had swallowed the potion, he released him. Belac's world spun. He could smell the color of the rocks and taste the insides of his own eyelids. *Everything is so bright!*

The world faded to shadow. The off-white tunnel walls lost their magic, and the elf could not taste anything at all. A dim light came from farther down the tunnel. *I should go that way.* A hand on his shoulder stopped him from getting up.

"Give it a moment," Rolan told him.

As Belac regained his senses, the ringing in his ears abated. "What did you do to me?"

Rolan was suddenly impatient. "I rescued you from prison."

Belac stood. "I am not rescued yet."

"Do you want to wait here and prove me wrong?" Rolan asked.

Belac looked to the light at the end of the tunnel. "Ah… No."

"Right." Rolan marched off down the tunnel.

Belac bent down and picked up his new sword and Vairug's shiny hand. *If I left Vairug's hand here, he would probably make us come back and 'rescue' it.* Belac did not understand why the metal hand was so important to the orc. It was broken. *I get why he would want a magic hand. I do. But a pile of twisted metal someone else has to carry around for him? Not so much.*

The tunnel led to a wide opening in the side of a cliff. Belac was met with the sight of ocean and sun. It was that moment that the elf finally felt rescued. He took a deep breath, expecting to smell the sea. *That's strange.*

"I don't smell anything," Belac said confused.

Rolan was dismissive. "You probably won't for a while."

"What?" Belac asked. "Why not?"

Rolan shrugged. "It happens sometimes if you drink too much of the potion I gave you."

Belac's head snaped toward the dwarf. "You say that like it's my fault!"

Rolan did not argue. "You were not cooperating."

Belac almost threw the orc's metal hand down on the rocks. "So, you poisoned me?!"

Rolan waved his hand absently. "You will be fine." Then he softly muttered, "Probably."

Belac held out Vairug's metal hand with the ruined harness hanging from it. He flipped the loose leather straps around the hand and then offered it to the orc. Vairug took the hand with a nod of thanks. Behind him stood two men at the edge of the cliff. Even if they had not been dressed as sailors, it would have been obvious from how they handled the rigging piled at their feet. *If they are working with Rolan, they are probably pirates.*

Belac scanned the small cave again. "Where is Ecard?"

Vairug nodded toward the edge. "He is already headed down."

Belac did not know how they were going to get down, but he suspected he would need his hands. He adjusted the baldric of his new sword and then slipped it over his head and onto his shoulder. One look at Vairug trying to juggle his mace and metal hand was enough to let Belac know the orc would need to be adjusted as well. He took the metal hand back and unwrapped the leather straps. He tied the two longest straps together and then hung the device on Vairug's shoulder with the straps crossing his chest and back.

Belac took a step back to get a better look at the orc. "That should work," he muttered to himself. An idea came to him.

"Wait." He took one of the other straps and tied it in a small loop. "See if that will hold your mace."

Vairug wiggled the mace into the loop and then nodded.

"Belac." Rolan waved the elf over to the edge of the cliff.

"How did you find this place?" Belac asked as he joined the dwarf. *There is no way he had time to make this himself.*

"The only difference between a well kept secret and a poorly kept one is how much it cost," Rolan explained while securing a wide leather belt around the elf's waist. He looked up and met the elf's eyes. "You owe me a boat."

"What?" Belac asked. *I don't have a boat!*

Vairug spoke up. "He still owes me a knife."

Belac looked at the orc. "I do not."

"You lost mine," Vairug insisted. "Back at the tailor in Tariel."

The guards took it! Belac shook his head. "That does not count."

Vairug held out his open hand, palm up. "Give me my knife back."

"I don't have your knife!" Belac told him.

Vairug nodded, lowering his hand. "Then, you owe me a knife."

"And a pair of boots," Rolan added.

"Now, wait there." Belac pointed at the dwarf. "I did not take your boots!" *They would not even fit.*

Vairug nodded. "You lost them in the bet."

"What?!" Belac shook his head. *Who makes a bet with a dwarf's boots?*

"In the race," Vairug reminded him. "You bet your boots."

"The good ones," Rolan added.

Belac remembered. He had explicitly refused to bet with his boots. "Lies and slander."

Rolan looked at him sideways. "Are you saying you did not lose the race?"

Belac had lost the race. *Technically.*

Rolan saw the look on the elf's face and nodded. "Right."

"No. Not right!" Belac had not bet his boots.

"That is how a race works, Belac." Vairug's cheek twitched as he suppressed a grin.

Belac shook his head. "No. I never bet my boots."

Rolan held up a hand. "Everyone that thinks Belac owes us a boat and a pair of boots, raise your hand."

Vairug raised his hand. "And a knife."

Rolan nodded. "And a knife."

Belac looked back and forth at them. *This is crazy!*

Rolan lowered his hand. "Now, everyone that thinks Belac does not owe us anything, raise your hand."

Vairug dropped his hand quickly.

Belac's hand shot up like he thought his vote would matter.

Rolan pushed him off the cliff.

Belac screamed something unkind as he fell.

Eight

Belac almost lost his new sword when the rope tightened. Had the fall stopped more abruptly, he would have. However, somehow the sailors above applied resistance to the rope tied to the ring of Belac's waist harness. The elf was safe, but he still would have kicked Rolan in the face if he could.

Once it became apparent Belac was not going to fall to his death, he came to enjoy the decent. The sky above and the ocean below were about as contrasting with prison as he could imagine. Hanging suspended between the two offered both peace and promise.

A two masted ship waited below, ready to smuggle him to freedom. A breeze whipped through the elf's hair and caused his bedsheet to flutter to the side. Belac wiggled his toes in the air. *I am going to need shoes.*

He had expected them to simply lower him into the sea, but a man on the ship reached out with a long crook and hooked the line. The elf was swung over to the ship and lowered onto the deck. The sailor unfastened the rope from Belac's leather waist harness and then tugged on the rope three times. He waited a moment before tugging on the rope again, and then the sailor tossed the rope overboard, trusting the men above to understand his message.

The sailor turned and smiled, showing off his missing teeth. "Best get below deck with the other."

Belac saw no reason why he could not wait in the fresh air, but he did not argue. He went below deck, past a small kitchen area, and found the main hold. Ecard sat on a coil of thick rope, staring at his hands. At first, Belac did not think the man realized he was there.

Then Ecard spoke. "I did not believe you."

The gravity of the man's confession set off a warning in the elf. Belac' left hand moved to his scabbard, securing it for a faster draw. He had wanted to save the man, but Belac was prepared to cut him down if he proved to be a threat. *I will need to be careful with the sword in here. It is a tight space, and I don't want the blade to get caught on anything. A short swipe, and then a thrust.*

Ecard looked up from his hands. "How could you be so sure?"

Belac relaxed a little, but he did not remove his hand from the scabbard. "Sure, about what?"

"That you would escape!" The man was untethering.

Belac was confused. "We did escape."

Ecard shook his head, his wild hair whipping about violently. "But how did you know?!" His voice quivered as if he were close to tears. "How did you know not to give up?"

Belac had not really thought about it. *I was not really there for very long.* Still, Belac did not think he ever would have given up. "I would have just kept trying."

"You think it is just that easy?" There was accusation in Ecard's question.

Belac shrugged. "I did not say it would have been easy." *Though, it kind of was.*

Ecard laughed mirthlessly and went back to staring at his hands. "And what if you had died?" His voice was soft and sounded lost. "What if you had died in that place without ever getting free?"

Belac did not see much point in the question. "Then, I would have never known I failed?" *Because, I would be dead. That is how being dead works.*

"To never know failure..." Ecard accepted the answer as if it were something profound.

A thump came from the deck above. Belac decided to leave Ecard to his own thoughts. He retraced his steps and returned topside, curious who had come down from the cliff. When he saw that it was Vairug, he considered pushing him off the ship.

Belac leaned out over the railing and looked down at the water. "Do you think you could swim with only one hand?"

Vairug frowned at the elf.

"Maybe we should take a vote," Belac suggested.

The sailor stepped away from the orc and tugged on the rope before throwing it overboard.

Belac raised his hand. "Everyone that wants to find out if Vairug can swim, raise their hand."

Vairug tilted his head to the side and stared at the elf.

The sailor looked like he wanted to be anywhere else.

Belac lowered his hand. "Now, everyone that wants to watch the orc drown in the ocean," he began to shout, "because he threw me off a cliff!" then he spoke calmly, "Raise your hand." Belac raised his hand back up dramatically.

Vairug straitened his head and looked down at the elf. "Rolan pushed you."

Belac pointed a finger at the orc, trying to think of an argument. "Your right."

"You know..." Vairug looked up toward the ascending rope. "Rolan is coming down next..." he said slyly.

Belac's grin hurt his face. He gazed up the cliff face, ringing his hand villainously as he waited for the dwarf to be lowered. He felt like a lion, waiting in its pit to be fed.

When Rolan was finally within reach, the sailor hooked the line. Belac silently took the crook from the man before he could pull Rolan aboard. The elf began to work the crook in a tight circle, causing the dwarf to swing wide.

Rolan's short legs kicked frantically as he tried to maintain his balance. "Stop it, Belac!"

Belac leaned out toward the dwarf. "Maybe we should take a vote!"

"Sodding ingrate!" Rolan shouted.

The rope slipped out of the crook and Belac stumbled, almost dropping it overboard. Rolan quickly regained control of his momentum and began to climb the rope as it continued to lower him toward the water. The dwarf began to swing back and forth, bringing himself closer to the ship. Belac looked around for help. Vairug was below deck, peeking up from the steps. Belac handed the crook to the sailor and ran.

Rolan landed on the deck with a thud. He untied the rope and then chased after the elf. *There is nowhere to go!* Belac did not want to jump into the ocean, but he knew he would be trapped if he fled below deck. He ran to the main mast and began to climb. The elf no longer felt like a lion. He felt like a treed house cat fleeing an angry badger.

"Dwarves can't climb trees!" Belac knew what he said made no sense.

He climbed up to the crow's nest and looked down expecting to see Rolan climbing up with a knife in his teeth. The dwarf stood at the base of mast, looking up. Belac knew what he was thinking. Rolan was trying to decide between cutting down the mast or setting it on fire.

Belac looked to the smaller mast, wondering if he could make the jump. *Nope. That would kill me.* He looked back down. Rolan was gone. It did not make the elf feel safer. He looked around, but Rolan was nowhere to be seen.

Belac watched from the crow's nest as one of the sailors was lowered from above. *How is the last one going to get down? There is no one left up there to lower him.* Instead of tossing the end of the rope overboard to be pulled back up, the sailors on deck tied another rope to it. One of them held the rope while the other wrapped a new rope around the ship's rail before binding the two ropes together. They tugged on the newly bound rope and braced themselves. When it tightened, they let out the rope hand over hand. It twisted around the railing to slowly rise up the cliff, lowering the last sailor down. *Pirates are clever.*

When the last sailor landed on the deck, the others wasted no time untying him. They immediately began to set sail while he untied himself and pulled the other end of the rope back down. The men were professionals and it showed.

Watching them work, Belac had forgotten about the homicidal dwarf hunting him. Remembering with a start, the elf spun around in the crow's nest, scared Rolan might be behind him. The crow's nest was mercifully free of dwarves. Belac breathed a sigh of relief. He scanned the deck of the ship, searching for Rolan, but the dwarf was still nowhere to be found. Belac sat down in the crow's nest. He did not think for a moment that Rolan had forgotten about him. *A dwarf might forget how much they have had to drink, but they will never forget a grudge.*

As the ship pulled away from the cliffs, the full grandeur of Harborage came into view. High above were mansions of matching stone. While each was unique, they shared a design similar to that of the castle proper. What distinguished them most, were the vibrant colors of their elaborate rooves. Each was painted an exotic color of which Belac had never seen before. Basking in the light of the sun, the homes of the aristocracy were a declaration of life and prosperity.

Above them all, towered the castle Belac had recently escaped. He looked away from the fortress, his eyes following the coast. Farther away, the cliffs became lower and lower until they reached a city of nautical artisanship that stretched out along the shore. It was an assemblage of wooden buildings that could only have been shaped by the same masters that were responsible for the ships that filled the harbor. The harbor itself was an extension of the city, following the coast and causing Harbridge to seem like a city spilling into the sea.

It was a place unlike any other in the world, yet Belac was glad to leave it behind. He remained in the crow's nest as they continued out to sea, resigned to sitting up there until they reached whatever port they stopped at next. However, a port is not where they stopped. With Harbridge still in sight, if barely so, they met another ship.

Belac counted three masts on the larger vessel. At first, he worried it was there to arrest them. He dismissed the idea quickly. *Rolan would not have stopped for them if they were here to arrest us. He would have just blown them up or something.* The sails were dropped, and then lines were thrown between the ships so that they could be brought closer together.

Now, Belac had a dilemma. He looked down from the crow's nest to find Rolan staring back up at him. The dwarf knew Belac could not stay up there. So did Belac.

Belac looked from one ship to the other. "Maybe you should wait for me over there," he called down to the dwarf.

"Thanks," Rolan called back up in a friendly voice that was obviously false. "But I don't mind waiting for you here. Come on down."

"Promise you will not throw me in the ocean," Belac replied.

After a moment, Rolan loudly said, "No." His voice was no longer friendly.

I am not going down there. Belac looked to the other ship. *I really need to get a magic carpet.* His attention returned to the ship he was trapped on. Rigging ran from the top of the mast to the end of the boom. *If I can get to that wooden arm thing, I can jump over to the other ship.*

Belac swung out and wrapped a leg around a rope. His plan had been to slide down, but the feel of the rope against his bare leg changed his mind. He moved his hands to the rope and then let his legs hang below him. Shifting his weight, he swung from hand to hand as he lowered himself down the rope. The angle made the maneuver awkward, and he found himself having to move faster the farther he went. Unable to keep up, his hands slipped.

The elf fell backward with a shout. His shoulder clipped the boom and he fell into the ocean. The water felt like a slap to the face. Disoriented, Belac flailed below the surface. He could not distinguish up from down. *The ocean is trying to eat me!* The black anchor on his new sword suddenly felt like more than a decoration. As the sword pulled against him, it felt like an anchor in truth. *If the sword is pulling me down…* Belac struggled against the weight of the sword, realizing up must be the other way.

He broke the surface of the water, trying to breathe and spit out sea water at the same time. He splashed loudly as he fought to stay above the water. He would have lost his bedsheet if it had not been held down by the baldric of his sword and the thick leather belt he still wore.

"Help!" Belac shouted up between the ships.

A rope was tossed down from the larger ship. Belac grabbed the rope and allowed it to take his weight as he waited to be pulled up. After he caught his breath, the elf frowned. No one was pulling him up. He tugged on the rope three times. He waited while no one pulled him back up. He tugged on the rope again. *They are not going to pull me up.*

Belac swished around in the water, placing his bare feet against the hull of the ship. "If I get a splinter…" he grumbled as he used the rope to walk up the side of the ship.

When Belac neared the railing, he was forced to stop and consider. He needed to change the way he was climbing and was unsure how to go about it. Rolan leaned out over the rail. The dwarf smiled and waved before the line went slack.

Belac screamed something unkind as he fell.

Nine

"Why are we going back to Harbridge?" Belac asked of no one in particular. *I do not want to go back to Harbridge.*

"We are not headed back to Harbridge," an unfamiliar voice said from behind the elf. "At least, not at the moment."

It sure looks like we are headed to Harbridge to me. Belac turned away from the bow of the ship. He recognized the bald man immediately. "Hey! It's you. From the fire in Tariel." He pointed at the man. "I saved your life!"

The man tapped his nose and then nodded agreeably, spreading his arms wide. A pale blue tunic covered his rotund midsection in the style of Tariel. "And now, I have saved yours." His voice was a little higher than was common among men.

Belac appreciated that the man had the sense to wear trousers under his tunic. "You saved me?" *I do not remember seeing you in the prison.*

The man lowered his arms and leaned forward. "I contributed," he said conspiratorially.

Belac took him at his word. "Thanks. It makes me extra glad you're not dead."

The man laughed. "Yes, well, I always pay my debts."

"Wait." Belac realized something did not add up. "How are you not dead."

"From what I understand, I have you to thank for that," the man replied. "You and your large friend."

Belac shook his head. "I am not talking about the fire. How did you survive Tariel? The colossus destroyed everything."

"Ah," the man said nodding. "I see your confusion." He furrowed his brow. "I doubt this 'colossus' destroyed everything. Also, there would have been many who fled the city. Tariel is likely to have survivors that outnumber the dead."

Belac had no way of knowing what the colossus had done after the pond closed. It could have laid waste to the entire city in frustration and rage. He did not see how anyone left behind could have survived. "How did you escape? Is the pond working again? Did anyone else come through with you? What happened to the colossus?"

The man held up his hand, halting the elf's questions. "When I left Tariel, all was well. If someone other than Rolan Brightstone had told me of what transpired, I would have doubted the account."

Brightstone? Belac pushed the thought away. *I have more important concerns than Rolan's name.* "Then how are you even here?"

"Well, I used the pond," the man said as if the answer should have been evident.

How? Belac tried to make sense of things. "You knew it would be opened early?"

"There is a reason people call him 'Daikon Knowit,'' Rolan said joining them.

The dwarf's sudden appearance startled Belac. He was still worried Rolan was going to throw him back into the ocean. Belac had just started to get dry, and he was in no mood for another swim.

"They call me 'Daikon Knowit' because it is my name, Rolan." The man said unconvincingly.

"Sure, it is," Rolan sounded like he knew a secret.

Belac did not really care what the man's name was. "If we are not going to Harbridge, why does it look like we are going to Harbridge?"

Daikon seemed pleased to answer the question. "We plan to follow the coastline past the city. From what I understand, Rolan has arranged further transportation."

Belac assumed the wind had something to do with their heading, but it still looked like they were headed to Harbridge to him. "Then, where are we going?"

"Be careful asking Daikon too many questions," Rolan warned. "He keeps a tally in his head."

"Rolan…" Daikon said in mock affront.

Rolan stepped to the side and pointed with his hand to an open hatch. "Vairug has a change of clothes for you. He should be easy enough to find below deck."

Belac worried it might be a trap. He narrowed his eyes at the hatch.

"Or you can stay up here in a bedsheet," Rolan added irritably.

Belac turned toward the dwarf. "How did you know we would need clothes?"

"Both you and Vairug got pretty torn up escaping Tariel." Rolan shrugged. "And you lose stuff."

"I do not!" Belac argued.

"You are wearing a bedsheet," Rolan said dryly.

"I…" Belac stopped. *Okay, maybe I lose stuff.*

"Right." Rolan nodded.

Belac turned away and bumped into a sailor. "Oh! Sorry."

The sailor nodded absently, returning to his work. "The Deep be with you."

Belac took an indirect path to the hatch. There were more sailors on deck, and he did not want to distract them. He was worried he would cause one of them to make a mistake, and the ship would crash into Harbridge. *I do not want to go back to Harbridge.* He climbed down through the hatch, having to kick his bedsheet out of the way to keep from stepping on it. The climb down was short, but it made Belac question why any woman would tolerate a dress. *I hope Rolan got me trousers.*

The ship was larger than the last; however, it was still easy to locate Vairug. *The orc is usually quiet, but he is not exactly small.* Belac found him in a cramped compartment doing his best to pretend Ecard was not sitting in the room with him. Sitting on crates, Vairug was leaned back staring at the ceiling, while Ecard stared at the floor. *It is probably better if they don't talk to each other too much anyway.*

Belac stepped into the stuffy compartment, though it was an uncomfortably close space. "Hey um… Lord Vairdoe," he tried to remind the orc who he was supposed to be. "Rolan said you have some clothes for me."

Vairug leaned forward, reached down, and picked up a leather bag with its strap cinched tight. Without saying anything, he tossed the bag to Belac. The elf hoped that the clothes inside were nicer than what Vairug had on. *It's all brown.* The orc's short boots and long trousers were slightly different shades of dark brown. His wool shirt was of a lighter color, yet it too was brown.

"We need to get you another red sash," Belac said. He thought the crimson sash had looked nice on the orc. *It somehow made him look a little more sophisticated. Sure, he still looked like something that might rip your head off, but the sash helped.*

Vairug leaned back and returned to staring at the ceiling. "I do not think that is a high priority at the moment."

Belac uncinched the strap on the leather bag and then dumped its contents on the floor. "Nonsense," he said as he began to change clothes. "It is not enough to save the world. You have to look good doing it."

"Is that so?" Vairug asked though it was obvious he disagreed.

"Why would you just save the world?" Belac asked, "When you could save the world and inspire people at the same time?" *And be famous.*

Vairug tilted his head to the side so that he could look at the elf.

Belac knew that he was on to something. He tried to figure out how to explain as he spoke. "Saving the world is hard work." He had never thought about it, but it felt like he was explaining something he understood. "But if you look the part, you can inspire other people while you're at it. If you can do that, they won't just help you, they will go off on their own and keep trying to make the world a better place." *Hopefully a better place for us.* "What is the cost of a sash when compared to that?" *Besides, there has got to be some way to make money being a famous hero.*

Ecard looked up from the floor. "The elves are wise."

Vairug laughed silently at the man.

Belac narrowed his eyes at the orc.

Ten

"I am not wearing this, Rolan." Belac held out the crumpled cloth as if it might bite him.

Rolan did not take the cloak. "Then, you can freeze to death."

Belac narrowed his eyes at the dwarf. *He did this on purpose!* "It's green!"

Rolan did a poor job of trying to hide his grin. "Is it?"

"You know it is!" Just holding the cloak made Belac uncomfortable. He thought about throwing it into the ocean. Then he thought about throwing the dwarf.

"What do you know?" Rolan asked disingenuously. "It is green."

With the exception of the cloak, all of Belac's new clothes matched the browns Vairug now wore. Rolan must have made a special effort to find the richly dyed green cloak. *I bet he paid extra for it!* Belac wanted to wrap the cloak around a rock and beat the dwarf to death with it.

Vairug reached out and took the cloak without saying anything. When Belac turned to thank him, Vairug stuffed the cloak into the leather bag at the elf side. Vairug smiled, his tusks jutting out.

Belac did not thank him.

"Now get in the boat," Rolan said.

Belac turned back toward the dwarf and held out his hands. "I am in the boat." *Stupid dwarf.*

"No," Rolan corrected him. "You are on a ship." He pointed his hand out over the rear of the ship. "Get in the boat."

Belac leaned out over the rail. Two sailors waited in a rowboat suspended below deck level. The men looked thoroughly untrustworthy. "Maybe we should lower Ecard down first."

"He is not going with us," Rolan replied.

What? "Why not?" Belac asked the dwarf.

Vairug answered, "He is useless."

Belac narrowed his eyes at the orc.

"Vairug is right," Rolan tried to preempt an argument.

Belac argued. "We can't just abandon the man."

"Sure, we can," Rolan said dismissively.

Vairug nodded.

Rolan continued before the elf could speak. "Daikon will see him safe, and then the man can make his own way." He cut his hand through the air. "Ecard would be nothing but a problem for us if we took him."

Belac nodded grudgingly. *We can't give him the opportunity to question 'Lord Vairdoe.'*

Vairug gestured down to the main deck. "Does he know he is not coming with us?"

Clad in Belac's old bedsheet, Ecard was a wretched sight to behold. *Now that I am looking at him, I am kind of glad we cannot take him with us.* The man looked lost until he located them on the stern deck. As Ecard made his way up the steps, Belac noticed that the man was already moving around better. *I wonder how much of him will recover.*

Ecard looked from the orc to the elf. "You are leaving."

Belac did not know if the man had overheard something or if he was simply guessing. "We still have a dragon to kill."

Rolan made it clear the man would not be coming with them. "Daikon will see you safe."

Ecard's gaze returned to the orc. "And you, Lord Vairdoe, do you have any advice for me?"

Vairug was quiet for a moment before answering, "Do not forget to keep your pinky up when you drink." He held up his pinky as he had at the tailor in Tariel.

Ecard shook his head slowly. "You are the wisest men I have ever known."

Rolan coughed and turned away.

Belac grinned and stepped up onto the rail of the ship. "Be sure to remember that when you tell the story." He hopped down into the dinghy waiting below. *Having my sword strapped to my back definitely has some advantages.* If he had attempted the jump with a sword at his hip, it likely would have caught on something.

Vairug was more careful getting down. As the orc climbed into the boat with the use of only one functioning hand, Belac considered trying to help. *I would probably just get in his way. With my luck, he would end up pushing me overboard.* Vairug sat down on the bench in the middle of the dinghy, repositioning the mace sticking out of his bag.

Rolan vaulted over the railing and landed in the boat with them. *It is amazing that backpack never throws him off balance.* The dwarf stomped his foot twice and called back up, "Lower us down."

The rowboat lurched and then began to descend. Belac lost his footing and had to grab the side of the boat. He quickly lowered himself to the bottom and braced his feet against the other side. His scabbarded sword pressed into his back uncomfortably. *Worth it.*

Rolan stood firm as the dinghy shimmied in the air. After the boat settled into the water, the sailors unhooked the rigging and extended the oars. One of them began to whistle a jaunty tune while the other rowed them toward shore. The dwarf put his hands on his hips and stared off into the inland.

Belac relaxed and then sat up to better see where they were headed. He held up a hand to shade his eyes. *It is almost like the sun moves through the sky just so it can blind me no matter which way I am facing.*

On the other side of a rocky shore, were rolling hills of dry grass. More golden than green, the grass stirred in a cool breeze that Belac could feel already. They had passed beyond the busy docks of Harbridge, and the country that awaited them felt empty in comparison. Mountains in the distance crowded the shore and marked the southern border of Enevic.

The dinghy beached on the rocky shore, and the whistling stopped. The sailor at the bow hopped over the side and stabilized the boat. Rolan marched off the dinghy and continued inland.

Belac used the side of the boat to get to his feet and then hurried after the dwarf. "Thanks for the ride," he said to the sailor holding the boat.

"May The Deep be with you," the sailor replied.

Maybe they are not pirates after all. They seem nice enough. Belac thought for a moment. *And not one of them had on a red sash.*

After Vairug jumped down next to Belac, the sailor began to push the dinghy back into the sea. Together, Belac and the orc trudged across the rocks to catch up with Rolan.

"You are kind of in a hurry," Belac noted.

Rolan did not slow his pace. "It is getting late."

Belac had more questions. "Where are we going?" he asked as they walked up a grassy rise.

"There is a wagon waiting for us on the other side of the next hill," Rolan told him.

"What? Why?" Belac asked. *You better not be taking us back to Harbridge.*

Rolan answered the why. "Because I told them to."

Belac frowned at the dwarf. "Fine. But how do you know they are there?"

"I could see them from the ship," Rolan explained. "Why else do you think we stopped here?" He held out his hands, encompassing the countryside.

"I don't know," Belac said, getting a little irritated. "That is why I am asking you."

Rolan sighed. "I hired a wagon and a team to move it. They are waiting for us up ahead by the road. We need to meet up with them and then they can take us to our camp for the night." He looked over at the elf. "I would rather get there before it's dark."

Belac nodded. *That all makes sense.* "Then what?"

"Then, we sleep." Rolan sounded like he needed sleep.

Grumpy dwarf. Belac was about to press Rolan for more answers, but Vairug stepped between them.

"Will there be food at this camp?" Vairug asked.

"There had better be." Rolan shook his head. "If there's not, I might end up eating one of the horses."

When the wagon came into view, Belac was surprised by its size. He had expected it to be a modest flatbed with a canvas covering. What Rolan had arranged was a long wooden enclosure that looked more like a small house on wheels.

"I don't see any horses," Belac said. *Maybe they already ate them.* "I am not pulling that wagon, Rolan."

Vairug nodded. "Agreed."

Rolan pointed his hand off to the right. "Do you see the way those two hills come together there?" He moved his hand a little to the left. "There is probably a brook that runs through over there. If I had to guess, I would say the horses are on the other side of that hill getting watered."

"Guess all you want," Belac said. "I am still not pulling the wagon."

As they approached the wagon, a man with dirty blond hair and a smile hopped down from the driver's bench, shouting, "Rolan!"

"I see you," Rolan grumbled.

The man was dressed plainly, with a cream colored blouse tucked into brown trousers. A longsword hung from his back, and he moved as if he were accustomed to its weight. "Rolan! It is so good to see you!" he said louder than Belac thought was necessary.

Men began to exit the rear of the wagon. Belac counted six. All of them carried a weapon of some type.

"That is more men than I paid for," Rolan said in a conversational tone.

The men spread out to either side of the man who had issued the greeting. The formation made it clear he was the one who lead them. Belac took a couple of steps to the side, instinctually wanting to prevent the men from getting too far to his right.

The leader held his arms out to his sides, smiling. "I do not think payment is going to be a problem."

If the man is trying to put me at ease, he is bad at his job. Belac looked at the other men again. The weapons they carried were not sheathed or put away; they were held in their hands, ready for use.

Eleven

"You are making a mistake, Larry." Rolan did not seem overly concerned by it.

The man took offence. "My name is not 'Larry!"

Rolan turned to the orc. "I thought his name was 'Larry."

Not-Larry pointed at the dwarf. "You know my name!"

Rolan returned his attention to the man. "Are you sure it's not 'Larry?"

"I know my name!" Not-Larry shouted at the dwarf.

Rolan held out his hands. "I thought you said, I knew it?"

"What?" Not-Larry was having trouble keeping up with the dwarf's banter.

Rolan loosened the straps of his backpack. "Here," he said removing the pack.

Not-Larry stared at the dwarf in confusion. Rolan walked forward and tossed the pack to him. Not-Larry caught the pack and Rolan buried a knife high on the inside of the man's thigh. Before the other men could respond, Rolan darted toward the ones on his left.

Vairug responded immediately. Holding his leather bag down with his left forearm, he attempted to pull free his cogged mace. He let out a growl of pain when an arrow punched into the left side of his chest.

Belac tried to draw his sword as he moved farther to the right and away from the violence. The sword was too long for the blade to clear the scabbard. Frantically, he slipped his head out of the baldric and drew the longsword, dropping the scabbard as soon as it was free.

A man came at Belac with a rapier. Having years of experience using such a slim blade, Belac knew to expect the lunge. He did not engage the blade, instead waiting for the man to commit before stepping to the side with a backhanded sweep of his longsword. The blade slashed through the man's bicep, rendering the arm useless. Belac reversed the swing, and the tip of his blade cut into the side of the man's neck. Belac continued to follow the blade's momentum, turning to face the wagon. *I have to stop the archer.* He did not know if the man with the rapier was dead, but Belac could not stop to finish him. Rolan would be a challenging target for the bowman. *The dwarf is fast, and short, and he moves like a crazy person.* Vairug, however, would be hard to miss.

Belac leapt up onto the driver's bench of the wagon and swung his longsword in a horizontal arch over the top of the cabin. The blade hacked through the back of the bowman's left ankle. The man cried out in pain and alarm before falling backward off the side of the wagon.

From his elevated position, Belac looked back to see if Vairug still lived. The orc grappled with one man while another with an axe attempted to circle around them. Vairug ripped the barbed arrow out of his own chest and stabbed his opponent in the neck. The man fell to his knees, pulling Vairug down with him. The man with the axe positioned himself to attack the exposed orc.

With a cry of fury, Belac jumped from the wagon, his sword held high above his head. Using the strength of both arms and the force of his fall, Belac brought the blade down in a savage blow. The sharpened steel landed above the man's shoulder and tore through his torso at an angle.

Belac looked over the man he had just cut in half, past the orc on the ground, and to the dwarf standing among the bodies of the fallen. From behind the wagon, a man with a shortsword charged at Rolan. The dwarf's back was to the man, and Belac did not know if Rolan could turn in time to save himself.

Without further thought, Belac threw his sword, shouting, "Rolan!"

Rolan dove forward as Belac's sword flew end over end. The blade intercepted the man, spinning him around after sinking into his chest. Rolan rolled over one of the corpses before coming to his feet at the same time as the man hit the ground. *I can't believe that worked.* Belac had only been attempting to disrupt the man's charge.

The elf looked down, breathing hard. The dirt under his boots had turned into a bloody sludge. *I am glad I still can't smell anything.* Vairug rose, growling at the pain in his chest. A pathetic moan came from the man with Belac's sword sticking out of him.

Rolan walked over and kicked the man in the head. The man recoiled, but was too hurt to fight back. Rolan put a foot on the man's chest and took hold of the sword's leather wrapped hilt. The steel scraped on something as Rolan pulled the blade free.

The man groaned in torment and then began to sob, "No. No. No…"

Rolan plunged the sword back into the man, ending his pleas. The dwarf jerked the blade back out and then stepped over the dead man. He held the sword up. "You know, you are not supposed to throw these?"

Now, who is the ingrate? Belac spread his arms wide. "It looks like it worked to me."

"But now what are you going to do about him?" Rolan pointed with his other hand.

Belac spun around to see who was behind him. He fell backward, landing on his backside. Scooting away, he searched for the threat though there was no one behind him other than Vairug.

A black anchor came into view on Belac's right. He turned his head and found Rolan holding out the longsword for him to take. Both the dwarf and the sword were smeared with blood. When Belac reached for the hilt, he saw that he too had blood on his hands.

"Die in a fire," Belac said, taking the sword.

Rolan said nothing. Obviously, he felt as if he had made his point. *Oh, I get the point. Next time, let the dwarf die!*

Rolan stepped around the dead and picked up his pack. Instead of returning it to his back, he opened the top and rummaged around inside while he walked to the orc. *I hope he has something that can fix Vairug.*

The faint sound of something dragging over dirt caught the elf's attention. Belac turned to his left, looking under the wagon. The bowman was crawling across the road, dragging his bloody stump behind him. Belac scampered under the wagon, chasing after the man. *I should have just walked around.* On the other side of the wagon, Belac stood and then approached the man cautiously.

The bowman rolled onto his back and stared up at the elf. Belac looked down at him without pity. The man had used his own belt as a tourniquet, but his face was blanched white and waxy.

The man held his hand out feebly. All he could manage to say was, "Peace."

Belac shrugged. "Sure," he said, and then stabbed the man in the chest. After pulling the blade free, he held up the sword and considered the blood. *I need to find something I can use to clean this off.*

Belac walked around the front of the wagon toward the first of the men he had killed in the fight. The man had died on his knees with his face pressed to the ground. Using the back of the man's shirt, Belac cleaned his sword as best he could. He then retrieved his discarded scabbard and slid the blade home.

Belac looked over the field of dead. *I don't feel anything.* He did not care that he had just helped kill nine men. He did not feel the need to rationalize it or explain it away. His foes were dead. Belac's thoughts would have troubled him if he had taken the time to analyze them. Instead, he walked over to the kneeling dead man, and kicked him over. He tugged off the man's boots, and then drew a small knife from its sheath on the man's hip.

Belac strode past the man he had cleaved in two, and joined his friends at the front of the wagon. Vairug was sitting on the side step to the driver's bench while Rolan bandaged the wound in his chest. Belac dropped the pair of boots in the orc's lap.

Vairug looked at the elf, confused. "What do you want me to do with these?"

Belac stabbed the small knife into the side of the wagon next to the orc. "Eat them."

Rolan laughed as the elf walked away. "You still owe me a boat!"

Belac had decided that he wanted a knife for himself. *And anything else I can find.* He began to search the dead but was mostly disappointed with what he found. Finally, on one of the men Rolan had killed, he found a dagger worth taking. He took the sheath as well, but the man's belt had been slashed in the conflict. On another of the men, he found a belt he thought would work. The belt had been used to carry a small leather pouch. Inside the pouch was a stone and striker and coiled bit of twine. He kept the pouch but tossed the belt aside.

The elf returned to the corpse of the man who had fought with a rapier. *I know he has one.* Belac unbuckled the belt and stripped off the rapier scabbard and the crude leather knife sheath. He slid on the small leather pouch and his new dagger before belting it below the wide leather waist harness he wore around his midsection. He briefly considered taking the rapier but decided against it. *A rapier is great when I am only fighting one or two people, but that is just not my life right now.* He thought about what he had fought recently. *Monsters, small armies, small armies of monsters…* He did not think his life was going to get easier any time soon.

He walked back to Not-Larry and removed the man's longsword. Belac did not take the time to inspect the quality of the blade, but the undyed leather that covered the scabbard and wrapped the hilt was well worn. He returned to the front of the wagon and placed the sword on the driver's bench.

Vairug asked, "Are you taking trophies now?"

Belac shrugged. "Sometimes, I lose stuff."

Rolan chuckled and clapped the elf on the shoulder.

Belac did not understand the approval, but he recognized it for what it was. He nodded toward the orc. "Is he going to die?"

"Eventually," Rolan said in a dry tone.

Vairug showed his tusks with a smile. "Would you care to make a wager on that?"

Rolan chortled. "Might as well make it three wishes."

Belac smiled with them. *That is a safer bet than the one I made.* He narrowed his eyes at the orc. *But I never bet my boots!*

Twelve

"Are you sure the horses are over there?" Belac asked.

"No," Rolan said. "But I don't think they pulled that wagon all the way out here with humans." He gestured back to the men they had just killed.

Belac nodded. "That makes sense."

"That is why I said it," Rolan replied shortly.

Belac narrowed his eyes at the dwarf.

A horse whinnied on the other side of the hill. Belac increased his pace, hoping to avoid an 'I told you so,' from the dwarf. The sun hit his eyes as he crested the rise. Looking down, Belac continued to walk toward the sound of the horses.

"Hey!" called the voice of a young man.

Belac looked up at the man. *Of course. They left a guard.* He was glad he only saw one. *The man is not much more than a boy.* Not-Larry must have left the youngest of them to watch the horses.

Thrack. The man's head snapped back, and he fell into the brook. He appeared even younger in the motionlessness of death.

Belac growled angrily.

"What?" Rolan asked impatiently.

Belac pointed at the dead man. "Do you know how many dead bodies I had to search to find a belt?" The man's belt looked so new it could have been made that morning. "I'm taking it." The elf walked over to the dead man and straddled the brook.

"You just said, you already found one," Rolan pointed out.

"I don't care," Belac told him. "I am taking it." The belt slid easily off the young man's corpse. "I will just take them all." Belac swept his arm out across the world, the belt flopping around in his grip. "All the belts!" He stepped away from the brook. "And then, I can build a castle out of them. And when people walk by, they can point at it, and they can say, 'Oh, no. Don't go over there. That is where the crazy elf lives that will kill you and Steal! Your! Belt!"

Rolan laughed.

One of the horses snorted.

Belac narrowed his eyes at the horse. He thought it might be laughing at him too. There were four horses, and he thought they could stand to lose one.

"Hey," Rolan said laughing. "It's not the horse's fault your crazy."

"I'm crazy?!" Belac's eyes went wide.

Rolan nodded merrily. "A little bit."

Belac threw the belt. It flew over the dwarf's head and landed in the grass behind him.

Rolan was unperturbed. "There goes your evil belt empire."

One of the horses whinnied.

Belac turned his ire on them, trying to ascertain the offender. "I can always make more belts out of horse hide!"

"Not unless you want to pull the wagon," Rolan told him.

Belac narrowed his eyes at the horses. "I can wait."

"Glad to hear it," Rolan said dismissively. "Grab two of the leads, and let's get out of here."

The horses all looked the same to Belac. Their dark brown coats with long black manes, tails, and furry feet often referred to as feathers, were simply too uniform for him to tell them apart. "They sure are big."

Rolan took two of the horses' leads. "They are Enevician."

I guess they are kind of pretty. Belac gathered up the other two horses, taking a lead in each hand. "Maybe I won't turn you into belts."

The elf had calmed down by the time they returned to the wagon with the horses. Vairug was waiting for them and appeared to be recovering quickly. *Rolan must have crammed some of that pink pasty stuff into the wound.*

Vairug inspected the horses admiringly. "These are beautiful creatures."

Belac offered him the leads. "You can have them."

Rolan protested. "You cannot give away my horses, Belac."

Belac shrugged. "Fine." He nodded to the orc. "You can only have my two."

"They are all mine," Rolan insisted.

"All horses?" Belac asked.

Vairug shook his head. "You cannot claim all horses."

Rolan frowned at them. "Just these particular horses."

Belac held up a finger. "You said these horses were Enevician."

"That's right," Rolan agreed impatiently.

Belac pointed at the orc. "That means they are his."

"What?" Rolan stepped around the horse he had just harnessed to the wagon. "How?"

Belac held out both of his hands toward the orc in an introductory manor. "Lord Vairdoe of Enevic."

Vairug stood up straighter and tilted his head back with an exaggerated air of nobility.

Rolan shook his head. "Give me a break."

"You ask for clemency?" Belac nodded his head. "I may be able to negotiate on behalf of His Majesty Lord Vairdoe."

"His Majesty?" Rolan asked unmoved.

Vairug stood there and attempted to look more noble.

Belac answered as if the question had been respectful. "I may be able to convince him to rent them to you." He tapped the side of his nose. "Once we have negotiated suitable compensation."

Rolan took another one of the horses and positioned it in front of the wagon. "Lords don't tap their noses like that."

Belac did not argue. "That is why His Majesty has me."

Rolan harnessed the horse and then looked at the orc. "And you want to rent me my own horses?"

Belac interjected, "Once we have negotiated suitable compensation."

Rolan gruffed. "Maybe you are lords." He took the lead of another horse. Harnessing the horse, he said, "How about we deduct the tariff from your transportation fees?"

"What?" Belac did not like the sound of that. "No."

"Yeah," Rolan said agreeably. "It would be a good start toward paying what you already owe." He took the lead to the last horse and moved it into position. "The cost of hiring the two ships was considerable." He began to harness the horse. "The interest alone is enough to bury you."

Belac raised his voice. "You were rescuing us!"

Rolan nodded while he worked. "And I am prepared to temporarily wave that fee."

Vairug deflated and looked at the elf disapprovingly. "You are a bad negotiator."

"Wait," Belac said. "What if we reward you with the horses?" He searched for the correct phrasing. "For services rendered."

"Deal," Rolan agreed, stepping away from the horses.

Belac smiled happily and nudged Vairug.

Rolan continued, "Now, we just need to discuss the cost of your further transportation."

Belac pointed at the dwarf. "Now, wait right there!"

"No." Rolan shook his head. "Can't wait here. All this death is going to draw the ghouls soon. I plan on being well away from here before that sun finishes setting."

He is just trying to scare me. "Ghouls?" Belac asked uncertainly.

Rolan nodded and then walked to the back of the wagon.

"Um," Belac said, following after the dwarf. "Maybe we can work something out."

"Right." Rolan opened the door to the wagon. "Now, get inside."

"You don't want one of us to ride outside with you?" Belac did not want to leave the dwarf alone if there really were ghouls coming.

Rolan shook his head. "There are going to be people searching for you two. Anyone that sees us will remember an elf or an orc. We are probably not going to run into anyone else out here, but if we do, no one is going to think twice about a dwarf driving a wagon toward the old Enevician mines."

"But..." Belac began.

"We don't have time for this," Rolan said, interrupting him. "It's getting dark. We need to move. Get in the wagon."

Belac frowned at the dwarf but then climbed into the wagon. Inside the cabin, there were long benches along either side that looked about as comfortable as a prison cell. In the front of the cabin, wooden barrels and boxes had been stacked and lashed to the wall. *This place is definitely unfit for a lord.* He chose the bench on his left and took a seat.

Vairug climbed into the cabin behind him. The orc's size made the space feel even more confined. He sat on the bench across from Belac and then Rolan closed the door. The inside of the cabin was left darkened, lit only by the faint traces of light that crept through the closed door and side panels.

Belac's eyes adjusted as they waited for Rolan to get the wagon moving. *I wonder how far we can get before night comes.* The stacked boxes rattled as the wagon bounced them around. Belac could already tell this was not going to be a comfortable trip.

"You gave away my horses," Vairug said accusingly.

Belac narrowed his eyes at the orc but did not argue.

They rode without speaking while Belac tried to organize his thoughts. The inside of the cabin grew dimmer as they were jostled around. Vairug seemed content with the relative quiet.

Finally, Belac confessed, "I thought he left us."

After arriving at the Temple of the Ancient in Harbridge, Belac and Vairug had immediately been arrested. Rolan had backed away from them, blending in with the excited crowd. While there had been nothing the dwarf could have done to help them, Belac had felt abandoned. He had never expected Rolan to come rescue them.

"He did leave us," Vairug said matter-of-factly.

"I know," Belac struggled to explain, "But he came back."

"He did that too," Vairug allowed. "You are not wrong that he left. But you are wrong, if you think he did it because he is a coward. Rolan is not a coward."

"No, that is not it." The idea that the dwarf might be a coward had never even occurred to Belac. "I just didn't think he was going to come back."

Vairug grunted, but said nothing more.

Belac thought the only reason Rolan was able to continue as far into the night as he did was that the moon replaced the sun. After the wagon was brought to a halt, and the cabin door opened, the dwarf stood bathed in moonlight.

Rolan pointed his hand to a cloth sack on the floor of the cabin. "Toss me that bag."

Belac picked up the sack, but instead of throwing it, he handed it to the dwarf. "What's in it?"

"Hoods for the horses," Rolan told him.

Belac followed the dwarf out of the wagon. "So they won't run off?"

The wagon had been stopped in the grass on the side of the road just before its course veered off to the left. The horses were still harnessed and Belac got the impression Rolan was going to leave them that way for the night.

Belac felt like the horses deserved some relief after pulling the wagon. "Shouldn't we at least take off the harnesses?"

"No," Rolan said in a tone that would allow no argument. "It would be dangerous for them if we did." He began to put the hoods over the horses' heads. "Also, there is a chance we will need to run tonight. They need to be ready to go if we do."

The night seemed peaceful to Belac. "Why would we need to run?"

"I was not joking about the ghouls," Rolan told him.

"Then, why are we stopping at all?" Belac was incredulous.

"It is not safe to continue at night." Rolan finished hooding the horses.

Belac gestured to the road. "We got this far all right."

Rolan stepped away from the horses and waved the elf to the back of the wagon. "That was using the road. This is as far as we are taking the road."

Belac moved as the dwarf directed, but asked, "So you want to sleep while there's ghouls running around?"

"In the wagon. Yes." Rolan took hold of the door.

Belac crawled inside the cabin, feeling like bait in a trap. "How are we all going to fit in here?"

Rolan followed the elf inside, closing the door behind himself. "You and I each take a bench, Vairug sleeps on the floor."

Vairug made a grunt only the dwarf could interpret.

"You can sleep on the bench if you want to Vairug, but you are not going to fit," Rolan replied impatiently.

Vairug grunted again.

This time Belac thought he understood. *It sounds like "Fine. But don't expect me to like it."* The elf felt much the same way.

As they laid out for the night, Rolan said, "You are going to have to be quiet, Belac."

"What?" Belac felt a little insulted.

"I'm serious, Belac." Rolan's tone matched his claim. "The ghouls won't care about the horses, but you have to be quiet."

"Why don't they care about the horses?" Belac asked.

"Because they do not smell like people, and they are not dead," Rolan explained. "The ghouls should have plenty to eat without bothering us, but you have to be quiet."

Belac's curiosity was not satisfied. "But what..."

Vairug spoke over the elf. "Should we gag him?"

Rolan answered, "It might be better to just stake him down in the middle of the road."

Belac decided that curiosity would be easier to ignore than hungry ghouls.

Thirteen

Sleep was not something the elf found that night. In undismissible fear, he had strained his hearing in an effort to discern what might be coming to kill them. The only sound he could be sure of was that of the sharp wind that howled as it blew past the wagon. However, Belac could have sworn that masked beneath the wind, he could hear the sounds of pattering feet and the gnashing of teeth. All the while, strange shapes had created fluttering shadows in the moonlight that crept into the cabin.

When Rolan sat up suddenly on the bench across from him, Belac almost screamed.

"Are the zombies here?" Belac asked in fright.

"Ghouls are not zombies," Rolan replied.

"Whatever." Belac looked around in the dark wagon. "Are they here to eat us?"

Rolan rubbed the sleep out of his eyes. "They should be gone by now. Why don't you go check?"

Belac did not want to be the one to stick his head out the door just to see if something bit it off. "...It's still dark out."

"No," Rolan corrected him. "It is dark in here. It's early dawn out there. You should be able to see."

That means they can see me! Belac knew the argument would not add up with his last one, so instead he suggested, "Maybe we should wait a little longer." *Like until one of you two go first.*

Rolan moved to the front of the cabin and began to rearrange boxes. "Sure. But try not to think about waterfalls while you wait."

What do waterfalls...? "Die in a fire," Belac told him sourly.

"Not if I stay close enough to hear the waterfall." Rolan slammed a box down on the bench.

Vairug growled at him from the floor.

Belac looked toward the door in the back of the cabin. *No choice now... Evil little dwarf.* He got up and stepped around Vairug as he made his way to the door. He cracked the door open and looked outside. Rolan had been right. Belac could see outside, if not well.

Vairug grabbed the elf's ankle and went, "Rarrr!"

Belac threw the door open in his haste to get away. He tried to turn while jumping away and fell backward out of the wagon.

Lying on his back in the trodden grass, Belac stared up at the dim sky while the orc laughed at him. *I don't have my sword.* He wanted to be mad at Vairug, but was too angry with himself. *What if there had been zombies, or ghouls, or whatever? What if there had been something out here waiting to kill me? I did not even remember to bring a sword. What was I going to do? Face monsters with nothing but a dagger and a belly full of fear?*

Belac climbed to his feet and then reached over the orc to take his longsword with the black anchor. He did not say anything to Vairug. Belac was not mad at him, but he was not going to thank the orc for the reminder either.

The elf looked around the outside of the wagon, searching first for present threats, and then for signs that any may have been there previously. He expected to find trails of footprints surrounding the wagon, but there was nothing in the vicinity that suggested anything had stalked them in the night. *Did Rolan make up the story about the ghouls?* He considered why the dwarf might do that. *Maybe he thought it would be funny.* Belac frowned. *Or he just wanted me to be quiet so he could sleep.*

Whether or not there had ever been ghouls in the night, there was nothing the elf could see that worried him at the moment. He slipped the baldric over his head and hung the sword on his back. His hair got caught under the strap, so he took the time to straighten it as best he could without a comb. He ran his fingers through the long black mess until he got out the worst of the tangles, before tying it in a knot behind his head. *I am going to need to make a comb or something.*

Remembering waterfalls, he scanned the landscape for a convenient tree. Finding nothing suitable, he returned to the back of the wagon. Vairug had not moved, but Rolan was already preparing for the journey ahead. The dwarf slid steel darts into his leather pouches, replacing what he had shot with ammunition he pulled from a box on the bench inside the cabin.

"Hey, Rolan..." Belac coughed. "There are no trees."

Rolan waved his hand dismissively. "Then use the side of a hill."

Belac shrugged and then did as the dwarf had instructed. When he returned to the wagon, Rolan was busy rearranging boxes once more.

"What now?" Belac asked the dwarf.

Rolan stepped around the orc and hopped out of the cabin. He handed the elf a waterskin and a waxed paper package. "You take this and climb up on top of the wagon. Go ahead and eat, but keep an eye out while you do. Watch down the road the way we came. If you see any movement or dust in the air, call out." He knocked on the side of the wagon. "Time to get up Vairug. I need you to give me a hand."

Vairug sat up. "That is not funny, Rolan."

Rolan shook his head. "I've told you Vairug, I am not changing the way I speak every time one of you two get something chopped off."

Belac's eyes went wide. *I don't want anything chopped off!*

Vairug frowned at the dwarf.

"Now get up," Rolan continued. "Harnessing the horses was simple enough, but we need to brush them down, and you can reach the top of their backs easier than I can."

Vairug growled, but he got up and stepped out of the cabin.

Belac went around to the front of the wagon and used the driver's bench to climb up on top. He sat cross-legged, facing the rear so he could watch the road while he ate. The sun had begun to rise over the ocean on his left, but he saw no evidence that anyone from Harbridge was coming to kill them.

The trail rations that Rolan had provided tasted like nothing. Belac realized it was not the rations. *I still can't taste anything.* He sniffed the air. *Nothing.* He thought about the night he had spent trapped in the cabin with Rolan and Vairug. *Maybe I should be glad I can't smell or taste anything.*

After he finished his breakfast, he continued to watch the road while Rolan and Vairug prepared themselves, the horses, and the wagon to move. They worked quickly and were ready to go by the time the sun was fully in the horizon.

Belac called down from the top of the wagon, "Shouldn't we feed and water the horses or something?"

Rolan climbed up onto the driver's bench to better speak with the elf. "We will. But first, I want to get to that river up ahead."

"I don't see a river," Belac said.

Rolan pointed towards the mountains with his hand. "Do you see those trees?"

Belac looked in the direction the dwarf had indicated. "No, I don't see anything but those bushes there." He pointed.

Rolan lowered his hand. "They're not bushes. What you are seeing is the tops of trees on the other side of a hill."

Belac nodded his understanding.

Rolan continued. "We can't stay on the road, so I am going to have you walk out in front of the horses and look for holes we might fall into or rocks we might hit. Keep us moving toward that stand of trees, but pay attention."

"What do we do if there is a hole or something?" Belac asked.

"Lead us around it if you can," Rolan explained. "If you can't, we will need to pull out the planks under the wagon."

Belac thought that sounded easy. *Not as easy as riding on a wagon.* "Why do I have to walk?"

"You and Vairug are going to take turns," Rolan gestured toward the orc. "He still needs to eat, so you go first."

Belac noticed the dwarf did not mention himself. "What about you?"

"I am driving the wagon," Rolan told him. It was a statement of fact. "Just lead us to the trees. Then we can feed and water the horses, and Vairug can take over while you ride up here with me."

Belac frowned. "Fine. But if a monster killer rabbit or something jumps out of a hole and bites off my leg, and then I bleed out and die, I am going to blame you."

Rolan gave a short nod. "I can live with that."

Belac climbed down from the wagon and positioned himself in front of the horses. He made sure he was far enough out that Rolan would have time to change course, but not so far that he could not yell at the dwarf if he wanted to. Once they began to move, Belac found that he enjoyed the walk.

There were a few times that he redirected the wagon. One of which was simply to see how it would work when he did. The other times may or may not have been necessary, but the elf chose to error on the side of caution.

"Better an extra step than a broken foot," Belac quoted the old saying to himself.

He was just about to congratulate himself on how good a job he was doing leading the wagon, when something occurred to him. *I don't know where we are going.*

Fourteen

"Where are we going?" Belac asked.

Seated next to him on the wagon, Rolan pointed with his hand toward the mountains ahead. "That way."

"No, Rolan." Belac did not even bother looking where the dwarf had pointed. "We took care of the horses, we crossed the river, no one is trying to kill us." He swept his hands in an X in front of himself. "No more excuses." He spoke as forcefully as he could. "Where are we going?"

Rolan looked at the elf sideways. "No, really. That way."

Belac pointed toward the immense gray mountain range. "That way?"

Rolan nodded. "Right."

"Toward the mountains?" Belac pressed irritably.

Rolan nodded again. "Right."

"Why?" Belac shouted. "What's in the mountains?" *And if he says, 'rocks,' I am going to...*

"Giants," Rolan said simply.

Belac looked at the mountains. "...Giants?" He remembered the colossus in Tariel. He remembered the destruction and the sheer unstoppable size of the thing.

Rolan reminded him of something else. "We need one to forge the sword."

Belac turned his head toward the dwarf, but his eyes did not want to leave the mountains. "How do you even know they are there?" *I don't see any giants.*

"Serath says they're there," Rolan told him. "If Serath says they're there, they are there." He sounded sure.

"You spoke to Serath?" Belac asked relieved. "How did he make it out of Tariel? Where is he?"

Rolan shook his head. "No, I have not seen him since we took the pond. I do not know where he is now."

Belac's relief evaporated. "Then, maybe we should wait on him." *And if he never shows, I never have to face a giant.*

"No," Rolan replied, but he did not sound as if he thought the idea was necessarily a bad one. "Serath said that time was an issue. We can't just wait. I am sure the colossus in Tariel is going to interfere with his plans some, but we can do this. If we can find the giants and convince a smith to come with us, we will be ready to head to the volcano when Serath finds us."

Belac's eyes had finally focused on the dwarf. "You say that like you are ordering a sandwich!" He lowered the pitch of his voice mockingly. "If we just order Serath something to eat now, he can join us when its ready. That way, we can save time and ignore the fact that Serath might be dead."

Rolan frowned at the elf. "I don't sound like that."

Belac spread his arms. "Sorry, I didn't have any gravel to gargle first."

Rolan shook his head. "And, Serath is not dead."

"How could you possibly know that?" Belac thought the dwarf was kidding himself.

Rolan's confidence did not waver. "I know Serath. He's not dead."

Belac recognized the dwarf was too stubborn to have a proper discussion about it. "Fine," he allowed. "But how are we even going to find the giants without him?" He regretted the question as soon as he asked it. *They are giants.*

"Serath told me where they are," Rolan explained. "It should not be too hard to find them."

"Serath told you?" Belac asked. "When?"

"We don't all spend our time drinking, sleeping, or getting into trouble," Rolan replied.

Belac nodded. "I know. You people are boring."

Rolan snorted.

Vairug called out, "Go around!" waving his hand to the side.

Rolan steered the horses around a depression that would have gotten the wagon stuck.

Belac waited until the dwarf had them back on course before asking more questions. "So, let's say we find the giants." He emphasized, "And they don't eat us." He paused for effect. "How do you plan on convincing one of them to come with us?"

"Right…" Rolan said. "About that…"

"You don't know!" Belac pointed at the dwarf, happy to see him uncertain about something.

"We will figure something out," Rolan said irritably. "We will just need to talk to them and find out what they want."

Belac could not believe how bad this plan was. "What could a giant possibly want from us?" He emphasized, "Other than to eat us."

Rolan shrugged. "I don't know. They are probably going to want us to plunder some ancient ancestral tomb or something. It could be anything. We just have to talk to them first." A thought came to him. "Maybe I can offer to broker a peace agreement between them and Harbridge."

Belac gestured back the way they had come. "Harbridge wants to kill us!"

Rolan looked at the elf sideways. "Maybe we don't tell the giants that."

I should have stayed on the ship with the pirates. Belac wondered if pirates had to take an oath.

"Don't worry about it," Rolan continued. "I am sure we can find some way to convince them."

"And then what?" Belac asked in a doomed voice.

Rolan shrugged. "And then we head back to Harbridge and wait for Serath."

"I don't want to go back to Harbridge." Belac was starting to think the dwarf's plan was intentionally bad. "Harbridge wants to kill us."

Rolan waved his hand dismissively. "Don't worry about it. I have a place we can hide."

Belac threw up his hands. "How are you going to hide a giant?"

Rolan looked at the elf. "I don't understand the question."

"It's a giant!" Belac yelled so loud Vairug looked back to check on them.

Rolan grinned like he knew something the elf did not. "What do you think a giant is?"

Now, Belac did not understand the question. "…A giant. Like the colossus, but with a beard."

Rolan chuckled. "No."

"What do you mean, 'no?" Belac asked. "That is what the word 'giant' means!"

Rolan shook his head. "They are not that big."

Belac did not believe him. "Then, why are they called 'giants?"

Rolan thought for a moment. "They might be a little bigger than an ogre, but not by much."

Belac remembered the ogres. "That does not seem very… giant."

"That is what happens when people talk about things they don't really understand." Rolan shrugged. "Some of them have beards, if that makes you feel better."

Belac frowned at the dwarf. "Then, why are people so scared of giants if they are not… I don't know… giant?"

"You mean, other than the whole 'people not understanding things' thing?" Rolan took a deep breath and then let it out slowly. "If you ask Serath, it is because they are better than other people."

Belac did not try to hide his disbelief. "How?"

"In just about every way there is." Rolan did not sound pleased by the admission. "They are bigger, stronger, smarter, and more resilient than anything else you would still think of as people."

Belac shook his head. "Then, why don't giants rule the world?"

"That is where things get kind of complicated," Rolan said. "Serath says it has to do with ingenuity."

Belac smiled. "The giants have too much ingenuity?"

Rolan shook his head. "No, not enough."

Belac did not think that was a very good argument. "Then, how can you say they are better?"

"Serath says something like, and I'm quoting here, probably poorly, that ingenuity is 'the compensative response to inadequacy or the perception there of.' The man is a wizard, so don't expect him to be easy to understand." Rolan took another breath. "I think what he is saying, is that because giants are better than everyone else, they don't need to make as many things." He turned to the elf. "Things' make a big difference in a power struggle."

Belac was unconvinced. "You are saying people only make things because they are weak?"

Rolan shook his head. "No." He gestured above the elf's shoulder to the hilt of the longsword strapped to his back. "But would you carry that around with you, if you could kill people with nothing but the power of your mind?"

Belac realized that the argument did make a strange sort of sense. *I really don't like that it makes sense.* "Wait!" He focused on the dwarf's face. "Are you saying a giant can kill me with just its mind?"

Rolan chuckled. "No. I am just making a point."

Belac let out a sigh of relief. "What do you think?"

"I think Serath has some strange ideas." Rolan shrugged. "That does not make them wrong."

Belac asked a more pointed question. "Do you think the giants are better than us?"

"I think 'better' is subjective," Rolan told him.

Now, that was something Belac could agree with. He grinned. "You know, that is just a clever way of not answering my question."

Rolan returned the grin with a sly one of his own. "Thanks."

Fifteen

"But, what if the ghouls eat him?" Belac asked

"He will be fine," Rolan said dismissively, standing up and walking away with the waterskin he had just filled in the stream.

"I will be fine," Vairug confirmed before he resumed brushing the horses.

Belac was becoming more convinced the ghouls were fictitious. "Is that because there are no ghouls?"

Rolan walked past the elf. "They probably won't come this far from the road. Besides, he can sleep in the wagon. Even if they do come out this far, the ghouls won't bother him if he sleeps in there."

Vairug tried to reassure the elf. "Don't worry, Belac. The ghouls are not going to eat me."

"That's right," Rolan agreed. "If something eats him, it probably won't be the ghouls."

Belac looked around nervously. The scraggly trees that lined the creek did not offer many places for something to hide, but he was not ready to trust even the trees.

"Nothing is going to eat me, Rolan." Vairug sounded a little offended.

Belac was still concerned. "It just feels wrong to leave you behind."

Vairug stepped away from the horses. "Are you coming back?"

Belac looked up at the massive formation of rock the dwarf wanted them to climb. "I hope so."

Vairug nodded. "Then, focus on that. I will be fine."

Rolan called from behind the wagon. "We are not leaving until tomorrow morning. You can say your goodbyes then."

Belac shrugged. *Yeah, okay.* He pointed at the horse brush in the orc's hand. "Let me see that."

Vairug tossed him the brush and then put his hand on one of the horses. "Be careful with this one. It will bite you."

Why does everything want to eat me? Belac reached back and untied his hair. "It is not for the horses."

Vairug frowned. "That is exactly what that brush is for."

"Not right now, it's not." Belac said brushing the tangles out of his long black hair.

"You should just braid it," Vairug told him. He held up his own thick braid to show the elf.

Belac dismissed the suggestion. "I like it tied back in a knot. It stays out of my way and does not get caught on anything." *And it's pretty when I let it down.*

Rolan walked over to join them. "I could just cut it off for you," he offered.

Belac looked at the dwarf's butchered hair. "No." He pointed the brush at him. "Bad dwarf!"

Rolan snorted and walked off to prepare for the night.

Belac handed the brush back to the orc. "I need something to eat."

"There are some trail rations in the wagon." Vairug nodded toward the dwarf. "Rolan says we should not start a fire."

"No fires!" Rolan called out.

Belac did not care if the food was fresh or not. *I still can't taste anything anyway.* He ate and readied himself for the night as the sun set in the distance. In the fading light, he crawled into the back of the wagon and laid out on his side of the cabin. After staying awake the night before, sleep came easily. If he dreamed, he did not remember, and if things moved in the night, he did not notice.

A box slamming down on the opposite bench woke him.

Vairug growled from the floor.

Belac looked at the dwarf, sleepily. "There are nicer ways to wake people up."

"There are less nice ones too," Rolan argued.

Belac was too groggy to argue with the dwarf. He sat up and took his black scabbarded longsword in hand. Being careful not to step on Vairug, the elf made his way to the door. As Belac stumbled out of the cabin, he felt a small amount of pride in remembering to bring the sword with him.

Rolan spoke from within the cabin. "You can't keep sleeping in your boots, Belac."

"What?" Belac shook his head. *It is too early for this.*

"Your feet are going to rot," Rolan explained. "Whenever you can, you need to take your boots off while you are sleeping. You need to air your feet, your boots too."

Belac knew the dwarf was right. He had just not been thinking about it. *With my luck, I will survive all the monsters, just to die of foot rot.* Belac nodded. "Your right," he said and then set off to greet the morning.

The elf walked around the camp, such as it was, and searched for signs anything had been there in the night. Finding nothing, he strapped his sword to his back and continued to move around the camp, stretching and preparing for the climb ahead. Belac preferred to sleep through the morning, but he had to admit they could be peaceful. *Though, sleep is peaceful too.* The morning had a quiet promise to it that was simply not present at any other time of the day.

Belac stopped next to the creek and watched the water flow from the mountains. The gentle sounds of the water made him thirsty, so he knelt down to drink. Something shot at the elf from his right. He rolled to his left and then came to his feet gripping the hilt of his sword. The squirrel stopped short and barked at the elf before turning and running up a tree.

"At least we know you are awake," Rolan said from behind the elf.

Belac had not heard the dwarf approach. "We need to get you a bell or something."

"Sure." Rolan nodded. "I can ring it when I need you to go fetch something for me."

Belac frowned, but then noticed the two waxed paper packages the dwarf was holding. "Is that breakfast?"

Rolan handed him both packages. "Stuff one of them in your bag. You can eat the other one now, but be quick about it. We need to get moving." He pulled the strap to a waterskin off his shoulder and offered it to the elf. "Here. Take this."

Belac took the waterskin, trying to balance the packages in his other hand but dropped one of them on the ground. He narrowed his eyes at the package. *Just for that, I am going to eat you first.*

"Try to get in the habit of drinking from the skin and then refilling it in the stream," Rolan advised.

Belac lowered the waterskin to the ground and then stuffed the package he held into the leather bag he wore at his side. "Why bother? It is easier to just drink from the stream."

"It will cycle fresh water into the skin," Rolan explained. "Also, it makes it easier to spot killer squirrels."

Belac nodded. He did not think the dwarf was really talking about squirrels. *It sounds like a hassle, but it might be worth the extra effort if it helps me not die.* He sat on the ground and picked up the dropped package. *You thought you could escape.* He pealed open the waxed paper and began to eat his tasteless breakfast. "Where is Vairug?" he asked between bites.

"He is still in the wagon," Rolan said irritably. He turned his head to the wagon and raised his voice. "He can sleep the whole time we are gone if he wants. But if something happens to the horses, he is pulling the wagon back to Harbridge!"

Belac grinned at the thought of Vairug trying to pull the heavy wagon by himself. *I wonder if I could get Rolan to make me a bull whip.*

"Are you through eating?" Rolan asked.

Belac shook his head and took another bite. "See? Still eating," he said with his mouthful. He started to choke on the dry food and had to wash it down with a drink from the waterskin. The water was warmer than he would have liked, but he was more concerned with not choking to death.

"Don't forget to fill that back up," Rolan said, gazing off toward the mountains.

Belac finished eating, drank from the waterskin, and then refilled it in the creek. After getting to his feet, he asked, "Are you sure Vairug is going to be okay here by himself?"

"No," Rolan said unapologetically. "But someone needs to stay with the horses. Lorance was supposed to stay here with two other men, but you saw how that turned out."

"Lorance?" Belac did not recognize the name. "You mean Larry?"

Rolan chuckled. "Yeah. His name was Lorance."

Belac was confused. "You said his name was 'Larry.' I don't think 'Larry' is short for 'Lorance."

"It's not," Rolan agreed. "I just wanted him off balance."

"Maybe that explains why he wanted to kill you," Belac said ruefully.

Rolan shook his head. "He must have figured he could make more killing me than helping me."

"Why?" Belac did not think the dwarf would have told the men he hired that they were involved in a prison break.

Rolan looked at the elf sideways. "Not everyone likes me."

Sixteen

"So, we are not climbing the mountains?" Belac was fairly certain the dwarf had pointed to the mountains.

Rolan shook his head. "Why would we climb the mountains?" Gray rock shifted under his boots, but the dwarf never seemed to lose his footing.

Belac looked up at the massive mountains on either side of them. "To get to the giants?"

"What would giants be doing on the top of a mountain?" Rolan asked.

"I don't know," Belac said. *I don't know what giants do.* "Eating goats?"

Rolan chuckled.

"Fine!" Belac said irritably. "Then, where are we going?"

Rolan gestured to the mountains around them.

Belac narrowed his eyes at the dwarf. The elf's foot slipped on a loose rock, and he had to grab the dwarf's shoulder to keep from falling. Despite Rolan's claims they would not be climbing a mountain, the route they took brought them higher with every step. Belac could already feel the cold beginning to slow his reflexes. The elf looked down at the leather bag he carried on his side.

"Just put it on," Rolan told him and then resumed his march into the mountains.

Belac groaned. He knew the dwarf was right. He pulled the cloak from his bag, careful not to lose the waxed paper package inside. "You did this on purpose!"

Rolan called over his shoulder. "If I did, don't you think I would know that?"

"What?" Belac looked away from the cloak and toward the dwarf. "What are you talking about?"

Rolan stopped and turned around. "Never mind." He pointed his hand at the cloak the elf held. "Just put it on."

Belac removed his sword and then used the baldric to lower it to the ground with the top of the scabbard resting on his foot. He shook out the thick, green, winter cloak and draped it over his shoulders. The thing made his skin crawl. He fashioned the cloak in place though what he really wanted to do was rip it off and throw it in Rolan's face.

"Don't blame me when something terrible happens!" Belac kicked the sword up into his hands and then slipped the baldric over his head.

Rolan shook his head but said nothing. Instead, he turned to resume moving onward. The dwarf froze.

Farther ahead, at the top of the rise, stood a masculine silhouette of pure white. Wild white hair and pale skin, the giant stood naked in the cold. Lifting a two-handed great hammer, the giant charged at them roaring. His thunderous voice echoed through the mountains and seeped into Belac's bones.

The elf stepped back, only to slip on the loose rock and fall backward. He tried to scoot away but got tangled with his cloak and longsword. Belac could not take his eyes off the giant's bulging muscles and unbridled rage.

Rolan reached for his springer and pulled it free. The dwarf gave no indication he would give ground to the giant.

The rocks fell away beneath the giant's feet, dropping him into a hidden hole. His roar changed from one of rage to that of surprise. "OH, SHAAAA!"

It happened so suddenly, Belac did not know if it had been real. He looked over at the dwarf. Neither of them moved in the silence that followed.

A voice called up from the hole.

Belac could not make out what it said, but Rolan walked over to the edge of the hole and looked down cautiously. Belac scrambled to his feet and hurried to join the dwarf.

Rolan called down into the hole in a language the elf did not understand.

After a moment, a deep voice replied, "Yes." The giant sounded resigned.

Rolan sat down next to the edge of the hole, smiling. "You seem to have gotten yourself into some trouble."

The giant yelled something angrily in the language Belac did not understand.

Rolan's smile only broadened. "I guess we could just leave, if that is what you want."

After another moment of silence, the giant called up, "What do you want, Dwarf?" He spoke in a way that suggested Dwarven was too soft a language for him to speak properly.

"Me?" Rolan asked in mock surprise. "What I want, is to help you get out of that hole."

"I would be willing to assist you in that." The giant's deep voice was guarded.

Belac leaned over the edge to see the giant. The drop was dangerously far, even for a giant. Inside was a rounded cave with dark tunnels too small for the giant to have crawled through. Dust filled the air and created a visible shaft of light that angled down into the darkness. Rocks had fallen on the giant, and his leg was bent in the wrong direction. The giant gazed up from behind a bushy white beard, no longer frightening in his vulnerability.

Belac called down, "We are looking for a smith."

Rolan frowned at the elf but said nothing.

"I am a smith," the giant claimed.

Rolan snorted.

Belac agreed with the dwarf. "That seems rather convenient," he said sarcastically.

"This does not seem convenient to me, Dwarf!" the giant replied angrily.

"Hey!" Belac said offended. "I am not a dwarf!"

This appeared to confuse the giant. "Then, what are you?"

Rolan spoke up. "Someone that is going to leave you to die in that hole, if you don't be nice!"

"I'm an elf," Belac told the giant.

"An elf?" The giant was more confused. "What are you doing here?"

"I told you," Belac explained again, "we are looking for a smith."

"You have found one." Either the giant understood, or he no longer cared. "Now, get me out of this cave."

Belac was not ready to do that just yet. "How do I know you won't try to eat me?"

Rolan put a palm to his face and shook his head.

"Why would I want to eat you?" the giant asked irritably.

Belac looked around. "I don't see any goats!"

Rolan laughed.

The giant said nothing for a moment and then called up, "I want to talk to the dwarf again."

Belac bristled. "Too bad! You're the one stuck in a hole! So, if you want out, you are going to have to talk to me!"

The giant mulled that over quietly before replying. "Very well. Go find my brother Morkan. He will help you get me out of this cave, and then we can discuss why you need a smith."

Belac narrowed his eyes at the giant. "How do I know he won't try to eat me?"

The giant sighed. "Tell him Ghoram sent you, and that I need his help. He will not eat you."

Belac looked at the dwarf.

Rolan shrugged.

Belac leaned back over the edge. "How do we find him?"

"Continue to follow the path until it splits," the giant instructed. "When you get there, take the path to the right. Be sure to make yourself known."

Belac stepped away from the edge. "Do you think we can trust him?"

Rolan shook his head. "It does not matter. We came to speak with the giants. No matter how this works out, helping him helps us."

Belac nodded. *And if he is a smith, we can't just let him die.* "We have to help him."

Rolan stood up and walked around the hole.

"Wait." Belac pointed to the dark opening. "What if there are more of these caves under the path ahead?"

Rolan knelt down and touched the edge of the hole. "Do you see these? They're tool marks. That means something made this deliberately."

Belac did not find that reassuring. "It also means there could be more of these things. I do not want to get trapped in a hole, waiting for unlikely travelers to find us."

Rolan stood up again. "There might be more of them, but they probably won't fall in on us."

"Why not?" Belac was not convinced.

Rolan kicked at the edge of the trap. "This had to be made for a giant. Both of us are a lot lighter than he is." He nodded toward the hole. "If we don't walk right next to each other, and we pay attention to where we step, we should be fine."

Belac did not like that the dwarf's plan to avoid a trap was to walk into the trap. "That does not sound safe, Rolan."

Rolan shrugged. "If it makes you feel better, the giant made it all the way out here before he fell into one of these."

That did actually make Belac feel better. "Why are you so sure this was made for a giant?"

"What else could it be for?" Rolan asked. "If the trap had been made for something other than a giant, the giants would have made it."

Belac grinned. "Do you think he could have fallen into his own trap?"

Rolan shook his head and sighed. "I hope not."

Belac lost his grin. "Why?"

Rolan stared at the elf, stonefaced. "I really don't like having to ask stupid people for help."

Seventeen

"There are too many rocks," Belac complained.

Rolan responded irritably, "You can't not step on the rocks, Belac."

"Watch me!" Belac replied. *I am not falling in a hole!*

The elf walked along the edge of the path, careful to only step on solid ground. *The crazy dwarf can wade through the loose rocks if he wants, but when he falls in a hole, I am going to point at him and laugh.* He thought for a moment. *And then get out of the way before he shoots me.*

"I should have left you with the horses," Rolan grumbled.

Belac looked up from the ground. *That is a good idea! Why didn't I think of that? I could be with the horses, sleeping in the wagon while Vairug freezes in the mountains and worries about falling in a hole.* "Why did you bring me?"

"Because, you are The Dragon Slayer," Rolan told him.

Belac nodded. *That does kind of make sense.* "But..."

Rolan held up a hand. "Quiet."

Belac stopped speaking. He stopped moving. The elf listened searchingly but could hear nothing other than the hollow sound of the wind sweeping through the mountains.

The path split a short way ahead. From the right, a giant strolled toward them. His exact size was difficult to make out at a distance, but he carried a two-handed great hammer resting on his shoulder and walked as if he were in no hurry.

"Hello!" Belac called out loudly.

Rolan turned and looked at the elf furiously.

Belac held his hands out to his sides. "He said to make ourselves known."

Rolan frowned and turned back toward the giant.

The giant had stopped where the path split. He stood with the heavy metal head of his great hammer planted on the ground in front of his feet. His hands rested on the shaft in a way that suggested patience, if not peace. Swollen muscle and pale skin, the giant blocked their path as surely as a mountain.

I think I would rather try to climb a mountain. Belac tip-toed around the dwarf, being careful where he stepped. He waved to the giant. "Hello there."

The giant said nothing until the elf approached. "Are you here to fight?" His deep voice sounded older than that of the other giant's.

Belac shook his head quickly. "No!" He stared at the giant wide eyed, worried he had made a mistake.

The giant was huge. He leaned over the great hammer glaring down at the elf. The top of Belac's head only came to the bottom of the giant's chest. Unquestionably male, the giant wore nothing except a thick leather strap wrapped tightly around his left forearm. His wild white hair and complexion matched his brothers, but this was the first time Belac had looked into a giant's eyes. Washed of color, the irises were a ring of white inside another of black. The effect made the giant appear insane.

"Why not?" the giant asked.

Because I don't want you to kill me! Belac shook his head some more.

"We should fight," the giant rumbled.

Belac continued to shake his head, trying to think of something to say. He pointed at the giant. "You are not allowed to eat me!"

The giant leaned back. "I will enjoy your death."

Belac stepped away. "Gordan said you wouldn't eat me!"

"Gordan?" the giant asked. "Do you mean Ghoram?"

Belac held up a finger. "Yeah! That's the one!"

The giant shook his head slowly. "Ghoram would not say that."

"He did!" Belac assured him. "Your Morgan, right?"

"Morkan!" the giant growled.

Belac took another step back, nodding. "Morkan, right." He held up his hands. "Ghoram needs your help."

This seemed to sober the giant. "He would not send you."

Belac made a conscience decision that he was not going to take another step back. "Your brother is stuck in a cave."

Morkan said nothing. He simply stood there, staring at the elf with his insane eyes.

"He fell into a hole and broke his leg," Belac continued. "He told us to find his brother," he gestured to the giant and was careful to say his name correctly, "Morkan." Belac decided that if the giant moved aggressively, he was going to rush forward and try to burry his dagger in its kneecap. *And then I am going to run.*

Morkan tilted his head to the side and grinned, the combination making him look more insane. "Did he threaten to eat you?"

Belac shook his head. "No. I… I just kind of assumed."

The giant laughed, and Belac almost took another step back despite himself.

"Take me to my brother." Morkan hefted his great hammer to grip it beneath the heavy head.

Belac held up a hand to forestall the giant. "You are going to need a rope."

Morkan made a rumbling sound deep in his throat. "Wait here." He turned and ran back up the path he had been guarding.

"That could have gone worse," Rolan said not quite approvingly.

Belac jumped at the sound of the dwarf's voice. He put a hand to his chest, over his racing heart. "Why didn't you say something?"

Rolan shrugged. "He did not want to fight me."

"He could have killed me!" Belac said accusingly.

Rolan raised his eyebrows and nodded as if to say, 'I know.'

Belac narrowed his eyes at the dwarf.

Rolan grinned.

Belac turned his attention to the path the giant had taken. "Do you think he is getting a rope?"

"What else?" Rolan asked.

"I don't know," Belac shrugged. "Maybe he went to get a giant army." *I don't think that sounds right.* "An army of giants?"

"Giants don't have armies," Rolan said dismissively.

"Whatever." Belac did not care what the dwarf called them. "A giant angry mob of giants that wants to kill us."

"No." Rolan did not sound concerned. "He believed you."

Belac looked back to the dwarf. "You think?"

Rolan shrugged. "You're not dead."

"That's…" Belac nodded. "That's a good point." *The giant would not have needed an army to kill me.*

Rolan grunted in agreement.

"Hey, Rolan." Belac sounded a little uncomfortable.

Rolan responded, "What?"

"Um…" Belac coughed. "Why are they naked?"

"That is a bad question," Rolan told him.

Belac did not think it was a bad question. *People are supposed to wear clothes.* "Why? Is it rude to ask?"

"No." Rolan shook his head. "But you don't need a reason to not do something. Well… not unless you have another reason to do it, but that is sort of my point."

"What?" Belac felt like the dwarf was trying to be confusing.

"They don't have any reason to wear clothes," Rolan said more concisely.

Belac thought this might be part of the argument that the giants were better than everyone else. "They don't get cold?"

"Did he look cold to you?" Rolan asked.

Belac coughed. "No. No, he did not."

Eighteen

"Stop staring at me, and show me where my brother is." Morkan's deep voice was not winded despite his run. He had returned without his great hammer, carrying instead a heavy coil of leather rope.

Belac coughed. "Um… Yeah." He turned and started walking back the way they had come. "But be careful, or you might fall into another one of the traps.

Morkan followed after the elf. "Did you make these traps?"

Belac shook his head. "Of course not!"

"We cannot even be sure that there are more traps," Rolan added.

Morkan seemed to believe them. "I will be careful."

As they retraced their steps, Rolan asked, "Do you know who might be trying to trap you?"

"It might be you," Morkan said.

"It is not us," Belac told him.

The giant offered no sign of agreement.

"You know?" Belac said a little perturbed. "You are not very friendly."

Rolan chuckled.

Morkan's frown could be heard when he spoke. "I will consider being friendly when I know my brother is safe."

Belac pointed. "He is in that hole over there."

"I see it." Morkan confirmed. He stepped around the elf and hurried toward his brother, his long gait moving him ahead quickly.

"Be careful!" Belac called after him and then grumbled, "Stupid giant."

Morkan leaned over the edge of the cave opening and called down to his brother in a language Belac assumed was Giant. *What would that be called? Giantese?* The giant deep voice did not sound concerned. It sounded like the giant was mocking his brother.

Ghoram yelled something back. He did not sound concerned with his brother's safety either.

Morkan laughed and began to ready the leather rope.

Belac leaned over the edge of the hole. "Did you miss us?"

Ghoram said something in Giant that made Rolan and Morkan laugh.

Something moved in the cave. A small shape emerged from one of the dark tunnels that surrounded the trapped giant. It began to take form as it moved closer to the light. It was shaped vaguely like a person and was dressed in hides, but its flesh was covered in pale blue scales, and it had a thick tail. Black, soulless eyes gleamed as the light illuminated its reptilian face.

Belac pointed. "What is that?!"

Morkan shouted something to his brother.

Ghoram turned and threw a rock at the creature. It dodged fluidly and then let out a hissing bark. It carried a primitive spear, and its malicious intent was obvious.

I can't let it kill the smith. Without a smith, there could be no magic sword. The quest would be over. There would be no way to stop the dragon. *There would be no Dragon Slayer.*

Belac grabbed the end of the leather rope and slid it through the ring on his waist harness. "Hold the rope!" Gripping the rope in one hand, he jumped into the cave.

The rope tightened and Belac swung inside the cave instead of crashing against the rock floor. His green cloak fanned out under his sword as the elf was spun around. He released the rope and fell the rest of the way into the cave. The distance of the fall was short enough for him to land safely, but he felt the shock run up into his shins.

Remembering the last time he had tried to draw his sword, Belac lifted the scabbard over his head before pulling the blade free. He faced the creature with the sword in his right hand and the scabbard in his left. *What is that thing? It's like a... creepy, blue, lizard goblin.* The creature was no taller then Rolan, yet it attacked Belac without hesitation. It hissed at the elf and began to thrust wildly with its spear.

Belac was able to fend off the thrusts, but they were too fast for him to counter. Movement on his right warned him he was being flanked. *I do not have time to dance with this thing.* He knocked the spear aside with his scabbard and thrust with his longsword. The blade sank deep into the creature's chest and the tip of the sword was pulled down when it fell.

Belac put his foot on the creature's chest and pulled his sword free just in time to swing the blade in a wide arc toward another of the creatures as it leapt at him. The blade caught the creature in midair, hacking through its arm and into its chest as it flew past.

Belac pointed his sword at the injured giant and called up to the opening of the cave. "Get him out!" *And then get me out!*

More of the creatures were coming. The elf had no way of knowing how many there would be. *If I am too defensive, I could be overwhelmed.* He looked at his sword. *I will need to rely on the blade's reach.*

Guttural hissing echoed from the dark tunnels around him. While fear could make their numbers sound larger than they were, Belac knew there were too many of them for him to face alone. *I don't need to kill them all.* He took a deep breath. *Just enough to survive.*

One of the creatures rushed out of a tunnel on Belac's left. He pivoted and brought the end of his sword down on the scaly blue head. He controlled the momentum of the blade with a figure eight pattern and hacked into another reptilian face approaching on his right. *I cannot wait for them to attack first.* He took a step forward and swung the sword down at another of the creatures. Tiny, wicked teeth glistened as the creature hissed in defiance. It attempted to block with a spear, but the force of Belac's swing was too great and the elf's blade tore into the creature's torso.

More of the guttural hissing filled the rocky cave. Belac spun to face the danger behind him. Ghoram had tied the leather rope under his arms and was being slowly lifted toward the light above. Barely off the ground, he dangled like bait on a hook. Blue scales and vicious teeth moved in the shadows on the other side of the giant.

I have to stop them. Belac sprinted at an angle to his left. He ran up the wall of the cave and then kicked off, turning to his right. With a backhanded swing, he brought his sword down in a diagonal sweep that cleaved into the back of a reptilian skull. He continued to move forward, swinging his longsword at another of the creatures. The creature screamed something Belac did not understand before the blade bit into its face.

The remaining creatures turned from the giant and surged at the elf. Belac stepped away from the rising giant in hopes he would draw them away. With an awkward motion he deflected a thrusting spear to his right and then slammed his empty scabbard into the side of the creature's head. He brought the scabbard back to the left, deflecting another spear while he stabbed at the staggered creature. The blade sunk deep, but the elf was quick to jerk the sword free before it could be pulled down.

A spear's tip gouged into Belac's left side. He shied away from the pain and swung his sword up in a diagonal back cut that slashed open his attacker's chest. More of the creatures poured into the cave from the dark tunnels. Hissing barks and flashing teeth promised the elf more pain.

Small rocks fell from above as Ghoram was pulled out of the cave. *One less thing to worry about.* While Belac would no longer be distracted with protecting the giant, the creatures too were now of singular purpose. Soulless eyes tracked the elf as the creatures moved to surround him.

Belac raised his sword high into the air and shouted in the Elven tongue, "I am not food!" His azure blue eyes were alit with madness as he charged into battle.

Before he reached the first creature, a silvery bolt shot through its skull. The shot had come from above and to the left, so Belac moved left. With a forward aggressive back cut, he slashed at blue scales as he passed by. Another bolt shot down into the pack.

Belac pressed forward as the creatures tripped over their own dead. He brought the sword down in a diagonal backhand that cut one of the creatures in half. A silvery flash shot down from above. Belac stepped past the creature he had cut in half and swung his sword into another. The blade hacked into flesh but was slowed by the hides the creature wore. The sword's edge was beginning to dull, and Belac was beginning to tire.

A clawed hand covered in blue scales gripped the elf's left arm. He tried to shake himself free, but the claws tore into him, drawing blood. Rolan continued to shoot down from the edge above, but the creatures were crawling over the corpses of their dead to get to Belac. The elf slammed the cross-guard of his sword into the reptilian head of the creature that held his arm. The cross-guard punctured the creature's skull, and Belac's arm was suddenly released. He ripped his sword free and slashed to his right. The blade cut into a creature's chest but caught on its spine. Belac's sword was wrenched from his hand as the creature was shoved aside by another. The oncoming creature took a bolt to the head and fell limply.

Rolan's strong voice ordered, "Grab the rope!"

Belac transferred his empty scabbard to his right hand and swung it like a club. The polished steel chape of the scabbard smashed into a scaly blue face. Belac wrapped his left arm around the leather rope and then tugged on it three times in quick succession. The rope tightened, and he began to rise toward the opening above.

He used the scabbard to knock away an overextended thrust of a spear, the motion causing him to spin gracelessly.

The elf kicked in the air, trying to regain what control he could. He flailed with his scabbard, deflecting the thrusts of spears as he was lifted higher.

A sharp pain in the back of his left thigh informed Belac that he had missed one of the spears. He swung his scabbard behind him blindly. The attack connected with something, but it was too chaotic for him to know what he had hit. *I hope I took out one of its eyes!*

Once the elf had been lifted beyond their reach, one of the creatures threw its spear. Belac swatted the spear away with his scabbard, but he knew more would soon follow. The creatures hissed their fury at the pray that might escape them.

Belac's left hand dragged on chiseled rock. He twisted around to face the lip and pushed away with the scabbard clenched in his right fist. A spear flew past his boots as he swung backward. He whipped his feet up to brace himself against the crudely shaped rim of the opening. Another spear flew past behind him as he was pulled the rest of the way from the cave.

Belac stumbled away from the hole before turning around to glare at it. He kicked a loose rock and sent it tumbling into the cave. *I am not food!*

Nineteen

"Your battle cry is, 'I am not food?" Rolan laughed.

"Die in a fire," Belac replied.

Rolan continued to laugh as he treated the elf's wounds.

"It sounds better in Elven!" Belac argued defensively.

Rolan stopped laughing long enough to say, "That is only because no one is going to understand what you are saying!"

Morkan spoke over the dwarf's laughter. "We cannot remain here." Despite his assertion, the giant did not sound frightened.

Rolan agreed with the giant. "Can you move your brother?"

"I can move myself!" Ghoram told the dwarf angrily.

Morkan ignored his brother's outburst. "His leg is too injured to walk on, but with my assistance, I believe we can manage."

Ghoram said something irritably in Giant.

"Right," Rolan responded. "Which means we should not have to listen to you complain along the way."

Morkan laughed.

Belac felt exhausted. "Just give me a moment."

Rolan shook his head. "You have had a moment."

Ghoram said something in Giant that sounded snide.

Rolan nodded toward the giant. "He's right. The scalics will know a way around. They might take the time to organize before they come for us, but they will come for us. We need to move."

"Scalics?" Belac asked. "The creepy-blue-lizard-goblins?"

Rolan shook his head. "We are not calling them that."

"I don't care what we call them," Belac said. "Scalic' works for me." *It takes less time to say anyway.*

The loose rocks underfoot shifted as Morkan helped his brother to stand on his uninjured foot.

Ghoram said something in Giant that sounded remarkably unappreciative.

Belac spoke in Elven, "Do giants speak Elven?"

"Probably not," Rolan replied without bothering to speak in Elven.

In Elven, Belac suggested, "Maybe I should speak nothing but Elven until they realize I don't speak Giant."

Rolan replied in passable Elven, "Do you think that is a good way to make friends?"

Belac frowned. *He is right. We are here to ask for help. I am just being petty.* He stood and turned toward the giants. "You should let us go first and check for more traps."

"Good idea," Rolan said in response to both conversations.

Belac and Rolan began walking up the path, leaving Ghoram and Morkan to shuffle up behind them. Belac could tell that Rolan did not expect them to find another cave trap. *This still gives us the opportunity to seem more useful than we actually are.* Despite Rolan's apparent lack of concern, Belac was careful where he stepped. *We need to show the giants that we are doing more than just walking up the path. …Also, I really don't want to fall in another hole.*

"Hold up," Rolan said when they reached the split in the path.

Belac stopped and turned around to check on the trailing giants. They had not fallen into any traps, but Belac understood why Rolan wanted to wait for them.

"You still think the scalics are going to attack," Belac surmised.

"Oh, they are going to attack," Rolan assured him.

Belac looked at the dwarf. "Why are you so certain?"

"Scalics are extremely territorial," Rolan explained. "The giants started a war when they moved into this part of the mountains."

"Do you think the giants knew?" Belac asked.

Rolan shrugged. "They had to know it would come from somewhere. If not the scalics, then the Harbridgers, or something else."

Belac did not understand the dwarf's assertion. "Who expects to be hunted by creepy-blue-lizard-goblins that live under the rocks?"

"We are not calling them that," Rolan said reflexively.

"Fine." Belac saw no reason to argue about it. "Scalic. Whatever."

"If it was not scalics, it would be something else," Rolan explained. "Nothing likes living around giants."

"Why?" The giants did not seem too bad to Belac. *If they would just put on clothes…*

Rolan shrugged. "They're giants."

Once upon a time, the answer may have been enough for the elf. That was before his best friend happened to be an orc. *If you think the world is simple, it's not. You are.* He looked at Rolan, another friend.

"You don't have a beard," Belac said.

Rolan looked at the elf sideways. "So?"

Belac shrugged. "Everyone knows that dwarves have beards." He hoped the dwarf would understand his point.

Rolan frowned in thought for a moment. "A wise man once said, 'Extremism is the intellectual inability to distinguish nuance."

Belac thought the dwarf was agreeing with him. He smiled. "It was Serath, right?"

Rolan turned and started up the path to the right.

Belac caught up to the dwarf and circled around to face him. "I'm right! It was Serath!"

Rolan grumbled, "It was Serath."

Belac nodded. "That sounds like something a wizard would say."

Something splattered on the elf's left shoulder. Without thinking, Belac reached up to his shoulder to investigate. His hand smeared the white paste across the green of his cloak. He pulled his hand away disgusted and looked to the sky in search of the perpetrator. A bird that he thought may have been an eagle flew high in the sky.

Belac looked at the white mess on his hand and then held it away from himself, unsure what to do about it. *Ugh. I want this off.* He tried to sling it off his hand to no avail. Finally, he simply wiped his hand on the side of his cloak.

Rolan grinned. "That is supposed to be lucky."

Belac narrowed his eyes at the dwarf. "Bad luck is still luck."

Rolan chuckled. "You think you have bad luck?"

Belac shook his head. "No. I think this stupid cloak you are making me wear has bad luck!" He pointed a mostly clean finger at the dwarf. "And you know why!"

"It's green?" Rolan asked in mock speculation.

"It's green!" Belac confirmed angrily.

With Ghoram's arm over Morkan's shoulders for support, the giants had continued their approach and were now close enough to join the conversation.

Morkan questioned them in a tone without inflection. "Why are you arguing?"

Rolan nodded toward the elf. "He thinks it is my fault a bird marked him."

Belac shook his head. "It did not 'mark' me, Rolan. It…"

Morkan cut the elf off. "How could that be his fault?" He looked at the dwarf. "Do you command the raptor?"

Belac narrowed his eyes at the dwarf. *He had better not!*

Rolan shook his head smiling. "I did not even see the bird."

Ghoram said something in Giant.

Rolan looked at the elf. "Do you want to tell them?"

Belac suddenly felt exposed. "What I want, is for us to get moving." He pointed behind himself with his thumb. "We need to stop standing around here, and get somewhere safe."

Rolan nodded, frowning happily. "You heard The Dragon Slayer. Let's get moving." He marched off past the elf.

Belac turned and followed the dwarf up the path, eager to leave the conversation behind.

In obvious disbelief, Morkan asked, "You claim the elf is a dragon slayer?"

"The Dragon Slayer," Rolan corrected the giant.

Morkan laughed, almost dropping the other giant.

Ghoram spoke, this time in Dwarven. "Do not laugh brother. I have witnessed." The phrase seemed to have a deeper meaning. "The elf is fierce."

It did not go unnoticed that the giant had spoken in Dwarven. *He wanted me to hear that. He wanted me to understand.* Still, Belac felt as if he were missing something. He stopped and faced the giants. "Then, will you help me?"

Morkan's insane looking eyes went wide. "To kill a dragon?"

Despite how similar Ghoram's eyes were to his brother's, they looked more tired than insane. "Not even a giant could kill a dragon."

"I don't need you to kill it," Belac told him. "I just need you to make me a sword."

"The lands of man have many swords," Ghoram replied cryptically.

Belac's clear blue eyes met the giant's insane rings. "I need a special one."

Ghoram did not look away. "One forged by a giant."

Joining them, Rolan said, "That is why we are here."

Morkan gazed intently at the elf. "You wish to be legend."

Rolan answered for the elf. "Maybe a giant can't kill a dragon. But a legend can."

Ghoram's attention never left the elf. "Then, you will have your sword."

Twenty

Belac looked back at the giants that followed a short way behind them. "Do you think they are really going to make the sword for me?" he asked the dwarf.

"That is what they said," Rolan replied.

Belac turned his attention to the dwarf. "People can say anything they want. That does not make it true."

Rolan chuckled.

Belac narrowed his eyes at the dwarf. "What is so funny?"

"You. Accusing other people of lying." Rolan laughed. "I watched you convince three countries that an orc was the long lost king of Enevic."

Belac frowned. "I never said he was the king."

Rolan laughed some more.

It bothered the elf that Rolan thought of him as a liar. When Belac thought about Rolan, he felt like he could trust him. *He has always been honest with me. Even when I did not like it.* Belac regretted that he had not made the dwarf feel the same way toward him. He felt as if he had lost something and did not know how to get it back. In his mind, he heard the wizard's words. *"Everything you do."* He thought he might finally be starting to understand what the wizard had meant when he said everything had a cost.

Belac dismissed the unpleasant thoughts. "I asked what you thought. Not, what they said."

Rolan nodded. "I think they said they would forge the sword for you."

Belac imagined the dwarf falling into a trap and getting eaten by creepy-blue-lizard-goblins. "And, what do you think about what they said?"

Rolan shrugged. "I think that is the most we can hope for right now. We asked for help. They said, 'yes.' Were you expecting a signed contract?"

Belac wondered how long it would take him to dig one of those cave traps by himself. *It would only need to be big enough for a dwarf.*

Rolan clapped the elf on the shoulder. "Don't worry about it so much. When we get to the giants' camp, I will sit down with them and work out all the details."

Belac thought he understood what the dwarf was telling him. "You want me to let you do the talking."

"I want you to let me negotiate," Rolan corrected him. "After that, you can talk as much as you want to."

Belac considered arguing, but decided to trust the dwarf. "Is there anything I should not say?"

Rolan nodded. "There is a lot you should not say."

Belac frowned and repeated something the dwarf had said often. "You are going to need to be more specific."

Rolan chuckled. "Maybe don't tell them that you keep getting thrown in prison."

As they continued on, the mountains began to crowd closer until they were steep cliffs rising to either side of the path. There was plenty of space for the giants to walk, but the undeniable size of the mountains made Belac feel small. They reminded him that there were things in the world far greater than he was. *I don't like it.*

The faint sound of hammering began to echo through the pass. *We must be getting close.* Belac wondered how Rolan and he would be received by the other giants. He thought back on how they had met Ghoram and Morkan. *Hopefully better than that.*

As it turned out, the giants did not have a camp. What they had were giant walls of steel that lined a portion of the cliff face on both sides of the mountain pass. Oversized doors and shutters of gleaming metal made it obvious the giants did not welcome visitors. While all the doors on the left were shut tight, a set of sliding double doors stood open farther ahead on the right. Orange light and the sound of hammering came from the open doors. It was impossible for Belac to know how far into the side of the mountain the complex encroached; however, he felt it was safe to assume it would be sized for giants.

Belac glanced at the dwarf. "This is more than a camp, Rolan."

Rolan nodded. "Your right. This is not something temporary. The giants plan on staying."

Belac looked back to the dwarf. "Is that a problem?"

Rolan shook his head. "Not for us." He shrugged. "It is just not what I was expecting."

That sounded like a problem to Belac. "What were you expecting?"

"Leather hides and caves," Rolan said.

Belac pointed to the open doors leading into the metal wall on the right. "That is sort of a cave." *A cave with a metal wall in front of it is still a cave.*

"It is the permanence," Rolan tried to explain. "That is what is important here."

"Why?" Belac asked. "You said the mountains belong to Enevic, and they are all dead." *Well, except Ecard. But that man is not any threat to the giants.*

Rolan shook his head. "The mountains might technically belong to Enevic, but the giants are not supposed to be this far south. If the Harbridgers find out the giants are here, they will have to do something about it. The giants know that." He gestured to the metal walls. "And they are preparing to stay anyway."

"War," Belac predicted.

Rolan nodded gravely.

It occurred to Belac that the dwarf might be overlooking something. "They may not let us leave."

Rolan tilted his head to the side and frowned as if he had tasted something sour. "That's possible, but I don't think we have to worry about that."

"Because we helped them?" Belac guessed.

Rolan shook his head. "We are not humans." He gestured to himself. "That means we are not Harbridgers. I can probably convince them to let us go."

Belac did not find that very reassuring.

Rolan continued, "Besides, they agreed to forge the sword for you. They can't do that and keep us here."

Belac looked at Ghoram and Morkan as they approached. *I hope giants are honorable.*

Rolan nudged the elf. "I am going to help them inside and then see what I can work out. You can rest here for a bit, but I expect they will want to talk to you too."

Rolan went to help the giants, but there was nothing for him to do other than holding open one of the steel doors on the left. He followed the two giants inside, leaving Belac alone in the shadowed mountain pass.

The elf waited patiently for all of a dozen heartbeats, before walking over to the open double doors to investigate. The hammering sounded like a smithy to Belac. *Maybe they have more than one smith.* If given the choice, he would have preferred a giant smith without a broken leg.

As expected, Belac found that the doorway led to a smithy. A cave had been cut into the rock of the mountain side and then smoothed into a large chamber. The smithy was sweltering hot despite the ventilation shafts cut into the high ceiling above. A giant stood on the other side of a glowing forge, shaping steel.

Belac watched as the giant hammered the glowing metal, but could not discern what was being forged. The giant set down its hammer and tongs and then stepped away from the forge. It removed a heavy leather apron and set it aside. The giant stared down at the elf inquisitively.

Belac had meant to say, 'hello.' Truly, he had. However, standing before the unclothed giantess, he forgot how to formulate thought. He stared at her unimaginably perfect proportions and realized that her size only made them easier to appreciate.

"You have come a long way to stare at me," she said.

It took every bit of self-control Belac possessed to move his gaze up to the giantess's face. Her long white hair had been pulled back and it drew his attention to the insane rings in her eyes. *Even those are beautiful.* He could not remember how to speak.

"How are you here?" she asked.

Belac did not understand the question. He may have been able to explain 'why' he was there, but even that would have been difficult at the moment. His eyes began to travel down.

The giantess seemed unconcerned by his attention. "Speak, Elf."

"Belac," he managed to say.

"Belac?" the giantess repeated. "It that the Elven word for…"

"Nope," Belac interrupted her. "That's me. That's my name. Belac. I'm an elf." *Stop talking.* He looked back up at her face and smiled.

"I am Breana." There was a depth to her voice, though it was no less feminine for having it. "Why are you here, Belac the elf?"

He almost said it was to see her, but stopped himself. "I came to ask the giants to make me a sword."

Her high cheekbones seemed to harden. "The giants are not for hire."

Belac shook his head. "Ghoram already said he would help."

"Ghoram?" She looked like she had been slapped. "Ghoram told you he would forge a sword for you?"

Belac nodded. "I need it to kill a dragon."

Breana laughed.

Belac would have been willing to brave the mountains just to hear that laugh.

Her smile was a lovely thing to behold. "I did not know elves were funny." She shook her head. "No one kills a dragon."

Twenty-One

Belac attempted to stand taller. "Well, I'm killing one anyway," he told the giantess.

Breana gestured to the elf. "You think you are going to kill a dragon?" She laughed again.

Belac had to force himself to keep his eyes on the giantess's face. *It is a beautiful face.* He nodded. "Yes."

She stopped laughing but continued to smile. "How are 'You' going to kill a dragon?"

Belac had been ready for the question. "With the sword Ghoram said he would make for me," he explained. "That is why we are here." *Though, I would have come just to stare at you.*

Breana shook her head. "You will need more than a sword to kill a dragon. Ghoram is not a wizard." She laughed at the idea.

"Not a problem," Belac told her. "I already have one of those." *Well… sort of. …maybe. …I hope Serath is not dead.*

Breana appraised the elf as if she thought this might be another joke. "You have a wizard?" She tilted her head in disbelief. "A wizard?"

Belac chose not to be offended. "How else am I going to make a magic sword?" He held his hands out to his sides. "I need a giant to make the sword, and I need a wizard to make it magic."

"You're insane," said the giantess with the insane looking eyes. "Ghoram would never agree to this."

Belac dropped his hands and frowned. "He already has." The elf smiled. "He said he witnessed my bravery, and now he is going to help me become a legend." *I may have left out some of the conversation.*

Breana was no longer smiling. "Ghoram said he witnessed you?"

Belac nodded agreeably. "After I saved him from the creepy-blue-lizard-goblins."

"You are insane." She shook her head. "How did you get here?"

Belac thought the question odd. *Maybe it is because I told her I have a wizard? Maybe she thinks I have a magic carpet or something.* "I walked." *I really need to get a magic carpet.*

Breana was unsatisfied with his answer. "How did you find us?"

"Oh!" Belac nodded. "Serath told us where to look. That's the wizard." He gestured back to the open doors. "And then Ghoram told us how to get here."

Breana shook her head. "Ghoram would not tell you that."

"He needed us to find Morkan," Belac explained. "Ghoram fell into a cave and broke his leg. We needed help to get him out."

Breana attempted to restrain a grin. "Ghoram fell into a cave?"

Belac nodded. "It was a trap. The scalics made it." He realized he had not told her what a scalic was. "Those are the creepy-blue-lizard-goblins."

"The things you say you saved Ghoram from?" Breana sounded unconvinced.

Belac decided that the giantess was too pretty for him to be mad at. "I jumped into the cave and fought them while Ghoram was pulled to safety." There was more than a trace of pride in his voice.

"You fought creepy-blue-lizard-goblins with your bare hands?" Breana asked as if she were pointing out a hole in his story.

Belac removed his empty scabbard and showed it to her. "I had a sword."

"You had a sword?" she asked, still not believing him.

"I lost it fighting the scalics." Belac returned the empty scabbard to his back. He pulled aside his cloak and pointed to the bloody tear in the side of his shirt. "They poked me a few times too."

Breana leaned down to inspect the wound. "Why would you fight to save Ghoram?"

It sounds like she is starting to believe me. Belac considered saying something to make himself seem braver than he was. *"Everything you do."* The elf decided to tell her the truth. "He said he was a smith."

Breana leaned back and looked down at the elf. "All giants are 'smiths." She said the word 'smith' as if it were a pejorative. She gestured to the empty scabbard on his back. "You already had a sword. Why would you risk your life to get another one?"

Once again, Belac considered bravado. He could have told her he had been unafraid. He could have claimed he was someone who would imperil his life for a stranger. He could have even suggested he enjoyed the thrill of combat. Instead, he told her the truth. "The sword I need has to be made in a special place, and it has to be made by a giant."

While she may not have believed him, the giantess seemed intrigued. "Why must this sword be forged by a giant?"

Belac shrugged. "Serath says that the sword has to be made by a giant for the ritual to work. Serath is the wizard," he reminded her. "It also has to be made out of starmetal."

Breana laughed again. She turned and rested one hand on a workbench as if she needed the support to keep from falling over.

Belac enjoyed watching her laugh. *I would be willing to watch her do just about anything.*

Breana looked at the elf with a tear in her eye. "I think I might keep you. Are you always this funny?"

If anyone was going to keep Belac, he would have wanted it to be the giantess. *The problem is, she sounds like she thinks I'm a pet.* He was flattered, offended, and disconcerted all at once. Not knowing what to say, he simply continued to watch her laugh.

"I see you have met Breana," Morkan said from behind the elf.

Belac turned toward the voice. Next to Morkan, stood Rolan. The dwarf stared stupidly at the giantess as she laughed. *I can't say I blame him.* Belac suddenly felt like he himself had been caught doing something he shouldn't.

"Morkan!" Breana began to speak to the other giant in their own language. She sounded like she was telling him a joke.

Morkan waited patiently.

Breana paused, and then spoke as if she were explaining the joke.

When she stopped, Morkan replied in Dwarven, "What the elf says is true."

Breana looked at the elf and spoke in Giant incredulously.

Morkan looked at the elf as well, though he spoke in Dwarven. "No. We cannot help them. Ghoram is too injured to travel, and I must remain in case of conflict."

Belac felt lied to. "You agreed to help me." *So much for the honor of giants.*

Breana said something angrily in Giant.

Morkan said, "I am willing to forge a sword, but I cannot leave our home." It was uncertain whom he was speaking to.

Breana gestured vaguely to her right and shouted in Giant.

Morkan replied in Giant, his tone no longer patient.

Breana pointed at the giant and began to berate him. Belac did not understand what she was saying, but her scorn was unmistakable.

Rolan evidently agreed with her. "I think that is a wonderful idea."

Belac had forgotten the dwarf was there. *Not my fault. That woman is distracting.*

Breana looked at the dwarf as if she had not noticed him before. "Who are you?"

Rolan walked over to the giantess and looked up into her eyes. He was tall for a dwarf, but he stood no taller than her hips. "My name is Rolan. And I think you are absolutely right."

The giantess's smile seemed to light the room. She nodded and then turned away.

Morkan said something in Giant. He did not sound pleased.

Breana ignored him. She took a large hide satchel from one of the workbenches and began to stuff tools into it.

Still speaking in Giant, Morkan said something that sounded like a threat.

Rolan's response was not friendly.

Belac was beginning to think Giant was not a friendly language.

Breana turned to look at the dwarf but said nothing.

Rolan was staring at Morkan as if he were about to climb up there and cut out the giant's eyes. Belac did not know what would happen if they fought, but he was sure that he would not have bet against Rolan.

Morkan threw up his hands, shouted in Giant, and then stormed out of the smithy.

Rolan continued to stare at the doorway until they heard another metal door slam shut. He turned around and said, "We need to leave now."

Belac did not understand how everything had gone wrong so fast. "We can't just leave, Rolan. We need a smith. We have to convince one of them to come with us."

"We have a smith," Rolan stated plainly.

Belac was confused for a moment. *He thinks he can make the sword himself!* Belac shook his head. "It has to be a giant."

Rolan gestured behind the elf. "We have one."

Belac turned around, still confused. Breana slung her satchel over her head and ran the strap across her chest between her breasts. Belac remembered her words. *"All giants are smiths."*

Breana picked up a long leather cord and began to wrap it around her left forearm. "If the men are too weak to bear our honor, then I will."

Twenty-Two

Belac followed behind Rolan and Breana as they journeyed through the mountains. And while the view was pleasant, Belac really wanted someone to explain what had just happened. Rolan and Breana had continued to speak with each other after leaving the giants' stronghold. *The problem is I don't speak Giant.* Belac thought for a moment. *No. The problem is that they refuse to speak a proper language!*

Belac decided to say something. "Do one of you want to tell me what just happened back there?"

"No," Rolan said without turning.

Breana nudged the dwarf but laughed. She turned to look back at the elf, smiling. "What do you not understand, Belac?"

Belac knew the giantess was trying to be nice, but he thought she might not comprehend what 'not understanding' was. "How about we start with why Morkan suddenly wants to kill us!"

Rolan grumbled, "I think Morkan probably always wanted to kill us."

Breana frowned at the dwarf in a way that seemed more like a smile. "Morkan simply did not wish for me to leave." She glanced back toward the elf. "So then, he behaved like a fool."

"Yeah, I got that part," Belac said irritably.

Breana frowned at the elf. It did not resemble a smile in the least. "Then, what do you not understand?"

Belac threw up his hands. "Why are you coming with us?!"

Rolan answered. "We need a smith," he said in a matter-of-fact tone that made the elf want to kick him in the back of the head.

"I know we need a smith, Rolan!" Belac gestured back toward the giants' stronghold. "Surely, we could have found another giant to come with us that was a..."

"A what?" Breana stopped and glared at the elf.

Belac halted at the challenge in that glare. He almost turned around and ran away. "A..." He coughed. *Do not say a 'a man.'* "A... A less important person."

Rolan laughed.

Belac narrowed his eyes at the dwarf.

Rolan stood with his arms crossed in a posture that clearly relayed that the elf was on his own.

"Oh?" Breana asked in complete disbelief. "You would rather have your sword forged by someone that is less important?"

Belac held up his hands in surrender. "I mean, someone less important to Morkan. If he did not want you to go with us, he could have just sent a different giant instead."

Breana's glare became a look of suspicion. "There is no one else to send. Lamana and Helana are away." She shook her head and leaned forward. "Even if they were here, they would not go with you."

There are no other giants? Belac tried to make sense of what he was being told. "Then, why are you coming with us?"

Rolan grumbled, "We need a smith," but to the elf it sounded like, *"shut up before you change her mind."*

Breana answered for herself. "Ghoram promised to forge your sword in payment for saving his life." She pointed at the elf aggressively. "I will not be the daughter of an oath breaker!"

The daughter? Belac grinned. "I saved your father!"

Breana said something irritably in Giant before turning around and continuing down the path.

Belac waited until the giantess was far enough away that he did not think she would hear him. "Are we really going to let her make the sword for us?" he asked the dwarf.

Rolan stopped smiling but kept his arms crossed. "That woman is stronger than any human man that has ever existed. She is older, wiser, and more experienced in the forging of metal than any human smith. We are not only going to let her make the sword, we are going to thank her for doing it." The dwarf turned and walked off after the giantess.

Belac's concern was not that Breana was a woman. *The problem is that she is just too pretty.* Weapons and war were ugly things to the elf. He felt that their creation was better left to ugly people. If Belac was going to face a dragon with nothing but a sword in hand, he wanted it forged by the ugliest and meanest person he could imagine. He felt like Breana was simply too good to create the weapon he needed.

Nothing seemed right to Belac. Serath was supposed to be there. Vairug was supposed to be there. And Breana was supposed to be an insane, terrifying giant of war. Something was wrong. Something was responsible for all this; and Belac had a definite idea what that was. *It is this stupid green cloak!* He knew it to his bones. *When I get out of these mountains, I am going to set this thing on fire!* In discontented silence, the elf began a determined march out of the mountains. He had a cloak to burn.

Belac caught up to Rolan and Breana at the opening to the cave trap. The giantess was staring down into the hole studying something while the dwarf waited patiently.

Breana turned at the elf's approach. "You jumped in there?" Her tone did not suggest it had been bravery.

Belac pulled back his cloak and gestured to his harnessing belt. "I sort of swung halfway down and then fell the rest of the way. There was not a lot of time to plan."

Searching for conformation, Breana looked from the elf to the dwarf. *She thinks I am a liar too!*

Rolan nodded. "He jumped."

Breana returned her attention to the darkened hole. "And then you fought in there?"

Belac nodded though he knew the giantess could not see him. He did not think she really wanted an answer anyway. He joined her next to the hole and looked down into the darkening cave. The bodies of the dead scalics were no longer there. Whatever had taken the corpses away had also taken his sword. The cave had grown dark in the fading of day, but Belac knew that the rock below would be stained with blood long after he had quit the mountains.

"What are you smiling at?" Breana asked him.

Belac had not realized he was smiling. In Elven, he said, "I am not food."

Rolan chuckled. "Let's hope they remember that." He walked around the hole to continue down the path.

Breana followed after the dwarf. "What did he say?"

She could have just asked me. I am standing right here!

Rolan answered with amusement. "The resolving battle cry of the Elven House of Melavar."

"Hey!" Belac shouted. "Who said you could go around telling people my name?" Then he added, "Rolan Brightstone."

Rolan looked back and frowned at the elf. "You wanted to be a famous dragon slayer but not have anyone know your name?"

"I…" Belac had not considered that. *What I want, is for no one to come and try to kill Belac Melavar!*

Breana smiled at the dwarf. "Your name is 'Brightstone?' That is a beautiful name."

Rolan grumbled. "That is not my name. It's my family's name. I am not allowed to use it."

That seemed strange to Belac. "Why not?" *Even I can use my family's name if I want to.*

Rolan shrugged dismissively. "Dwarven culture is complicated. We use a caste system. That makes names a bit more significant than they are for other people."

Breana was careful with her question. "Did they find you unworthy?"

Rolan shook his head. "It is more complicated than that. Every system, every culture, will have those that suffer for it. It would be great if that suffering were limited to the people that deserved it, but that is just not how it works."

How can he be so calm? While Belac could not have articulated the thought, what bothered him was the idea that an entire civilization was willing to collectively decide to deny the truth of who a person was. "Why are you not more upset?"

Rolan shrugged again. "It was a long time ago, Belac." Amusement bled into his voice. "I was not always so... understanding."

Belac had never thought of the dwarf as someone who would be 'understanding' if wronged. "What changed?"

Rolan sighed. "I traveled the world. And I found that there was more to it, than my own misfortune."

Twenty-Three

Rolan growled.

Even though Belac walked three paces behind, he worried the dwarf might turn around and bite him. He considered the dwarf warily. *I am not food!*

Breana did not seem worried she would get bitten. She looked around at the gray mountains that surrounded them. "Are you mad at the rocks?" she asked playfully.

"I smell a fire," Rolan said irritably.

Breana sniffed at the air with her perfectly shaped nose. "I smell it too."

Rolan nodded. "So does everything else around." He increased the speed of his stride. "I said no fires."

As Belac hurried after the dwarf, he was suddenly worried about the absent orc. *Dragons breathe fire.* "Do you think Vairug got eaten by the dragon?"

On reflex, Rolan said, "There is no dragon, Belac."

Easily matching his pace, Breana looked down at the dwarf. "If there is no dragon, then why do you need a magic sword that can kill a dragon?"

Rolan frowned up at the giantess. "Fine. There is a dragon. There is just not a dragon right here, right now." He pointed down the path with his whole hand. "There is just a reckless orc, doing something stupid."

Breana smiled down at the dwarf's frown. "You travel with an orc?" she asked with an amused surprise.

Rolan returned his attention down the rocky path. "It's complicated," he said dismissively.

"No, it's not," Belac disagreed without thinking. "Vairug is our friend, and he wants to help us kill Danorin."

"Danorin?" Breana asked with less amusement in her voice.

Belac nodded. "That's the dragon."

Breana did not need the explanation. "I know what The Danorin is." She shook her head. "I hope you die bravely."

I don't! Belac decided that they needed to get another giant. He did not want one that expected him to die. He wanted one that would let him ride on its shoulders while they charged into battle screaming in defiance. *Wait a moment... That sounds an awful lot like dying bravely.* "Well, I hope we come up with a better plan than that."

When they finally reached the base of the mountain, Vairug was nowhere to be seen. Belac looked out over the rolling hills of golden grass. *Where would he go?* Belac revisited the idea that the orc may have been eaten. *I guess something other than a dragon could have eaten him.*

Vairug stepped away from the wagon and walked over to join them. *Oh, yeah. The wagon.* The orc stopped a short distance away and stared openly at the unclothed giantess. Rolan glared at him, but Vairug did not seem to notice. *Completely understandable.*

Belac gestured to the orc. "Breana, this is Vairug. He's an orc." Belac then gestured to the giantess. "Vairug, this is Breana. She is a giant."

Vairug did not look away from the giantess. "The giants are very pretty," he said by way of introduction.

Rolan grumbled, "Not all of them." He marched past the orc. "We got lucky."

Breana looked at the orc like he was a puppy that had just done a backflip. "Hello, Vairug."

Rolan kicked dirt at the remains of a small fire. "I said no fires, Vairug."

Vairug turned calmly to face the dwarf. "I kept it small. It is daytime; no one saw it. And the smoke will not travel to the road."

"I could smell it," Rolan argued irritably.

"The wind is blowing toward the mountains." Vairug shrugged. "I caught a squirrel and wanted to cook it."

Belac pointed at the orc dramatically. "You ate my squirrel!"

Vairug looked back at the elf as if he thought he were crazy. "Then, put your name on the next one."

He ate my squirrel. Belac did not understand why it bothered him so much. He thought about it for a moment. *I guess I can forgive him. The squirrel was kind of rude anyway.*

Breana walked toward the dark Enevician horses. "Those are beautiful."

"Don't eat them!" Belac said, remembering the story of the giant that had eaten the king's horse.

Breana gave the elf a perturbed look. "Why would I eat them?" She ran her fingers through one of the horses' black manes. "They are such beautiful creatures."

"Yes," Vairug said. "Beautiful."

Belac did not think the orc was referring to the horses. *Am I the only one that wanted an ugly giant?!*

Rolan waved negligently toward the setting sun. "We need to bed down for the night. I want to have this wagon ready to move before dawn. And that means waking up early."

Belac gestured to the wagon. "I don't think we can all fit in there, Rolan. Where is everyone going to sleep?"

Rolan nodded toward the giantess. "Breana is going to keep watch and make sure we wake up early enough to get this wagon moving on time."

Belac considered the giantess. "Don't giants need to sleep too?"

"She can sleep in the wagon tomorrow on the way to Harbridge," Rolan told him. "But if her uncle shows up in the night looking for her, I want her awake."

Her uncle? Belac was confused for a moment. *Morkan!* He felt like he really should have put that together sooner. *If Morkan is Ghoram's brother, and Ghoram is Breana's father, then that makes Morkan Breana's uncle.* Morkan's behavior suddenly made more sense to the elf. *He did not want his niece to go running off with two strange men she had just met.* Belac almost laughed.

Rolan frowned at the elf. "You are not going to think it is funny if you wake up to an angry giant."

Belac recalled the threatening, insane look of the giant's eyes, but he did not think that Morkan would try to kill them in their sleep. The elf kept his smile and walked past Rolan to where Breana stood with the horses. Belac removed his baldric and then unbuckled his cloak. He held the heavy green cloth out to the giantess.

Breana took the cloak with a questioning look.

Belac nodded to the cloak. "You can lay it out and have something to sit on."

Breana's smile had a slight touch of surprise in it. "Thank you, Belac."

The elf shrugged and tried not to blush. *I just want to get rid of the thing.* He glanced at the remnants of Vairug's small campfire. *And I don't think Rolan is going to let me burn it.* Belac smiled shyly and nodded to the giantess before turning and walking over to the back of the wagon. He tossed his empty scabbard inside the cabin and then sat down in the doorway. He dug into the bag at his side and pulled out the wrapped ration. *I should have eaten this earlier.*

Belac still could not taste anything. He sniffed at the food. *Maybe that is a good thing.* He could not smell the rations, but he did not think they would have smelled appealing if he could. *I just hope my taste comes back in time to have a real meal.*

Rolan walked up to the elf and stared at him for a moment. "You are in the way."

Belac's back straitened. *That is kind of a hurtful thing to say.*

Rolan waved impatiently. "Move."

"Oh!" Belac scooted to the side so that the dwarf could step past him.

Rolan went inside the cabin and began to arrange things for the night. The sound of the boxes being moved around was loud in the closed space, but Belac did his best to ignore it. He finished eating and then crawled into the wagon.

Taking a seat on one of the benches, Belac asked, "Do you know where my other sword is?"

"The one you stole from Lorance?" Rolan questioned in response.

"I did not steal it," Belac argued. "He was already dead when I took it."

Rolan chuckled. "So, if a couple of guys kill you and then take your coin purse, you would not call it stealing?"

"I would not call it anything," Belac said. "I would be dead."

"Right." Rolan nodded. "But that is still a seriously big loophole."

"Fine." Belac changed tact. "I am just borrowing it. If Lorance wants his sword back, all he has to do is let me know."

Rolan held up a hand to stop the elf. "So, if a rotting corpse walks up to you and says," he held out his arms and spoke in a slow, deep voice, "Give. Me. My. Sword." He dropped his arms and laughed. "You are going to just hand it over to him?"

Belac laughed with the dwarf. "I never agreed to give it to him hilt first."

Twenty-Four

That night, Belac dreamed of Emily. They were once more in the nillanan's domain. This time, they were alone. This time, things were different.

The world felt washed away and nothing seemed true except Emily. The princess stared back at him from across a stone table, complete trust in her eyes. Golden hair framed the noble features of her face, and Belac wanted nothing more than to reach out and touch the delicate skin of the cheek beneath. She was an icon of innocence too lovely to behold. He looked away.

Instead, he studied the magic charm in his hand. It was a thing without form or substance; however, its power was undeniably real. He held the power of life and death itself. Life for one, and death for another. He had chosen life; life for himself. And in so doing, he had chosen death for another. He had chosen death for Emily. *I killed her.*

Belac's lost gaze returned to the princess. They were now on the mechanical lift, rising slowly to the freedom above. Emily was dead in his arms. Her lifeless eyes stared back at him. *A blue that could have been the sky…* He wept, and tears rained down on her face.

Never had the elf known such sorrow. Even when he had held her in his arms last, he had escaped the depth of his emotion. Now, he drowned. There was nothing but sorrow. *Soon, there will be nothing left of me.* Belac clung to the memory of Emily as if he clung to himself.

The world rocked, and strange noise pressed in. Belac felt like his heart was being washed away with the dream.

"…Attack!" a woman's strong voice cried out.

The dream was shaken away as a gruff voice ordered, "Get up!"

Belac's eyes opened to darkness and confusion. He could hear scuffling outside the wagon. Rolan turned away, put his hand on Vairug's shoulder, and vaulted feet first over the orc. He landed in front of the door and threw it open before flying out into the night.

Moonlight lit the inside of the cabin and brought with it a sense of reality. Vairug rose from the floor, his cogged mace glinting as he charged out of the wagon.

Belac's heart was racing, but his thoughts were still slow. *I need to move faster.* Whatever was happening, he did not want his friends to have to face it without him. He grabbed his boots and began to tug them on as fast as he could.

The sounds of battle and guttural hissing informed the elf what awaited him outside. *It's the creepy-blue-lizard-goblins!* The horses screamed and then Belac heard the sound of something heavy hitting the ground.

Remembering to take his new sword with him, Belac scampered out of the cabin. The moon was so bright, the elf almost needed to shield his eyes. He had stepped into yet another surreal world; one of black and white contrast that left the colors of life forgotten.

Belac drew his sword and then tossed the empty scabbard back into the cabin. He felt the uneven leather wrapping the hilt of the sword digging into his palm. *I hope this sword works as well as the last one.* He immediately changed his mind. *Better! I hope it works better!*

Rolan's voice called out in the night. "Vairug! Get the horses!"

Belac did not know how Vairug was going to do that with only one hand while also carrying a mace. *Can orc's juggle? Who would not want to see an orc juggle?* The scalics that attacked Belac afforded him no time to consider it further. The suddenness of their attack reminded the elf that he needed to pay more attention to not dying. Had they not hissed at him, Belac may have died unaware, thinking about an orcish carnival.

Belac swung his sword up and to his left, the back of the blade cutting into a hissing face. Black blood sprayed from pale scales bleached by the moonlight. Taking the hilt in both hands, Belac turned the swords momentum in the air above him and brought the blade down and through the torso of another scalic. He lifted the sword back up above him and then twisted sideways as he dodged a spear thrust toward his midsection. Swinging the sword down, he hacked into the back of the attacking scalics neck, severing its reptilian head.

Wanting to finish the last of his attackers quickly, Belac thrust his long blade at the remaining scalic's chest. A crude spear pushed the sword away; however, Belac continued to press forward. He slammed his hip into the scalic, knocking it off balance before sweeping the blade of his sword up and clipping the side of the creature's head. The blow was awkward, but the blade bit into the scalic's skull with a wet crunching sound as it tore away a slab of bone and brain.

Belac spun around in a circle, searching for more threats. He could hear the sounds of fighting, but the only other person he could see was Vairug. *The others must be on the other side of the wagon.* The orc held the lead of a frightened horse and was directing it toward the front of the wagon. Another horse lay dead on the ground next to more slain scalics, a spear jutting from the animal's side. *Rolan must be harnessing the other two.*

Guttural hissing came from the other side of the wagon, angry and insistent. *That leaves Breana to fight alone!* Belac raced to the left side of the wagon, running toward Vairug and the last horse. The sparce trees lining the creek made the approach feel less exposed. He wanted to help Breana, but he did not want to die doing it. *I can't be much help dead.*

More guttural hissing on his left warned Belac of another attack. Rising from the creek bed, four scalics surged out fangs first. *I have to stop them from getting to Vairug!* Belac changed course and rushed at the scalics.

His first swing was wild, and the scalic he had intended to kill dodged easily. The creature twisted and countered with a thrust of its spear. Belac was able to swat the crude thing aside, but he knew focusing on defense would only get him killed. He stepped in dangerously close to the scalic and wrenched his sword down into where its neck met shoulder. The blade cut deep into the creature and caught on rib and spine. Blood gushed across Belac's front and splattered against his teeth.

He put his shoulder into the dying scalic and threw it bodily toward two of the others as he pulled his blade free. As Belac turned with the throw, he saw that a scalic had gotten behind him. He let the momentum of the turn flow up into the sword and then brought it down on the scalic. The blade cleaved through the creature, the thick hides it wore doing little to slow the steel.

Belac's commitment to the swing left him bent forward with his sword held out behind him. He looked back past the blade and saw the oncoming scalics. Leaping away, the elf rolled over the upper half of the scalic he had cleaved in two. He came to his feet swinging his sword in a wide arch as he turned to face the vicious things. The blade swept through the air between him and the scalics, halting their advance. Belac stepped into the momentum he had created and swung his sword overhead in a one-handed grip. It felt like his shoulder was being torn from its socket, but the extra reach allowed his blade to slice through another reptilian face.

The remaining scalic let out an enraged hiss and lunged at the elf. Belac's left hand joined his right on the sword's hilt in an underhanded grip. He used the sword to guide the spear aside and then drove his blade into the scalic's chest. He pinned the creature to the ground and then stomped a booted foot down on its slim, scaly neck.

Holding the scalic down with his foot, Belac jerked his sword free. *I hope Breana saw all that.* His attention snaped toward the front of the wagon. *Breana!* He remembered his need to save her.

It was then that Belac witnessed the giant. Ahead of the wagon, farther into the night, Breana was surrounded by scalics. Most of the creatures were dead, their broken bodies scattered around her. She fought naked, with nothing but the leather cord wrapped tightly around her left forearm, and a blacksmith's hammer gripped firmly in her right fist. Her hair had come undone, allowing the white strands to gleam silver as she moved in the moonlight.

Where she moved, scalics died. Her hammer tore through the creatures, ripping away gory chunks of flesh and bone. With every strike, one of the scalics fell. Though they were fearless in their assault, they could not stop her swings. The giantess had already killed more of the creatures than Belac had; and yet still, she faced more.

As Belac stared transfixed, he realized Breana was not slowing down. He saw no sign of fatigue or faulter. *How can she…* The rhythm of her swings only increased. While another would tire from such extreme exertion, she seemed to breathe in the death, and feed it to her rage.

Belac did not care what she looked like. Breana was a terrifying giant of war.

Twenty-Five

"Why are the mountains on fire?" Belac pointed toward the mountains with his sword. He glanced at the giantess before quickly looking away.

Breana's white skin was painted with blood and gore like a canvas depicting the horrors of war. The insane rings in her eyes shown with an excitement the night could not hide. It was the first time Belac did not want to look at her.

Breana's voice was far too calm for a woman who had slaughtered so many. "It is more of these scalic things." She swept her arm out to the dead around her.

I know that! Belac glanced at the giantess again and decided he did not need to explain that to her. He felt safer looking at the army coming to kill them. The mountains were alight with countless flames of ember orange that had lit in a wave across the rocky prominence. *Every one of those flames is a creepy-blue-lizard-goblin that wants to kill me.*

Breana's smile could be heard in her words. "Think of it as dragon slaying practice."

I would really rather start with wooden cutouts. Or maybe a padded leather dummy on puppet strings. Belac took a deep breath to steady himself. "If I die before I kill a dragon, will people still call me 'The Dragon Slayer?"

There was no fear in Breana's voice. "Survive this, and your name will be sung in legend."

"No deal." Belac shook his head. "For this, I deserve a song even if I die."

Breana's laugh was almost enough to make him forget his terror of her.

The dots of fire began to pour down the mountainside. The scalics moved quietly, but their numbers were too great for them to be silent. *Even had they come without the torches, we still would have heard them.* Belac considered the torches. *The moon must be bright enough for the scalics to see without them. The torches are to frighten us.*

That the scalics wanted him frightened changed things for the elf. True predators did not want their pray frightened. It made the scalics seem less monstrous to Belac. *Monstrous or not, they still want me dead.*

Rolan shouted from behind the elf, "Belac! Get on the wagon!"

Belac and Breana turned to see the dwarf standing on the driver's bench with Vairug seated next to him. *Yes, please.* Belac decided he really did not want a song. He ran to the wagon, not caring how cowardly he looked.

Belac tossed his sword on top of the wagon's cabin where it landed with a clangor. He followed after it, scrambling past Rolan on the driver's bench. Belac snatched up his sword and then wedged his foot under a luggage rail. He looked at the fiery scalic horde in the distance. *Why is the wagon not moving?*

Rolan pointed his hand away from the mountains commandingly. "Breana, lead us to the road. Follow our tracks as best you can, but watch out for anything that will break a wheel. We need to move fast."

Yes. Fast. Belac nodded emphatically. *Why is the wagon still not moving?* He looked from side to side, though no one else was there. *Am I the only one who realizes that the wagon needs to be moving?!* He slammed his hand down on the roof of the cabin. "Let's go!"

Rolan plopped down on the driver's bench and flicked the reins. The wagon lurched forward and began to turn to the right. The motion jostled Belac, and his face bounced against the roof of the cabin. He yanked his foot free and rolled over before lodging it back under the luggage rail on the opposite side. Sitting up, the elf expected his fear to abate as they fled. It did not.

The closest of the scalics broke away from the main horde and sped toward the wagon. Belac did not know if they were an advance force, or simply the warriors too eager to wait, too blood thirsty to allow their enemy to escape. *Whatever they are, those will be some of their most dangerous.*

Belac swept a fallen lock of his long black hair behind his pointed ear. "They are still coming, Rolan!"

Will three horses be fast enough? The elf glanced behind himself toward the surviving horses. Breana loped ahead, leading them away and to safety. Belac looked back to the flaming army of scalics racing toward him. He decided he would prefer to have the giantess on the other side of the wagon. *I want her between me and those things!*

The scalics were faster than the horses. Using their thick tails for balance, the reptilian creatures ran bent forward. *It looks like they are slithering through the air.* Each of the scalics brought with them a crude spear in one hand and a blazing torch in the other, the open flames giving their pale blue scales an orange hue in the night.

Staring at the hellish sight, Belac realized something. *The fight is not over.* Safety was not something he would be given freely. Escape would require more combat. Leather creaked as he tightened his grip on the hilt of his sword. *Lizards and fire.* He looked up, his azure eyes cutting through the moonlight. *Dragon slaying practice.*

Belac pulled his foot free from the railing once more and rolled forward onto his knees. He made his stance as wide as he could, using both his feet and knees for balance. The wagon shook beneath him, but Belac was determined to fight. If a song were to be sung, it would not be of an elf that had cowered in the night.

A burning torch flew up and landed on the wagon. Belac picked the torch up and threw it back down at one of the scalics. The fiery head of the torch slammed into the unfortunate scalic's skull. Its hiss of pain was joined by others of threatening malice.

A spear flew past Belac. *I should try to dodge those.* He heard claws dig into wood on his right. Turning toward the sound of the climbing scalic, Belac held his sword out to his left in preparation to swing. When the scaly head popped up, his blade hacked through it.

This time, Belac saw the scalic that threw its spear. It twisted while running and hurled the weapon with an alien grace. Belac dropped onto his back, the spear flying through the air where his chest had just been. Behind him, claws dug into the wagon. Rolling onto his stomach, Belac swung his sword at the climbing scalic. The swing was weak, but it was enough to dissuade the creature. The blade cut into its jaw and sent it spinning away from the wagon.

Following the swing, Belac rolled onto his back. A spear thudded into the side of the wagon. *We are not going to escape if we don't move faster.* He sat up and got his legs under himself. He looked back toward the pursuing horde. Discarded torches had set the grass on fire. The spreading patches of flame might slow the larger force, but it would not stop the wagon from being boarded.

All around him, Belac heard claws digging into wood. Relentless in their chase, the scalics had set the world on fire for the chance to taste elven blood. *I am not food!* Belac knew he could not wait for them to all come at him at once. He leaned over the side to see if he could stop one there. A scalic clinging to the side of the wagon hissed up at the elf and thrust a spear toward his face. Belac turned away from the spear and swung his sword at the scalic blindly. The steel shuddered in his hand as his blade cut through scales and skull.

Another scalic rose from the back of the wagon, thrusting its spear without hesitation. Belac slapped the spear aside with his left hand and then buried the length of his blade in the scalic's bony chest. Blood spattered across Belac's face as the creature attempted to hiss.

Two more of the scalics climbed onto the wagon's roof. Expecting their attack to be immediate, Belac wrenched the impaled scalic between himself and its kin. The elf's back slammed onto the top of the wagon as their weight pressed down onto the dying scalic. Struggling to hold back their reaching claws, Belac braced his feet on the impaled scalic and kicked the tangled mass of frenzied reptiles away from him. His sword slid wetly from the scalic's chest as the creatures were thrown over the side. However, the force of the shove pushed Belac back and he rolled off the rear of the wagon.

With luck born of desperation, Belac grabbed the end of the luggage rail. Holding on almost broke his wrist, but he slammed into the back of the wagon instead of the ground speeding past below. A scalic ran toward him, preparing to thrust with its spear. Belac's sword swept out in a wild backhanded swing that hacked into its reptilian snout. The scalic was sent off balance and it tripped, tumbling to a motionless stop.

Hanging twisted from the back of the wagon, Belac stared at the burning hills. Hazy smoke and spreading flames had joined the scalic's cause. It was as if the night itself were angry. Fire and fury hungered for the elf. *I need a new job.*

Twenty-Six

Belac spun around to face the wagon. *Why do I want to be a dragon slayer anyway?* He tossed his sword up on onto the wagon's roof. *That has got to be the worse career choice in the history of the world.* He reached up and grabbed the end of the luggage rail with his now free hand. *I might as well have chosen to be a...* He paused, trying to think of something more dangerous than a dragon slayer. *...A nothing! Nothing is more dangerous than being a dragon slayer!*

Belac whipped his body and then braced his feet against the back of the wagon. He pushed off with his legs and pulled with his arms, vaulting himself onto the top of the cabin. The wagon lurched and he had to grab the luggage rail again to keep from falling over. Bent forward on one knee, holding onto the railing for support, he looked up to find a reptilian warrior holding a sword.

Hey! That's mine! Staring at the scalic, Belac decided that if a lizard could smile, that is what it would look like. "Stupid, thieving lizard!"

Rolan reached back with a knife and stabbed the scalic in the side of its rib cage. The scalic pulled away from the blow and then collapsed to its knees. Belac rushed at it and grabbed the hilt of his sword. He pried the weapon loose and then shoved the scalic off the wagon.

Belac shouted at the dwarf, "Where have you been?!"

Rolan gestured irritably ahead of the wagon. "I've been keeping the scalics from killing the horses." He held up his springer as evidence.

"Well, that's! ..." Belac stopped shouting. "Okay, that was probably a good idea."

Rolan growled and then leapt onto the cabin with the elf. He stood on the center of the roof, his short legs easily balancing him despite the wagon's jostling. With a professional focus, he proceeded to load and shoot his springer at the trailing scalics.

If he had done this from the beginning, maybe I would not have almost died six times! Belac did not know how many times he had almost died, but he was sure it was at least six. *Wait. If I am busy almost dying, and Rolan is shooting at the scalics, who is driving the wagon?* A quick glance showed Belac that Vairug held the reins. *Oh great. I'm riding on the back of a wagon while a one handed orc races it through the hills at night!* Belac looked back toward the horde of scalics chasing them. *And the hills are on fire!* He wanted to hop up and down in agitation.

Instead, Belac took a deep breath and watched Rolan kill scalics. *Even if we somehow manage to get away, the scalics could just follow the trail of their dead and find us.* Belac decided that if the only way he could find someone was to follow a trail of corpses that looked exactly like himself, he would need to reconsider his priorities.

Rolan turned away from the fiery death following them and put his hand on Belac's shoulder. He then used the elf to steady himself as he climbed down onto the driver's bench.

Belac glanced back toward the scalics. "I don't think they are giving up, Rolan."

Rolan holstered his springer. "If that fire does not stop them, the road might."

"The road?" Belac did not believe him. "Why would the road stop them?" He thought it sounded like the start of a bad joke.

"It is what it represents," Rolan began to explain.

"And what is that?" Belac asked.

Rolan frowned at the interruption. "Civilization," he answered and then continued his explanation. "The scalics are primitive, but they are not stupid. They understand how dangerous civilization is." He looked back at the elf. "And they know better than to wake sleeping dragons."

"I don't know why you are looking at me?" Belac said defensively. "If Danorin is asleep when it's time to kill him, I am not going to wake him up before I do it!"

Rolan grinned grudgingly. Leaning over to the other side of the bench, he nudged the orc. "Slow us down."

Belac understood that racing a wagon off road was perilous. *It is amazing we have not broken a wheel already.* He speculated that somewhere amongst the chaos, his hated green cloak must have been set on fire. *That is the only thing that could explain our luck.* Still, when the wagon began to slow, Belac almost panicked.

"Why are we slowing down?!" Belac's attention bounced back and forth between the slowing horses and the fires behind them.

Rolan answered calmly. "Not even Enevician horses can keep that pace up all night. We need to let them catch their breath. Besides, the scalics have fallen too far behind. They are not going to catch us." He looked back at the elf. "Not unless we run the horses to death."

"What?!" Belac asked. *That is not how a chase works! You keep running until your safe!* "What if there is another group without torches?"

Vairug answered, "Then, we kill them."

Belac narrowed his eyes at the orc.

Rolan did not allow for argument. "When we make the road, we can pick up the pace. That will put the most distance between us and the scalics."

Belac appreciated the goal if not the plan. "Why are they so determined to kill us?"

Rolan began to count on his fingers. "You interfered in a war. You aided their enemy. You killed kind of a lot of them." He gestured toward the fires still burning. "And you set their home on fire."

Belac pointed to the fire and smoke behind them. "I did not set that!"

Rolan nodded. "Feel free to go tell them that." He pointed with his thumb.

In a helpful tone, Vairug said, "I can stop the wagon if you want to get off and go back."

Belac narrowed his eyes at the orc again. "Did you know they tell stories about how funny orcs are?"

Vairug shook his head. "No." He sounded a little surprised.

Belac shouted, "That is because they are not!"

Vairug laughed. "Is that why I never hear about wise elves?"

Belac sputtered. "That..."

Rolan issued a sharp laugh. "Look at his face!"

Vairug turned in his seat to see the elf.

Belac let go of the luggage rail and gestured forcefully toward the horses. "Watch where you are going!"

Vairug made a show of peering ahead at the rolling hills of grass rippling in the moonlight. "Do you think I am going to hit a tree?" His gaze lingered on the giantess. "Though, if you insist..."

Rolan chuckled deeply. "Be careful, Vairug. That woman will rip off your other hand."

Vairug snorted. "As long as it is only my hand." He shrugged. "You can make me another one of those."

Rolan laughed at the idea, but Belac did not think it was funny. He could see it now. As they continued their quest, Vairug would have more and more of himself replaced until he was more machine than orc. *Maybe that is what will let him survive the dragon. Maybe he will be the only one that survives.* Belac thought of Vairug, more metal than flesh, standing alone among charred ruins. Belac could feel the tragedy of it. *Mostly because I would be dead.*

The elf sat quietly while his friends laughed. *We can't keep this up. One of us is going to die.* The thought of Rolan or Vairug being lost was no more preferable than being crippled himself. *How much can a person loose before there is no longer a reason to go on?*

Breana's voice drew the elf from his dark thoughts. "There is a river ahead!"

Rolan stood up and shouted over the horses, "We can cross it. It is more shallow than it looks."

Belac slapped the orc on the shoulder and pointed ahead. "Look. Trees."

Vairug growled, "I see them."

Elated they would escape the scalics, Belac turned to the dwarf. "This means we are almost to the road!"

Rolan nodded. "The river should also stop the fire if the wind changes."

Belac looked back. The fires still raged, but he could not actually see any of the scalics. He had not considered the direction of the wind. *If it had been blowing the other way, we could have been burned to death.* That settled things for the elf. *No doubt about it. That green cloak is ash.*

Twenty-Seven

"How many scalics do you think I killed with that fire?" Belac asked over the rumbling of the wagon.

True to his word, Rolan had increased their speed once they were on the road. While the horses could have run faster, their pace was fast enough that Belac felt safer every moment that passed.

Rolan answered inquisitively, "Now, you want credit for the fire?"

Belac shrugged. "Fire or steel, a dead scalic is still dead."

Jogging beside the wagon, Breana asked, "You started the fire?"

Belac did not think she sounded happy about it. "Only the first one." Then he added, "Sort of."

Breana harrumphed, but said nothing.

Belac noted that after all she had done, the giantess was not winded. She had fought what amounted to a small army and then ran ahead of the horses. However, when given the option to ride on the wagon, she had chosen to run alongside it instead. *Maybe giants really are just better.*

Something slammed into the lead horse. It was thrown violently off the road, pulling the other two horses with it. The animals fell in a tangled heap and the wagon was wrenched to the side. The wheels snapped and the wagon toppled into the road with a crash of broken wood.

Belac was launched from the roof to fly backward into the night. He yelled unintelligibly as he flew, his arms and legs flailing for balance. His yell ended abruptly when he collided with the road. He hit with his upper shoulders, and his feet were thrown over his head. He bounced and rolled gracelessly until he laid sprawled in the middle of the road.

There was a moment of nothingness, and then Belac woke to a world of pain. He did not know how many of his bones had been broken, but his body refused to move. *No.* It was a thought that denied all others. *No.* He did not understand what had happened, but he would not accept this new reality. He would move again.

"No." Belac's voice was a painful croak. His hand twitched and his shoulder spasmed. With the force of pure will, he pushed away from the road and rolled himself onto his back. For a moment, there was nothing in the world except him and his pain. *If it hurts, then I can still feel. If I can feel, I can move.* True or not, the thought gave him strength.

The horses were screaming but they sounded too far away. Belac focused on lifting his other hand. It hurt to move but the arm responded. He held his hand in front of his face and stared at the blood and grit smeared across his palm. The horses had stopped screaming.

The thing that attacked him was gray in the moonlight. Black eyes and bladed teeth rushed into Belac's view. Terrified into the present, he held the thing back with both hands, his pain forgotten. Dull fingertips dug into the elf's arms and the teeth moved closer in. Warm drool leaked down onto Belac's cheek as he turned his face away. The teeth continued to move closer until they were held back by nothing but Belac's left forearm against the monsters neck. Snarling, gargling sounds came from the thing as it bit at the air between them.

With frantic determination, Belac forced the numb fingers of his right hand to grip the hilt of his dagger. He jerked the blade free from its sheath and stabbed the monster in its naked gray chest. The monster continued to bite at the air, each snap of its jaw bringing teeth closer to the elf's face. As the monster bit, Belac stabbed, seeking to pierce its heart.

When the monster stopped biting, Belac did not stop stabbing. He rolled over on top of the vile thing and began to hammer his dagger into its chest repeatedly. The elf was snarling as he bared teeth of his own. He would have been horrified had he somehow saw how closely he resembled the monster in that moment.

Belac stood and stumbled away from the gruesome work. He only vaguely realized that he could stand. He stared down at the thing that had tried to kill him. *It has to be a ghoul.* Waxy gray skin covered a sexless humanoid form. Though masculine in bone structure, Belac would not have thought of the thing as a man even if it had not been absent of genitalia.

There will be more. Belac spun around, unsteady on his feet. The toppled wagon had been swarmed by ghouls and still more poured in from the hills to his left. The nightmarish things ran on their hands and feet with an unnatural gait, gray hairless skin gleaming in the moonlight. *Where did my sword go?*

Already up and fighting, Rolan stabbed a ghoul under its jaw while standing over the corpse of another. The dwarf leaned in with his shoulders and flipped the ghoul over his back using the knife as a handle. Not satisfied it was dead, Rolan then stomped on the ghoul's skull.

Vairug was lying next to the wagon, struggling to lift the broken mass off his long braided hair. With his wrist together, he pushed against the grip of his single hand. The wagon however, was simply too heavy for the orc to move.

Where is Breana?! A gray body flew over the wagon and landed limply in the road. Its chest had been caved in and it was missing an arm. Belac looked past the top of the wagon and saw a glimpse of something white. *And that would be her.*

Rolan ran to the struggling orc and knelt down next to him. He reached out with his knife and cut through Vairug's braid with a quick motion.

"Get up," Rolan ordered briskly before standing and then vaulting over a dead horse.

Vairug sat up, clutching the remains of his severed braid. He appeared more shocked than when he had lost his hand. A ghoul leapt onto the back corner of the wagon, black eyes directed at the confused orc. Thin lips peeled away from its bladed teeth.

Belac was running before he could think. He caught the thing in mid-air as it attempted to pounce on Vairug. Belac slammed the ghoul against the wagon and drove his dagger into its chest. Convinced a single thrust would prove insufficient, he stabbed the monster repeatedly. When the ghoul stopped fighting and Belac was sure it was dead, he stepped back and let the bloody carcass fall to the ground.

Belac turned to the startled orc. "Stop playing with your hair, and get up!"

Vairug's eyes hardened at the words, but he began to climb to his feet. Belac helped the orc stand and then followed Rolan around the front of the wagon, circling dead ghouls and the mangled horses as he made his way to the dwarf.

Rolan had moved ahead of Breana, tearing into the oncoming ghouls like a fish swimming upstream. The giantess followed in his wake, swinging her hammer over and around the dwarf. One misstep, and they would have killed each other.

I am staying over here. Belac was willing to fight, but he was not walking into that. Vairug bumped into him when he stopped, causing the elf to stumble and trip over a dead ghoul. Belac fell into the road, smearing something awful on his shoulders and back. He rolled away from the muddy mix of bodily fluids and glared up at the orc angrily.

"Hold them back!" Rolan ordered and then stepped aside for the giantess.

Without bothering to answer, Breana pressed into the fray. Hammer and fury rebuked the monsters' hunger. Though her advance was halted, the ghouls continued to die around her.

Vairug bent down and hooked his left wrist under Belac's arm, helping him to stand. Rolan ran past them, both hands digging into pouches on either side of his belt. He pulled a slim vial from each pouch and threw them at the wagon, first one and then the other. When the second vial broke against the liquid from the first, fire engulfed the wagon.

Rolan turned away from the flames, ready to continue the fight. However, the ghouls immediately shrank back as the night was burned away. They cried in strange gargling voices and retreated beyond the fire's glow.

Rolan called out, "We have to move!" his commanding tone drawing the others attention to the dwarf and the fire raging behind him.

Breana walked backward away from the ghouls. "How? Where can we go?"

Belac agreed with her. If the fire held back the ghouls, he wanted to stay there until the sun came up. *The sun counts as fire, right?*

Rolan was not interested in consension. "East." He removed his pack and set it down in front of himself. With quick movements, he pulled out a long wooden box and set it to the side. "We have to make it to the ocean." He slung his pack and picked up the box before standing. "We have to move now."

"Ghouls can't swim?" Belac asked hopefully.

Rolan ignored him. "Breana, you hold the rear, but don't stop to fight the ghouls. If someone goes down, pick them up and carry them to the front."

Breana nodded.

Vairug spoke proudly, "I will not need to be carried."

Rolan scowled at the orc. "If you don't want to be carried, then don't stop running."

Twenty-Eight

"Do you people have to set everything on fire?!" Breana asked as they fled through the night.

The flames had spread from the wagon to the dry grass behind them. And while the fire separated them from the ghouls, they would be no less dead if they were caught. Belac glanced back at the blaze and thought about the monsters on the other side. *I really do not want to get eaten alive by ghouls.* He never before would have believed that being burned to death was a preferable alternative to anything.

Vairug answered the giantess, "I have set nothing on fire."

Belac swiveled and then pointed at the orc as they ran. "Liar! You ate my squirrel!"

"Enough!" Rolan called back over his shoulder. "You can argue when we are safe."

As far as Belac could tell, they were never going to be safe. *The dwarf thinks he is clever.* He narrowed his eyes at the back of Roland's head. *You are not going to trick me with reason!*

"And you think the ocean is safe?" Belac asked. Drinking in taverns, he had listened to many sailors' stories. *The ocean is no safer than land.* Sea monsters, pirates, curses, and demons disguised as men were but the beginning of the dangers the ocean had to offer. *The ocean even has its own dragons!*

Rolan gestured into the air aimlessly with one hand. "Safe…er"

"Oh?" Belac's tone was sarcastic. "Because that is what people wish for before they sleep. Children everywhere close their eyes and say, 'I hope everyone I love is safe," he yelled the last part, "Er!"

Rolan's answer was amused. "The smart ones do."

Belac looked around for something to throw at the dwarf. Grass and shadows were the only things readily available. He considered throwing one of his boots, but he did not think Rolan would give it back to him. *At least, not nicely.*

They crested a hill, and Belac saw the ocean waiting for them on the other side of a rocky shore. Moonlight danced on the surface of waters too great to be tamed. *It just looks like one more thing that wants to kill me.*

Rolan maintained their pace, neither slowing at the reassurance of safety, nor speeding into its embrace. Belac felt like this was the time something would happen. He did not know what that would be, but he felt like they were too close to safety to reach it unimpeded. He expected the ghouls to head them off, or scalics to flank from the side. *Or a giant fiery ball of fire to fall from the sky and set us all on fire.*

When nothing bad happened, Belac decided that the only reason was that he had known it was coming. In his mind, the catastrophe was simply holding back until he was unprepared. *It is just trying to make me doubt myself.* He narrowed his eyes at nothing. *Stupid, sneaky, …badness!*

Rolan stopped at the ocean's edge. He took the wooden box he carried in both hands and twisted the top free. He tossed the smaller piece aside and slid a glass bottle from the open container. Inside the bottle nestled a miniature boat with a single sail. Rolan gripped the bottle by the neck and smashed it on a nearby rock. In a shower of shattered glass, the toy boat fell to the shore with its mast broken. Rolan dropped the empty box, then picked up the broken boat and threw it into the ocean.

As the miniature boat flew through the air, it began to grow in size. When it landed in the water a short way from the rocks of the shore, the boat was large enough to carry them all. The simple fishing boat was small, but it could no longer be called miniature.

Breana gasped in amazement.

Belac pointed and said, "Your boat is broken."

Rolan growled at the elf, "Get in." He waded out into the ocean without waiting.

Breana followed, happy to investigate the magical boat. Belac thought she might offer to help the dwarf, but Rolan lifted himself up and over the side before Breana reached him.

Vairug nudged the elf on the shoulder with his forearm then pointed with his wrist. "That does look safer."

Belac mumbled, "That is only because we have not set it on fire yet."

Vairug walked backward into the ocean. "That sounds like an agreement to me."

Belac decided that some sort of argument was necessary. "It's broken! What are we going to do? Sit in it and just float around all night?"

From aboard, Rolan said, "It has oars, Belac. Now, get in the boat."

Vairug added, "Or you can stay and wait for the ghouls."

Belac rushed past Vairug in his hurry to get to the boat. He climbed inside and stood staring back toward the shore. The glow of both fires could still be seen in the distance.

From behind him, Rolan said, "Hey, Belac."

Belac turned around and Rolan pushed him in the chest. The side of the boat pressed into the back of his calves and the elf fell out of the boat backward. Belac crashed into the ocean and sank into the dark water before he understood what had just happened. *Sneaky dwarf!*

Belac splashed above the surface, trying to breathe and spit out sea water at the same time. He looked up to see Rolan staring down at him. The dwarf had one foot on the side of the boat and was resting his weight on the raised knee with his arms crossed.

Rolan only smiled, but the elf could hear its meaning. *"Are you ready to stop playing this game yet?"*

Belac sputtered out sea water. "Hate you!"

Rolan's smile only broadened. "You needed a wash anyway."

While in the prosses of climbing into the boat, Vairug began to laugh so hard that he lost his balance and fell into the water with Belac. Unlike the elf, Vairug came back to the surface still laughing. Belac splashed at the orc, but Vairug only laughed harder. Though he laughed quietly, it looked like the effort might kill him.

Belac splashed at the orc again. "That's right, laugh yourself to death!"

An oar slid into the water behind the elf. In a conversational tone, Breana said, "I assume we are following the coastline to Harbridge?" She began to row the boat to sea.

Belac ducked away from the oar that glided toward his head. The boat accelerated sluggishly, but it was obvious to the elf that Breana meant to leave him behind. He grabbed the side of the boat and scrambled aboard as quickly as he could.

Vairug, having only one hand, found it more challenging to climb into the moving vessel. Belac reached over the side and helped the orc up. When Vairug was safely aboard, Belac rolled over and leaned against the inside of the hull, too exhausted to bother taking a seat.

Vairug stood, wobbled on his feet, and then sat down on a bench to keep from falling back into the ocean. The orc took a deep breath and looked up tiredly. His black hair had come undone, and it hung wetly against the sides of his face. Bathed in the light of the moon, he appeared remarkably human.

I wonder if I could talk him into filing down those tusks? Belac closed his eyes and relaxed, finally feeling safe. *I am still not telling Rolan he was right.*

In an irritated voice, Rolan asked, "What is it, Vairug?"

Vairug was ready with his response. "You cut off my hair!"

Belac opened his eyes, curious how this would be resolved. He did not think Vairug would fair very well if they fought on the boat. The dwarf's short legs would give him an advantage in stability and Rolan had twice as many hands. *Still... Vairug is really strong.*

Rolan frowned. "I saved your life." He gestured dismissively at the orc. "Besides, all that hair made you look like a girl."

Breana stopped rowing and covered her mouth with both hands. Belac thought it was adorable that the giantess was completely nude, but she felt like it was her smile that needed to be covered up.

Vairug looked like his eyes might pop out of his head. It was obvious he had no idea how to respond to such an accusation. He glanced to Belac, presumably for some offering of support. The elf was not even trying to hide his smile. *Now, I have to call him 'Sarah.'*

Vairug pointed his empty hand at the elf. "What about him?"

What about me?

Rolan shrugged. "He's an elf. He looks like a girl anyway."

"I do not!" Belac moved a lock of his hair away from his face with a delicate finger.

Breana's hands were now covering her entire face and her body was rigid in an effort to not laugh. Belac almost told her to get back to rowing, but managed to constrain his own stupidity. *I do not want to swim all the way back to Harbridge.*

Rolan continued, "You wore your hair pulled back anyway. Just tie it in a knot on top of your head or something and let's move on." When the orc did not answer, Rolan said, "Besides, hair grows back." He absently reached up and tugged on a longer tuft of his choppy hair, muttering, "It's annoying like that."

Breana resumed rowing while doing a poor job at not smiling.

Now that they were moving again, Belac had to ask, "Why didn't we stay at the wagon? The ghouls were scared of the fire. We could have just waited for daybreak." He looked sideways at the giantess while he spoke to the dwarf. "Did you just want to show off your fancy boat?"

Rolan shook his head, unoffended. "Ghouls don't like fire, but its not magic. Once their eyes adjusted to the light, they would have rushed us again. Only this time, we would have had to fight with a burning wagon behind us."

Vairug mumble glumly, "And you set it on fire."

Rolan looked at the orc. "What?"

"My hair!" Vairug growled. "You cut it off. And then you set it on fire!"

Twenty-Nine

Breana was adamant. "I am not wearing that."

Standing across from her, Rolan replied with forced patience, "Yes, you are." He had cut the sail from the broken mast, and he wanted her to wear it as a cloak.

Breana stood and picked up an oar like she was preparing to hit him with it. "I disagree."

"Woman…" Rolan took a deep breath, angled his head down, and turned it to the side in self-restraint. "It is not dawn yet. If someone sees us sneaking in through the harbor, they may not notice you are a giant. Distance plays tricks on people. But if anyone sees this," he gestured up and down at the nude giantess, "they are definitely going to notice."

Belac nodded but said nothing. The movement drew Breana's attention and she glared down at the elf. He offered her a smile of exaggerated friendliness and hoped she would not hit him.

Breana returned her stare to the dwarf, the insane rings in her eyes more threatening than the oar she held. "Let them notice!"

Rolan pinched the bridge of his nose. "That would defeat the entire purpose of sneaking."

Breana gestured with the oar. "You just don't want anyone else to look at me!"

"Exactly!" Rolan agreed with exasperation. "Anyone that looks at you is going to want to talk to you, or they are going to want to talk about you."

"Let them talk!" Breana leaned forward to glare at the dwarf more forcefully.

Rolan closed his eyes and repeated, "That would defeat the entire purpose of sneaking."

Breana threw the oar down. "Then, why don't you wear it!"

Rolan shouted, "Because I am not a giant naked woman!"

Breana stared at the dwarf as if he had just insulted her. Her silence was louder than his shout.

Rolan took another deep breath. "When we get to the storehouse, I will wear whatever you want, and you can dance naked in the loading bay. But unless you want to start a war with the whole city," he held up the canvas sail, "You are going to put this on."

Belac turned to Vairug and widened his eyes. The orc smiled and shrugged. Not wanting to miss anything, Belac quickly looked back to the giantess. She seemed to be thinking. *Not good.* Belac smiled. *Not good for Rolan, anyway.*

Breana stepped over the bench between her and the dwarf. She took the sail, draped it over her head, and then wrapped the sides around her shoulders. She sat down, saying, "Someone else will need to row." There was a calmness to her voice that sounded dangerous.

Rolan ignored her tone. "You heard the woman, Belac." He pointed his hand toward the oars. "Get rowing."

Belac stood. "Why do I have to row?" he asked while shuffling to the stern of the boat.

Rolan sat down across from the giantess. "My hope is that you get too exhausted to complain."

Belac sat down and began to position the oars. "And what happens when I don't stop complaining?"

Rolan chuckled. "Then, the three of us will get off at Harbridge, and you can keep on rowing."

Breana stifled a laugh and then kicked the dwarf for making her do it.

Belac glanced over his shoulder toward the sprawling docks of Harbridge in the distance. Though notably absent a lighthouse, the piers were lit with the flickering light of hanging lanterns. As he rowed, he wondered if they would be able to actually sneak into the city unchallenged. *I guess the sail Breana has on might work as a kind of camouflage in the harbor.*

The corner of the harbor they docked at was darker than the rest. Belac suspected they were not the only people that preferred to travel unnoticed. The pier was in disrepair and appeared to have been damaged in some kind of fire. *What were the smugglers moving that could burn through so much of the docks?* He considered the rocky shores they had passed and wondered how many smuggler's caches had been hidden in the shadows.

Rolan took hold of a dock mooring and held the boat steady while Breana climbed out. Vairug followed the giantess onto the pier with the hood of his charcoal brown cloak pulled low to hide his face. Looking at the two standing in the open with their identities so thoroughly concealed, Belac decided to do what he could to hide his own lineage. He reached back and tucked the tips of his ears into his long hair. It was an unsophisticated disguise, but he could think of nothing else that might help.

Rolan hopped onto the pier and Belac hurried after him before the boat could waft away. The elf turned around and considered the boat as it bobbed in the dark water.

Belac pointed at the abandoned vessel. "Don't you want to tie it up or something?"

Rolan shook his head. "It is not worth the effort. It is better if it floats off or someone takes it."

Belac looked at the dwarf askew. "You want to throw away a magic boat?"

Rolan shrugged. "You can not get it back in the bottle."

Belac remembered the shards of broken glass. "That seems like a pretty obvious design flaw."

Rolan disagreed. "Not if you want to sell more magic bottles."

The idea of someone with magic behaving so cynically bothered Belac. *Why be greedy if you have magic?*

Rolan waved the elf to follow him. "Come on. You can frown while we walk."

Belac scratched at the side of his head as he followed Rolan through the docks. The elf's hair tickled the tips of his ears more than he would have expected. *I hope we get to wherever we are going soon.* While the few people walking the docks were wise enough to avoid the darkened piers, Belac knew it was safer to keep his elven ears hidden.

Though the physical sensations were tolerable, there was something upsetting about being forced to be uncomfortable. *I can't believe I have to hide what I am just because of a bunch of stupid humans.* With a start, he realized he might understand a little of what Breana felt. *I wonder if there is something I can do to make her feel more comfortable.*

The storehouse that Rolan led them to was close to where they had docked. Like the rest of the buildings in lower Harbridge, it resembled an oversized ship that had been flipped upside down. The timbers were aged but the wood retained a luster that spoke to the caretaker's pride.

As Belac was beginning to find customary, Rolan barged inside like he owned the place. The door swung in and struck a hanging bell that rang throughout the small office. A lamp burned brightly, illuminating the tall man that stood up from behind a counter.

The man's eyes went wide with shock. "Rolan..."

Rolan walked around the counter and casually stabbed the man in the chest. The man fell to his knees and stared at the dwarf confused. Rolan shook his head disapprovingly and pushed the man away. Turning his back on the dying man, Rolan walked through an open doorway.

Belac glanced at Vairug, unsure what they should do. The orc held out his arms and shook his head, obviously at a loss. Belac looked back to the empty doorway, wondering if he should go help. There was the sound of scuffling and a heavy chair hitting the floor, and then silence.

Rolan came back through the doorway, blood dripping from his knife. He pointed his open hand at the door they had entered. "Lock that door," he said calmly as he walked to a large sliding door on the opposite side of the room.

Breana hastily shut the door, causing the bell to ring again. Vairug reached in front of her and pulled the bolt in place. *Are we keeping people out, or are we stopping them from getting away from Rolan?*

Wheels rolled in their track loudly as Rolan pushed the larger door to the side. He stepped into the open storeroom and navigated past shelves filled with boxes of merchandise. Rolan seemed to know where he was going, and he moved with a sense of purpose. Not knowing what else to do, Belac hurried after the dwarf. *Is he just going to kill everybody?*

A muscular man with a shaved head took one look at Rolan and froze. He dropped the crate he was carrying and held up his hands. "I did not know, Rolan." He shook his head and looked down at the floor. "They did not tell me until I came in this morning."

Rolan studied the man without offering any reassurance. He scratched at the stubble on his cheek and then pointed his hand at the man. "Stay there."

Belac watched as Rolan walked over to a shelf and began to rummage through the boxes. Belac thought the man may have had a chance at escape if he had chosen to run. The man was clearly terrified, but he waited obediently instead of running or attempting to fight.

Rolan walked back to the man and handed him a small multifaceted glass bottle with a dark brown liquid inside. "This is going to tell me if you are telling the truth. Drink it, and then tell me again how you did not know." He took a step back and held his knife ready to strike. "Try to tell a lie and you'll die for it."

The man nodded eagerly and downed the contents of the bottle. "I swear I didn't know, Rolan. I would have done something."

Rolan lowered his knife and nodded. "Go find two more men you know we can trust and bring them back here."

The man nodded deeply. "Absolutely. I know just who to get." He turned away to go but then stopped and looked back. "I am really glad you're not dead, boss."

Rolan nodded impatiently and then the man ran to do as he was bidden.

Belac leaned forward and looked to the side to see the dwarf's face. "You have truth potions?"

Rolan shrugged. "It was rum."

Thirty

Rolan led them through the cluttered maze of inventory and to a wall on the far side of the storeroom. He took hold of one of the tall shelving units and pulled. Both the shelves and a section of the wall swung smoothly into the isle, revealing a hidden room on the other side.

Belac waited with Breana and Vairug as Rolan walked inside and lit a brass lamp. The dwarf left the lamp sitting on an old, well-worn table in the middle of the room. He turned to face the others still waiting outside and then waved them into the room impatiently.

Rolan pointed his hand to his left. "The privy is through there." He then pointed his other hand to his right. "The beds are over there." He dropped his hands and nodded to his companions. "Go to sleep."

Vairug looked at the row of stout bunk beds lining the wall and then back to the dwarf. "It will be daylight any moment now."

Rolan nodded. "Exactly.' He pointed his hand toward the others as a collective. "None of you people can be seen. Hide here. Get some sleep. And then, you can move around in the storehouse tonight."

Belac yawned. He was so tired he almost did not argue. "Look at us, Rolan. We are filthy."

Rolan shook his head and nodded at the same time. "The sheets can be washed." Under his breath he added, "Or thrown away." Sensing the elf was not through arguing, Rolan raised his voice and continued, "I will have a tub brought in and you can bathe when you wake up."

Belac wanted to argue, but he looked at the beds and decided he wanted to sleep more. "Fine. But I get the top bunk."

Sounding exhausted as well, Vairug said, "There are six beds, Belac."

It took Belac a moment to come up with a response. "And you can't have them all!"

Vairug opened his mouth to say something, but sighed instead. He walked away from the elf and sat down on the lower bunk of a set of beds in the far corner of the room. *I don't think I have ever seen him look so tired.*

Belac walked over and took another look at the orc. When he was satisfied that Vairug was not dying, Belac climbed up onto the bed above him.

"What are you doing, Belac?" Vairug asked tiredly. "There are plenty of other beds to choose from."

Yeah. But if something comes in here and tries to kill me, I want you in the way. Belac smiled. "I can't protect you from the other side of the room."

Vairug laughed softly at the idea but said nothing.

Breana laid down on the floor between the table and a wall of shelves filled with dried food. She closed her eyes and her breathing immediately took on the slow rhythm of slumber. *I am going to have to remember not to step on her if I need to go to the privy.*

From the doorway, Rolan said, "And take off your boots." Without waiting for argument, he shut the secret door and left them hidden inside.

Belac kicked off his boots and let them fall to the floor with a clomp. *I would have forgotten to take those off.* The elf wondered how Rolan stayed so mindful. *He always seems to know what to do next.* Belac pinched at the gray wool blanket covering his bed. The fibers were coarse but strong. *It is all I can do to just deal with what is happening to me in the moment.* He stretched out on the bed and closed his eyes, unaware of the seed he had just planted in his own mind.

The bed shook. "Wake up," Rolan said.

Belac opened his eyes. He shook his head and muttered, "I will do it later." He closed his eyes and tried to go back to sleep.

Rolan took the elf's toe and squeezed it with his thumb. Belac shot up in bed, jerking his foot away from the pain. For a moment, he thought something might have bitten him. *I am not food!* Belac narrowed his eyes and peered over the side of the bed, searching for the dwarf. Even in the dim room, Belac's azure eyes were alight with cold intensity. *Evil little…*

Rolan was completely nude. Without the loose splotchy clothes that usually hid his shape, the dwarf was nothing but muscle and hair.

Belac fell out of bed in his haste to withdraw from the sight. He clutched at the mattress clumsily and managed to get his feet under himself before he hit the floor. He tilted his head backward and looked down, trying to keep only the dwarf's head and shoulders in view.

"Good. You're awake." Rolan said as if nothing had happened.

Belac did not know what to say. "Um… You're…"

Rolan pointed his hand at the bottom bunk of the set of beds next to them, drawing the elf's gaze lower. "Take that change of clothes and go wash up." He pointed to the open doorway with his thumb. "There is a tub in the storeroom next to the loading bay. Everything is already set up for you."

Belac glanced down at the pile of folded brown clothes before returning his focus to the dwarf's face. "Are you… ah… sure you don't need them?"

Rolan frowned. "It was either this, or listen to her call me an oath breaker."

From the table, Breana called out, "You are still not dancing!" Her smile was brighter than the room.

Rolan turned around. "I said, you could dance," he told the giantess gruffly. "I am not dancing."

Please, don't make the dwarf dance.

Breana, nude again herself, turned toward the dwarf. "Well, I think you should dance."

Belac closed his eyes. *She is going to make the dwarf dance.*

"Tough," Rolan told her. "I am not dancing."

Belac wanted to leave the room. *The problem is that there is a naked dwarf in my way.* He averted his eyes and crawled in between the beds of the bunk next to him. Careful not to look too far to his left, Belac reached over and took the folded pile of clothes. He stared at the flickering light in the open doorway as if it were salvation itself.

Though the elf attempted stealth, his exaggerated movements only made his exit more conspicuous. Despite this, Belac was able to flee the room without further trouble. *Don't see me. Don't see me. Don't see me.* He considered closing the secret door behind himself, but he did not want to chance drawing any attention.

The storeroom was lit by a series of small glass lamps that led him to a large copper bathtub waiting next to the closed doors of the loading bay. Belac looked from the tub to a wooden chair with a towel draped over its back. He turned around slowly, scanning the shadowed storeroom suspiciously. *This is not very private.*

He looked back to the copper tub and the steam rising from the water. *It looks like a trap.* Belac narrowed his eyes at the tub. Lamplight flickered against the polished copper. *I am missing something.* The elf set his change of clothes down on the chair and proceeded to walk around the metal bathtub. *I don't see anything green…* He kicked the tub and then hopped back away from it. He drew his dagger and waited for something to happen.

The copper tub reverberated with a soft depth, but appeared to be nothing more than a bathtub filled with steaming water. Belac thought the water looked a little too inviting. He took a step closer and cautiously leaned over the top to look down into the water. He quickly stabbed the water with his dagger and then hopped away.

Belac waited, ready for anything. He thought he could almost hear the flickering of the lamplight around him. After a moment, he allowed his guard to lower a little. *I think it is entirely possible that this is just a bathtub.* He stared at the steam rising from the water. *I am just going to have to risk it.*

Belac set his dagger on top of his change of clothes while he undressed and then, still unconvinced of his safety, took the dagger in hand once more. Climbing into the tub, sore muscles relaxed as the elf sank into the heated water. With his dagger held clutched to his chest, Belac laid back in the tub, and for a moment, thought that the relief might be something worth getting eaten for.

He imagined the copper bathtub growing fangs as it came to life, chomped shut, and swallowed him whole. *I take it back!* The elf shot up with a splash to stand dripping wet in the middle of the bathtub staring down at the water with his dagger held ready to stab the metal monster.

I think I might be going crazy. He lowered the dagger and stood up strait. *Is crazy contagious?* He thought that in some ways it must be. Belac dropped his dagger to the floor beside the copper tub. If it were his own insanity he was fighting, the dagger would be of little use.

The elf lowered himself back down into the water and repositioned more comfortably in the tub. He closed his eyes and allowed the warmth of the water to soak into him. As he inhaled and exhaled, he focused on the fact that it was he who willed the breath.

It is too much. The thought was small. Belac focused on the thought, trying to isolate the feeling. *I am going to die.* He wanted to dismiss it. He wanted to think about something else. He wanted to feel something else. His mind began to turn to food, to sex, to drink, to anything that would avoid that awful thought. *I am not enough.*

Belac took another deep breath. And then, lying comfortably in a bathtub, he did the single bravest thing he had ever done. He faced the truth. *I am not enough.* The thought was not small.

Thirty-One

Becoming 'more' was a lofty goal. Belac considered how he was going to go about achieving this, but he could come up with no easy answers. By the time he had finished bathing and changing into his drab, new clothes, he had just about decided that there may not actually be an easy answer to be found. *I think there should always be an easy answer.*

Belac knew that he did not want to die. He did not think this made him weak. *It makes me not stupid.* He also knew that as he was, he would get himself killed long before he ever slayed a dragon. *I guess I could just… not try to slay a dragon.* Belac shook his head. *The dragon needs to die.* The Danorin was not only a menace to the world, it was a threat that Belac did not believe would ever leave him in peace. And if he were being honest with himself, the elf did not want to let down Rolan and Vairug. He felt like it would be worse than merely disappointing his friends, it would be a betrayal. *No. The dragon has to die.* He nodded to himself. *Now… How do I be someone that can do that?*

When Belac entered the secret room, he completely forgot what he had been thinking about. He was so stunned by what he saw that for a moment, he could not think at all. Breana, naked as she preferred, was sitting on her knees next to the table while Rolan, also naked, braided her long white hair into two buns on top of her head. Vairug sat on the other side of the cluttered table eating small flat noodles from a bowl, seeming oblivious to the bizarre scene. *This can't be real.*

Breana touched the finished bun on the right side of her head and smiled happily. "Look how pretty it is!"

"Stop moving," Rolan said as he worked to braid the other side.

Breana held up a silvered hand mirror and inspected the complexly braided bun. "Why doesn't everyone wear their hair like this?"

Rolan shrugged. "Most dwarven women do."

Breana looked at the dwarf slyly. "Do the dwarven men braid their hair for them?"

Rolan huffed in amusement. "No," he said seriously.

The giantess's teeth gleamed in her smile. She looked so happy that Belac thought she might start bouncing up and down at any moment. *How long did I sleep?*

Vairug stopped shoveling noodles into his mouth long enough to say, "You should eat."

No. I should go back to sleep and hope the world makes more sense when I wake up again. Belac tossed his dirty clothes to the side. "What is it?"

Vairug swallowed and then answered, "Food."

Belac frowned at the orc but sat down in the chair next to him. "You did not ask what it was before you started eating it?"

Rolan spoke absently, "It's Salber."

Belac picked up a spoon and poked at the creamy gray noodles in the serving bowl. The flat noodles were smothered in a sauce thick with tiny bits of mushroom and shredded meat. *This actually looks alright.* He scooped some of the noodles into a smaller bowl and brought the dish up to his face.

Belac sniffed at the noodles and then growled, "Rolan!"

"What?" Rolan replied irritably.

Belac glared at the dwarf. "I still can't smell anything!"

"Lucky you," Rolan said dismissively.

Belac slammed his bowl of noodles on the table. "How is that lucky?"

Rolan pointed his hand towards the elf's discarded boots. "It does not smell great in here. Why do you think we have the secret door to our secret room wide open?"

Belac glanced at the open door. *I did not think about that.*

Rolan asked," You know what 'secret' means, right?"

Belac narrowed his eyes at the dwarf.

Vairug nudged the elf. "I know what it means."

Belac gave the orc a curious look.

Vairug's cheek twitched. "But I can't tell you."

Breana shook her head and laughed. "That's a bad joke."

Vairug shrugged and went back to eating.

"Stop moving," Rolan told the giantess again.

Breana tried to look at the dwarf without moving her head. "How long until it's finished?"

"I am doing the same thing to both sides," Rolan told her. "You were here when I did the other one."

Breana twisted her shoulders without moving her head and began to swat at the dwarf's legs.

Rolan turned to the side to insure nothing important was hit. "Stop moving."

Breana crossed her arms under her breast. "Well, hurry up!" She uncrossed her arms and picked up the hand mirror from the table. "I want to see what it looks like when you are finished." She angled the mirror to the right side of her head.

"You know what would make this go faster?" Rolan smiled. "If you would stop moving."

Breana swatted at the dwarf again, though there was little effort in it this time.

Belac closed his eyes and shook his head slowly. *Do I even remember a time when things made sense?*

Vairug asked, "Are you going to eat that?"

Belac picked up his bowl of noodles and moved it away from the orc protectively. "Of course, I'm eating it!"

Vairug frowned. "Then, you are doing it wrong." He scooped up a spoonful of his own noodles and held them up. "You have to put them in your mouth." He demonstrated, putting the noodles in his mouth and chewing dramatically.

And now, I am taking dining advice from an orc. Belac smiled with sudden inspiration. He reached over with his spoon and scooped up noodles from Vairug's bowl. Belac crammed the noodles into his own mouth, almost spitting them back out laughing.

Speaking while he chewed, Belac said, "You're right. That is how to do it."

Vairug glowered at the elf.

Belac's spoon darted out as he attempted to steal more of Vairug's food. The orc intercepted Belac with a spoon of his own. The tiny metal shovels clashed and then Belac and Vairug stared at each other over their locked spoons. With a fury of short movements, the two began to battle each other with the spoons. The dull muted clatter of spoons filled the room until Vairug leaned away, disengaging. Belac angled his spoon at the orc in a mockery of a fencing stance. Vairug's hand shot out and his spoon rapped the elf's knuckles.

"Aow!" Belac dropped his spoon and tried to shake the pain out of his hand.

Vairug reached over with his spoon and took a scoop of noodles from Belac's bowl. With a tusked grin, Vairug ate the noodles. He seemed too pleased by his victory to be upset with the elf.

From across the table, Breana said, "I feel like it would be best if we left that fight out of the song."

Rolan chuckled. "You don't want to sing about The Battle of the Spoons?"

Breana shook her head primly.

With obviously disingenuous affront, Vairug accused, "You would deny my glorious triumph?"

Breana laughed at the orc.

Belac said, "You can tell the story." He flexed his sore hand. "Just leave out the part about the spoons."

Rolan's chuckle was so deep that it sounded like a cough. "You think you are going to look better in that story," he emphasized, "without the spoons?"

Breana giggled. "I could sing of how the daring elf and the fearsome orc wiggled their fingers at each other."

Rolan laughed. "Until the elf screamed like a cat that just had its tail stepped on."

Belac narrowed his eyes at the dwarf.

Vairug nudged the elf and nodded toward the giantess. "She thinks I'm fearsome." He grinned proudly.

Belac shook his head. "Fine," he said exasperated. "You can just say we used swords." He mimed fencing with the orc.

Breana laughed fully. "You want me to sing a story about you getting into a sword fight with an orc over a bowl of noodles?"

Rolan put his hand on the giantess's shoulder for support as he laughed. "And losing!"

Belac narrowed his eyes again. *Stupid, naked dwarf!*

Breana began to sing,

"And they fought for the bowl in the hidden room.
When the elf stole what would the orc consume.
And they fought for noodles with swords in gloom.
Till the elf lost with a cat scream of doom."

Her song had been meant in jest. However, her voice was simply too beautiful to be funny. A stunned silence followed that quickly began to feel confusingly awkward.

Breana's voice sounded as irritated as any dwarf's. "You are allowed to laugh."

Rolan did. Then he patted her on the shoulder and said, "It's finished."

Breana put a hand to the left side of her head and used the silvered mirror to inspect the braided bun. Her smile was as wonderful as her song.

Belac scowled. "Can't you make us fight over something better than noodles?" *If I am going to die in a song, I don't want it to be over noodles.*

Vairug nodded, his tusks jutting playfully from his smile. "The elf can be fighting to avenge his pet squirrel."

Thirty-Two

Belac crossed his arms and stared at the dwarf seated on the other side of the table from him. "I need new clothes, Rolan."

Rolan swallowed his food before answering. "You have new clothes." He gestured to the elf. "You're wearing them."

Belac ignored him. "And a sword."

Still seated comfortably on the floor, Breana lowered her hand mirror and said, "I thought forging you a sword was the first part of our quest."

Rolan pointed at the giantess and nodded as he chewed.

Belac shook his head. "I can't wait for the magic one." *Too many things want to kill me.* "I need one now." He thought for a moment. "And a new bag. And another cloak." He pointed at the dwarf. "This time, one that is not green!"

Rolan quit eating and stared at the elf.

Belac continued, "And a …"

"Stop," Rolan said resigned. He pushed his bowl of noodles away and stood. "Come on." He waved for the elf to follow. "Let's go get you something to write on."

Belac liked this idea. *If I make a list, Rolan can't try to tell me he forgot something.* He hopped out of his chair and followed the dwarf out into the storeroom. *And I am going to write, 'NOT GREEN!' next to every single thing on the list!*

In the storeroom, two roughly dressed men were in the process of carrying the copper tub out into the loading bay. Belac grabbed the hilt of his dagger. *They are stealing the bathtub!*

"Calm down," Rolan told him. "They work for me." He looked sideways at the elf. "So, don't kill them."

Me?! I am not the one who goes around killing everybody! Belac narrowed his eyes at the dwarf.

As he led the elf past the men, Rolan asked, "Where did you think the bath came from?"

I did not really think about it. Belac shrugged though the dwarf could not see it.

Rolan continued, "Everyone else is clean. That means everyone else took a bath before you. Where did you think the fresh water came from?"

This time, Belac's shrug was more aggressive. *What do I care where the water came from?* "It was a bath, Rolan. I bathed."

Rolan shook his head and kept walking.

Belac felt offended by the dwarf's apparent disapproval. "What? Do you ask where the water came from every time you take a bath?"

Rolan halted outside the sliding door to the front room. He took a deep breath and said, "I am not saying you should ask, Belac. I am saying you should think."

Wheels rolled in their track as Rolan slid the door open. Belac wanted to argue with the dwarf but there was something in his words that almost seemed compassionate. *Is this what dwarves are like when they are being nice?* Belac shook his head and followed Rolan into the front room. *No wonder they don't bother doing it very often.*

The first thing Belac noticed in the room was the obvious lack of dead bodies. Belac was sure he had seen the dwarf kill someone in there. "What happened to the dead guy?" *Maybe they just piled him in the corner of the office with the rest of the people Rolan killed today.*

"Fish food," Rolan answered with a professional tone.

Belac grimaced. "I don't think I am going to be able to eat fish for a while."

Heading into the office, Rolan asked, "What do you think you were eating earlier?"

Belac's eyes went wide. "You fed me dead guy?"

"No." Rolan chuckled. "Fish."

"Oh." Belac shook his head. "Well, that's okay." He followed the dwarf into the office. "Don't feed me people."

"Sure," Rolan agreed absently. He walked to the other side of a large desk, pulled out a drawer, and took out a crisp sheet of paper. He slapped the paper on the desk before reaching back into the desk drawer.

"Wait," Belac said. "Is this your office?" He looked around the room. It was well appointed, with dark wooden cabinetry polished to a satin sheen. Nothing appeared to be out of place. *...No dead bodies...*

Rolan set a writing implement down on the desk. "It's one of them."

Belac pointed to the doorway with his thumb. "Then, why did you come in and start killing everybody?"

Rolan frowned. "Evidently, I am in a disagreement with another distributor." He waved his hand dismissively. "Don't worry about it."

Belac decided to worry about it. "What is the disagreement about?"

Rolan walked back around the desk. "Whether or not I should keep breathing."

Belac looked at the dwarf curiously. "That sounds like something worth worrying about."

Rolan shook his head dispassionately. "I will take care of it."

Belac did not need to ask how the dwarf would do that. He knew Rolan well enough to know that people would die and something would be set on fire.

Rolan clapped the elf on the arm. "Make your list. I am going to go finish eating."

As Rolan exited the office, Belac wondered how the dwarf could be so confident walking around in the nude. *Maybe he just knows no one is going to want to look at him unless they have to.* While naked dwarves were not a regular occurrence in Belac's life, he had encountered enough clothed ones to expect a hefty midsection. However, Rolan's physique was clearly defined. *The dwarf can't even get fat right.*

Belac walked around the large desk and took a seat in the highbacked leather chair on the other side. The chair was surprisingly comfortable. *I wonder how often Rolan actually sits here.* It was hard for Belac to imagine the dwarf working in an office day in and day out.

Belac picked up the uncut grease pencil resting next to the sheet of paper on top of the desk. *What is this thing?*

Obviously Rolan had intended for him to write with it somehow. *Why else would he have left it on the desk for me?* At the end of the slender black rod, hung a thin string. Belac tugged gently on the string, but nothing happened. *Maybe the string is not supposed to be there. I guess I could cut it off…* He unintentionally pulled the string at an angle and the string cut through the paper wrapping. At first, the elf feared he had damaged it, but as the loose paper unraveled, it exposed a waxy black core.

"That's genius!" Belac said aloud. He wondered how the dwarves had come up with such a thing. *There is no way humans would be smart enough to think of something like this.* He hoped Rolan would allow him to keep the marvelous instrument.

Belac began to make a list of everything he thought he would need for his quest. He was careful to include only the details he felt were most important. *If I am too specific, Rolan might just tell me he could not find what I wanted.* He tapped the grease pencil on the page in thought and then added a final request. *I probably should have put that at the top of the list.*

The elf stood and took his list from the desk. Before leaving, he appraised the room one last time. *It is a nice office, but Rolan does not belong here.* He thought that Rolan should be out exploring ancient ruins, or leading armies of the damned in some righteous crusade, or almost anything other than sitting in an office counting coins.

Belac retraced his steps through the storeroom. The loading bay doors were closed and the only sign there had been a bath set up next to them was a slightly damp floor. The workers, or whatever they were to Rolan, were nowhere to be seen.

Belac took a moment to consider the bath. *I guess… If someone saw the bathtub, they might question who it was for.* He nodded thoughtfully. *A secret room is a lot easier to keep secret if no one is looking for it.* Belac grinned, pleased with himself. He followed the glass lamps back to the secret room. *I don't know… Is it still a secret room if the door is wide open and there is a trail of lights leading to it?*

Rolan and Vairug sat at the table facing each other while Breana lounged on the floor. Her double braided bun made the giantess appear more youthful, and to Belac, she seemed more energetic despite how she lounged. He found it difficult to not stare at her.

He forced himself to look at Rolan. Belac suddenly smiled so broadly that it hurt his face. He could hardly believe what he saw. Rolan frowned as the elf laughed.

Belac pointed with the grease pencil. "Your hair!"

Rolan shook his head dismissively. "Shut up, Belac."

The dwarf's stubble had been shaved close and his hair had been cut even. Without his jagged, haphazard tufts of hair, Rolan looked even more naked than before.

Breana sat up and held her hand mirror out so that the dwarf could see himself. "Doesn't it look nice!"

Rolan growled, but he was gentle as he pushed the mirror away. "Give me the list." He held out his hand.

Smiling, Belac handed him the sheet of paper. *I bet she makes you wash your clothes next!*

Rolan scanned the list. "This is ridiculous." He held up the sheet of paper and looked at the elf scornfully.

Belac shook his head, disagreeing. "We are not mercenaries, Rolan. We are heroes. What we are trying to do is heroic." He held out his hands. "We need to look heroic."

Vairug spoke up. "I think you should listen to him, Rolan."

Rolan looked at the orc and pointed to the last item on the list. "He wants a giant bag of gold."

Vairug grinned. "How much does he want?"

Rolan handed him the list. "He doesn't specify. It just says, 'not green.'"

Vairug accepted the list and began to look it over. *Vairug can read?* Scholarly was not something typically associated with orcs.

Vairug lowered the sheet of paper. "How would you even carry a silk pavilion?"

Belac pointed. "Next thing on the list."

Vairug shook his head and flattened the sheet of paper on the table. He took the grease pencil from the elf and then, frowning like a disappointed professor, he proceeded to draw lines through Belac's desires.

Thirty-Three

Absent distraction, it does not take long for an elf to get bored. Belac, despite his parentage, was very much an elf. He spent some time exploring the storehouse, but Rolan had warned against opening any of the containers. While the dwarf had insisted it could be dangerous, Belac was convinced Rolan simply did not want him to find the liquor.

Still, Belac was not willing to risk having his face blown off. So, he paced around the storeroom until it began to feel like a prison. *It is not the size of the cell that makes something a prison.* He decided to return to the secret room and annoy people until someone found him something to drink.

Vairug was in the back corner of the room, laid out on a bed. Belac chose to let him rest. He did not know if the orc was asleep or not, but Belac remembered how tired Vairug had seemed before. *He is not going to know where the booze are anyway.*

The heavy table had been pushed to the side of the room, making space for Rolan to sit on the floor next to Breana. Adorned in nothing but the flickering of lamplight, the two spoke to each other in hushed voices.

Breana asked, "But, how would you…"

With a devilish smile, Rolan gave an answer the elf could not quite distinguish.

Breana replied with a surprised, "Oh!" and then said, "Oh…" her smile becoming wicked as well.

Nope. Belac turned on his heels. *I do not want anything to do with whatever that is.* He walked back into the storeroom, trying in vain to not think about what he had just witnessed. *He's a dwarf! She is a giant!* Belac shook his head, attempting to banish the image of Breana's wicked smile.

The elf was in the front room of the storehouse before he knew where he was going. *I need fresh air.* He crossed the room and unlocked the front entrance. Remembering how noisy the hanging bell had been, he reached up and held it out of the way as he opened the door. *I don't want the others to think someone is breaking in. The last thing I need is for a naked dwarf to come flying out of the dark with a knife.*

Closing the door without ringing the bell required some awkward maneuvering, but Belac managed to do it. *Getting back in is going to be more difficult.* The elf shrugged. *I will worry about it later.*

He tucked his ears into his black hair. Despite his bath earlier, the long strands were a mess. *I bet Breana has a brush or a comb I could borrow.* Belac had put both a brush and a comb on his list of wants, but he did not know when Rolan would acquire them. *After all the lines Vairug drew on my list, I don't even know if I will get one of them at all.*

Belac walked away from the storehouse with no real direction in mind. Hanging glass lanterns illuminated many of the docks along the sprawling harbor, though there was a disorderly feel to their spacing. The elf took a deep breath but found himself unsatisfied by it. The air was too thick to feel fresh. And while he still could not smell anything, he was convinced the air would stink. He turned at the next cobbled street and headed farther into the city in hope of finding fresher air.

Unlike the fringes of the harbor, the remainder of the city was left to rely on the dim moonlight that filtered through the clouds above. As he walked the streets, Belac began to realize that Harbridge felt alive in a way unlike any other city he had ever visited. While some cities seemed to die when the night settled in, others developed an energy that promised unknown excitement. In Harbridge however, if felt like the buildings themselves were slumbering.

The timber hulls seemed to breathe in the darkness, groaning faintly with the breezes that blew gently through the city. There was a quiet peace that offered the wholesomeness of a hamlet, irrespective of the city's size. What Belac appreciated most, was that this all made it remarkably easy to locate the nearest tavern.

Light and sound poured lazily from the open doors of an establishment under a sign that read, 'The Drunken Mermaid.' *Ha!* Belac laughed to himself. *No one that has ever actually seen a mermaid would want to drink with one.* His mind summoned an image of the ethereal beings that had swum in the underground lake. *I do not care how beautiful a woman is, fangs are a deal breaker.*

Regardless of the tavern's name, he would have gone inside had he the coin to buy a drink. Belac was fairly confident that he could convince someone to pay for his company. Though, not without drawing attention to himself. He was not as noticeable as a giant or a one handed orc, but he could not hazard the chance of someone mentioning the elf they had met. *It was a lot more fun being a hero than it is being a fugitive.*

"Hello there, Friend," said a man's voice in a mocking tone.

Belac spun to his left to face a group of four men. Even standing in the light provided by the tavern, the men's dark clothes blended with the wooden city. *I guess Harbridgers just really like brown.* Two of the men stepped closer, offering insincere smiles.

The one on the elf's left asked, "Are you looking for a drink?" His voice was as fake as the first's.

Belac said nothing. He did not know what the men wanted, but he was sure it was not to buy him a drink. *This is not an accidental encounter.*

"Why don't you come with us." the man on the right said. It did not sound like a suggestion.

The man on the left nodded agreeably. "We can get you a drink… We can all have a seat… We can all get to know each other…"

Belac did not like the way they spoke to him. It was obvious they were trying to intimidate him. That is not what they were doing. The elf shifted his stance so that none of the men would be able to get behind him easily. The men misinterpreted the movement, believing it to be in response to the mention of alcohol.

The man on the left smiled in truth. "You can have as much to drink as you want. Our treat."

The man on the right finally told the elf what this was about. "And then, if you want to talk to us a little about your boss…" The man grinned in a way that only a fool would trust. "You could walk away with a purse heavy enough to buy your own drinks."

"See," the man on the left added, "we're friends."

A moment passed and Belac said nothing. *I am going to have to kill them.* He knew they were not going to let him walk away.

The man on the left leaned to the side and presented his hip, displaying the short sword that hung there. "We're friends, right?" he said in an unfriendly tone.

Now. Belac grabbed the hilt of the man's sword with his right hand. With his left, he drew his own dagger and stabbed the man in the chest. Pushing the man away using the dagger still buried in his chest, Belac pulled the shortsword from its sheath.

Belac let the man fall from his dagger as he pivoted toward the man on the right. With a quick thrust, Belac plunged the tip of the sword into the other man's chest. Instead of running the man through, Belac jerked the shortsword back after piercing his heart.

Belac stepped toward the man who had stood behind the one on his left. The man held up his hands, wide eyed and confused. Belac swung the short blade down into where the man's neck met his shoulder. The steel caught in the man's ribcage and Belac released the hilt, allowing the sword to fall with the man.

The last man turned to flee, but Belac grabbed a fistful of his hair with his free hand and stabbed the man in the side of the neck. Belac stabbed the man twice more before they fell to the street together. Straddling the man's back, Belac brought his dagger down three more times, ravaging the man's neck.

A man shouted, and a woman screamed. Belac stood, feeling a little lightheaded. Another shout followed the first.

I should probably get out of here now. More shouts came from the tavern and then someone blew a whistle. *That secret room is seeming really nice right about now.*

Belac stepped away from the bloody bodies in the street and began to jog toward the docks. Farther ahead, two men with a red X across their chests dashed into the street carrying lanterns. They stopped and then one of them blew another whistle. The shrill sound was more than loud enough to announce their location to any other watchman nearby. *Not good.*

Belac turned and began to run back up the street. *I can sneak back to the storehouse once I get away.* Another whistle answered from the direction of the tavern. Realizing he was trapped, Belac ran between two of the buildings on his right.

It was then that it started to rain. What started as a mild sprinkle, quickly became a steady downpour. Belac felt like the world itself was trying to drown him. *It's a conspiracy!*

On the other side of the buildings, the elf was faced with a choice. He could turn right and head for the docks, or he could turn left and move deeper into the city. If he tried for the docks and could get around the watchmen, he would find safety in the storehouse. However, that would also risk leading the city watch back to his friends. After only the slightest hesitation, Belac turned left.

Rain ran down the sides of the nautical buildings and flowed into the street. Belac's boots splashed as he sprinted through the water and deeper into the city. A whistle blew behind him. *I made the right choice.* A lantern appeared in the street ahead of him and another whistle pierced the night. *Maybe not.*

Belac turned and ran between two more buildings. The way was blocked with crates, but he thought he would be able to climb over them. *This could work to my advantage.*

Without slowing, the elf leapt into the air and planted his foot against the center of the crates. Instead of vaulting over as he had intended, the crates collapsed and he crashed into a paved stable yard on the other side. He rolled over the crates and his back hit the stones with a splash.

"It's a conspiracy," Belac muttered aloud.

Whistles spurred the elf to action. He stood, realizing he had dropped his dagger in the fall. He scanned the stable yard, frantically searching for a way to flee, but the stables and the gates were all closed. Watchmen climbed over the crates, their whistles blowing shrilly into the rain.

Belac spun around, looking for his dagger. *I can't let them take me.* He did not believe Harbridge would allow him to escape imprisonment a third time. More watchmen entered the stable yard, lanterns emblazoning the scarlet X across each of their chests. Accepting his dagger as lost, Belac stepped away from the men of the city watch.

The elf's clothes were soaked through, and his long hair had come undone. Rain continued to fall, plastering the black hair to the sides of his face and exposing his elven ears. He pointed at the guards. "Okay!" He hopped up and down as he yelled. "Which one of you is wearing green?!"

Thirty-Four

Two of the watchmen looked at each other in confusion before returning their attention to the irate rain-soaked elf. Everyone in the stable yard was drenched and the deluge showed no sign of ceasing soon. One of the other watchmen blew his whistle. To Belac, the whistle sounded different than the others, though no one else seemed to notice.

One of the watchmen stepped forward and declared, "You are under arrest!"

Belac disagreed firmly. "No. I'm not."

The watchmen shifted uneasily in the rain, some of them pulling out truncheons. The odd whistle blew again. Belac stood his ground, ready to fight the next man that took another step toward him.

The first watchman to have spoken pointed his truncheon at the elf. "Put down your weapon!"

What? Are you afraid I am going to stab you with my ears? Belac held his empty hands out to his sides.

The gate to the stable yard shook loudly and then was forced open. Both Belac and the watchmen looked toward the breached gate. *More watchmen? Or a way out?*

A sandy haired man wearing a loose vest and short legged trousers stepped into the stable yard. He turned back and shouted into the night, "Over here!" He waved an arm above his head, beckoning. "This way!"

And here come the angry peasants with pitchforks. Belac considered trying to hide behind the guards. *Maybe I can even sneak away while everyone is distracted.*

A small army of men armed with shortswords and cutlasses surged into the stable yard. There was no questioning their violent intent. Belac turned to the watchmen, suddenly more than willing to be arrested. A watchman lurking in the rear brought his truncheon down on another watchman's head. The traitorous watchman did not stop there, but instead continued to hammer into his comrades from behind as they were focused on the charging mob.

Belac began to slowly walk backward away from the furious cries of battle. *Don't see me. Don't see me. Don't see me.*

The watchmen faced the armed men valiantly, but were quickly cut down. Belac watched with increasing concern as the army of men drove their blades into the bodies of the fallen to assure that none survived.

The lone watchman still standing clasped hands with the man who had opened the gate. They exchanged quiet words the rain disguised, though the watchman's allegiance was clear. The two men nodded to each other before releasing their grips and then the watchman turned away. The traitor stepped past scattered crates and the bodies of the dead alike as he marched off into the night.

Belac realized that all the other men were staring at him. *I think they see me.* The elf's eyes searched the yard again. *I could really use that dagger…*

The man who appeared to lead the others pushed through the crowd. He halted a respectful distance from the elf and then asked, "You are the foreign elf?"

Belac pointed at one of his own ears. He did not think Harbridge had any local elves.

The man nodded. "We are of The Deep. You must come with us." He tilted his head earnestly. "There will be more of the unborn."

Belac did not like the sound of that. "The unborn?"

The man gestured to the dead watchmen. "Those who have yet to know The Deep."

"So… More watchmen?" Belac asked for clarification.

The man nodded. "Yes. Among others."

Something about 'The Deep' tugged at Belac's memory. This was not the first time he had heard it spoken of. *The sailors that helped me escape from prison mentioned something about it.* At the time, he had simply not considered it. *It just sounded like something a sailor would say.*

Belac shook his head. "Sure." *What else am I going to do?*

The man nodded. "Follow close. We will see you away to safety."

Belac motioned for the man to lead on. *No reason to just stand around here.* He glanced at the slain bodies of the city watch. *And a lot of reasons not to.*

The man led Belac out of the stable yard through the open gate. The mob of armed men trailed along behind them protectively. Belac did not think it was a particularly sneaky way of escaping, but it worked well enough. *I am not dead, and I'm not in prison. So, I should probably not complain.*

They crossed streets and navigated back alleys until Belac was thoroughly lost. The darkness and the rain only added to his sense of dependency. *What is safety that comes from another?* To Belac, it seemed more like a form of submission. And while the relief offered by both could be comforting, they were not the same thing.

Whistles began to sound in the distance. *We are not moving fast enough.* Belac grabbed the arm of the man he was following, bringing him to a halt. *I should probably ask his name.* The man turned, a question on his face.

Belac gestured to the mob following them. "This is too many people. It makes us too easy to track."

The leader of the mob nodded and then stepped around the elf. He leaned close to one of the other men and spoke into his ear. Belac could not make out what was said, but the man nodded in acknowledgement. The leader turned back to the elf while the other man relayed his orders.

The mob's leader leaned in closer to the elf and gestured to the men behind them. "They are going to lead the unborn away."

Belac nodded. He was still uncomfortable with the term 'unborn,' but he thought the plan was a good one. "What is your name?"

"I am Gelb," the man told him.

"Well, Gelb, let's get out of here." Belac turned and resumed walking in the direction they had previously been headed.

Gelb hurried to take the lead, and they continued to move further into the city. Four men from the mob stayed with them, silently trailing in a loose formation.

"Where are we going?" Belac asked over the rain.

"To a safehouse." Gelb answered readily, though the details were of little use to the elf. "It is a building across the street from The Pelican's Perch."

Upon hearing the answer, Belac felt like his question may have been a rather stupid one. *I don't know where The Pelican's Perch is.* He wanted to hop up and down in frustration. *I don't know where anything in this cursed city is!*

"It is not far from where we are now," Gelb continued. "Once we get there, we have a plan to take you safely away."

Whistles were blown in seeming random directions as the arrant members of the mob went about their work misdirecting the city watch. The shrill sounds of the watchmen's whistles reminded Belac what the alternative was. *I guess I get to find out what The Pelican's Perch is.* He did not think it could be a worse place than prison.

Leading him away from a back alley, Gelb indicated to a modestly sized building. "This is the safehouse. We will have you safely away soon."

Belac found himself a little disappointed that he did not get to discover what The Pelican's Perch was. The safehouse itself was even more of a disappointment. When Gelb had described it as a 'building,' Belac had imagined it would be something larger than a tool shed.

The safehouse had been crafted by the same masterful shipwrights that had shaped the rest of the city. There was nothing about the building other than its size to distinguish it from the other structures. *It might even be a good place to hide.* Belac glanced back at the men following him. *If there were not six of us.*

"It is kind of small," Belac complained. *Though, it will be nice to get out of the rain.*

Gelb attempted to reassure the elf. "We will not be here long."

Without an eve to hide under, Belac was forced to stand miserably in the rain while Gelb unlocked the door to the safehouse. The man stood on his toes and reached up above the doorframe. He took hold of a hidden ring connected to a thin cable that ran into the wall. He pulled firmly, and the door opened with a metallic click. With his other hand, he pushed the door inward.

Belac followed Gelb into the safehouse and then stepped aside as the four other men crowded inside with them. The interior was dark, and the men stumbled into each other as they found a place to stand.

Belac's eyes adjusted as Gelb moved through the single room. The walls were bare and the furniture simple. Bed, wardrobe, dresser, table, and a short stool; nothing about the room seemed lived in. To Belac, it all made the inside of the safehouse look like an unused guestroom.

Gelb opened a dresser drawer and pulled out a folded towel. He offered the towel to the elf, saying, "You should dry yourself off."

Belac took the towel, shook it out, and began to dry himself, starting with his hair. His clothes were too soaked for the towel to try, but he did the best he could. Holding the damp towel out to his side, he realized none of the others were drying themselves. *I hope I was not supposed to share the towel.*

Belac tossed the towel onto the table. "What about you?"

"We have to go back outside into the rain," Gelb explained. "We would only get wet again."

Belac looked around the room. "And you want me to stay here?"

The shake of Gelb's head could barely be made out in the darkness. "No. It would not be safe for you to remain here." He stepped to the other side of the room and opened the narrow wardrobe that stood there. The inside was empty, and the walls were lined with a padded leather. "We will move you the rest of the way with this." He gestured to the inside of the wardrobe. "This way, you will not only be hidden, but out of the rain as well."

Belac glanced at the open wardrobe. *Rain or no rain, I am not getting in there.* He looked back to the man who suggested he should. "I am not getting in a box."

Gelb held his hands out toward the wardrobe. "This is the only way to move you safely." He touched the padded leather inside. "It is well padded." He pointed to a series of baffled slits. "And there are vents." He turned back to the elf. "You will be safe inside."

Belac stared at the man and said nothing. *I am not getting in the box, Gelb.*

"You will be comfortable, I assure you," Gelb persisted.

Belac maintained his stare. "That is not the point, Gelb."

Gelb tilted his head. "I do not understand."

Belac tilted his own head to match the man's. "You don't understand why I don't want to climb into a coffin?"

Gelb was silent for a moment. "You do not trust us?"

Belac said nothing.

"You are alone in a room with five armed men," Gelb told him. "Just this night, you witnessed us slaughter many of the city watch."

Belac's hand drifted to his hip, searching for the hilt of a dagger that was no longer there.

Gelb continued, "If we wanted to harm you, we could." He gestured to the open door. "But you can leave if that is what you want." He dropped his hand. "We offer you only aid."

Belac growled. He hated how convincing the argument was.

Thirty-Five

The waxed canvas tarp covering the cart was thrown aside, exposing the wardrobe. Rain beat against the wood, the sound muted by the padded leather inside. Lying on his back, Belac braced himself against the inside walls as his dark sanctuary was dragged from the cart. The wardrobe tilted into an upright position, shaking the elf's small world.

"Are we there?" Belac asked with premature optimism.

Gelb hushed him, saying, "Be quiet."

Belac was silent for a moment. *He would not need me to be quiet if we were already there.* Whispering loudly, Belac asked, "Where are we going?" *I probably should have asked that before I climbed into the box.*

The wardrobe tilted to the side and the bottom rose up as the men positioned it for carry. Belac's weight shifted inside, and he found himself resting uncomfortably on his shoulder. He wiggled around in search of a more tolerable arrangement.

One of the men carrying the wardrobe said, "You need to stop moving around in there."

Belac narrowed his eyes at the padded wall, knowing the man was on the other side. "Then, stop bouncing me around."

The man only grumbled in reply.

When nothing else was said, Belac asked again, "Where are we going?"

Gelb's answer was an obvious attempt to quiet the elf. "We are taking you to the temple."

Belac shook his head. *Bad idea.* "Last time I was there, things did not go very well."

Genuinely surprised, Gelb asked, "You have been to the temple?"

"They threw me in prison!" Belac explained. He did his best to sound like a grumpy dwarf and said, "How did you think I got to Harbridge?"

Gelb's tone became one of understanding. "You speak of the Temple of the Ancient." He spat audibly. "We would not take you there."

"Then, where are you taking me?" Belac asked, confused.

"You will be taken to the Temple of the Deep." Gelb's voice was solemn. "There you will be given the honor to judge… and be judged."

Belac did not like the sound of that last part. "Ah… You know what, Gelb? That sounds like an awful lot of trouble for you to go through. I, ah… You… You have already done so much to help me. I just… Ah… I would not want you to have to go through all that trouble."

There was no response.

Belac continued, "I have an idea. Why don't you just let me out here, and I can sneak off on my own?"

The rain pattered on the wardrobe as he waited for a reply.

"You will be taken to the Temple of the Deep. You will judge. And you will be judged." There was finality in Gelb's voice.

You see, Belac?! The elf was furious with himself. *This is why you don't let strangers lock you in a box!* He pushed against the doors of the wardrobe, attempting to force them open. Try as he might, the doors would not budge. Whoever had built the box had never intended for it to be used as a wardrobe.

Belac kicked at the doors. "Let me out!"

"Calm yourself," Gelb admonished the elf. "All will be well."

Belac kicked the doors again but accepted that he was not going to be able to break out of the box on his own. "Hey, Gelb, buddy." The elf smiled, hoping his captors could hear it in his voice. "Why don't you let me out of the box?"

The suggestion was ignored.

Belac clenched his jaw and gritted his teeth in an effort to keep smiling. "Come on, Gelb. Just let me out of the box." *And maybe I won't have to kill you!*

The wardrobe began to sway; moderately at first and then more drastically. The foot of the wardrobe crashed down and then the back was gently lowered. The swaying was replaced with a rocking motion that Belac recognized as the movement of a boat. His eyes darted to the vents in the wardrobe. *Water could get in as easily as air.* The Temple of the Deep suddenly had a much more ominous implication.

Gelb spoke to his men. "I will see him on from here. You have all done well this night. May the Deep be with you."

In disjointed harmony, each of the men replied, "May the Deep be with you."

The sound of oars slapping into the ocean could barely be heard over the thick pattering of the rain. The oars swooshed through the water as Gelb began to row them away. With each of his rhythmic strokes, the oars creaked against the side of the boat.

Belac wiggled around in the wardrobe, repositioning himself in an unsuccessful attempt to see through the vents. "Gelb."

Gelb ignored him.

"Hey, Gelb."

There was no response.

"Gelb?"

Nothing.

"Geeeeelllllb…"

Still nothing.

Belac shouted, "Gelb!"

"What?!" Gelb replied angrily.

"Are you going to drown me?" Belac asked disapprovingly.

"What?" Gelb did not attempt to hide his confusion. "What are you talking about? Why would I drown you?"

"The Temple of the Deep," Belac clarified. "Do I have to drown to get there?" *I really hope I am not giving this guy ideas.*

"Of course not." Gelb's voice sounded offended. "The temple is a place of light and truth." After a moment of silence he added, "You have some peculiar thoughts about the world."

Did he just call me crazy? Belac yelled, "Did you just call me crazy?!" He hammered his fist against the inside of the wardrobe. "You locked me in a box!" He kicked the doors. "Now, you're rowing me out to sea! Which one of us is acting like a crazy person?!"

"All will be well," Gelb said simply.

Belac's sarcastic reply had a slightly hysterical edge to it. "No… That doesn't sound crazy at all!" He yelled the last part so loud it hurt his throat.

"All will be well," Gelb repeated.

Belac crossed his arms and wished for all he was worth that he could turn into a gorilla-wolf-monster. *I would bust out of this box and rip Gelb's stupid head off his stupid shoulders.* The elf proceeded to spend an unhealthy amount of time thinking of all the ways he wanted to kill Gelb.

The rain suddenly stopped beating down on the wardrobe, bringing Belac immediately alert. Water still fell into the ocean, its sound echoing around them. *We are in some kind of cave.* The boat bumped into something with a deep thunk. Muffled voices approached the craft as its forward motion was arrested.

A man's cold voice spoke calmly above the others. "Is this him? Is this the foreign elf?"

Gelb answered, "I believe so. The commandments leave little doubt."

"Then, The Deep shines upon us." There was praise in the man's cold voice.

Gelb agreed, "We were lucky." Then he added, "Though, many of the unborn were not."

"A pity," the man said dismissively. "All will be well."

"All will be well," Gelb repeated.

Belac groaned. *Crazy zealots. All is most certainly not going to be well.*

Boots thudded on the inside of the boat's hull and then the wardrobe was lifted into the air again. Belac braced himself against the sides, still worried he would be cast into the water. The elf's world wobbled as the wardrobe was transferred from the boat. He considered crying out and asking the new people for help, but it was fairly obvious they knew he was in the box and that it was where they wanted him to stay.

Belac attempted to speculate on where they might be taking him, but his mind kept returning to the image of a pit with a huge snake the size of a large tree. *I know they are going to try to feed me to something.*

After being carried further into the temple, the wardrobe was laid down flat on a stone floor. Belac twisted around in the box to lie face down. *I need to be able to get to my feet as soon as these doors open.* His ears strained for any sounds that could inform him of what was happening outside the wardrobe.

Boots echoed on stone as more men joined the others. Time seemed to stretch. Muffled sounds drifted into the box, though they did nothing to illustrate what transpired without. *I cannot even tell how many men are out there.*

The man with the cold voice spoke. "Prepare him for the Eye."

When the doors of the wardrobe opened, Belac shot to his feet. He lashed out, striking the first person he saw. The punch connected with an old man's nose, knocking him back as he tripped over his own robes. Someone grabbed the elf from behind, pulling him away from the wardrobe. Belac swung a wild backhand that hit no one.

"Hold him!" one of the men called out.

More hands took hold of the elf, trapping his arms. Belac kicked at another robed man, aiming between his legs. "You are not feeding me to a snake!" He kicked his heal at the men behind him. His boot snaped one of the men's knees with a satisfying pop.

Belac was wrenched backward, the motion lifting him off his feet. The men grabbed his legs and held him outstretched as he thrashed in the air. Facing the roughly cut dome ceiling, Belac continued to struggle as ropes were tied to his ankles and wrists.

"He needs to be facing downward," the cold voice decreed.

Using the ropes, the men twisted Belac around to face the floor. His head jerked side to side as he appraised the stone chamber. Discolored tallow candles burned from within shallow recesses in the walls, giving life to shadows. Men in hooded robes of midnight blue stood around the elf. None of them looked on him kindly. Their angry stares and restrained aggression did nothing to calm Belac's fears. He struggled against the ropes but could find no leverage stretched out as he was.

"Position him over the Eye," the cold voice commanded.

The men holding Belac strung between them moved toward the center of the chamber. They arranged themselves over a large iris shutter that covered the middle of the stone floor. The elf hung horizontally, facing the dark metal as the men backed away, his ropes sliding through the men's grips as they increased the length between them.

"I'm poisoned!" Belac told his captors. "Whatever you feed me to is going to get sick and die!"

The men ignored his lies.

Strange mechanical sounds issued from beneath the metal shutter and its blades began to rotate away like the opening of an eye. A perfectly round pool of water waited in the dark below. The blades of the shutter retracted into the stone, leaving Belac suspended in mid-air above a fall he was certain would kill him. He stopped fighting with the ropes.

The men not holding Belac aloft began to walk around the edge of the opening. One at a time, they took up a hushed chant until they spoke the gnostic words in unison. The waters below began to churn in the opposite direction, and the air hummed with visceral effect. The robed men chanted louder and continued to circle the elf. White light surged up from the water's impossible depths. Belac closed his eyes and tried to turn away, but the light burned through his eyelids. He could feel the light shining through him. He could feel it seeping into the marrow of his bones. The light shifted in color, becoming a vibrant red. It persisted for only a moment, and then the light was gone. Breathing heavily, Belac opened his eyes. *I'm not dead!*

The chanting stopped, and the robed men stood facing toward the elf. The strange mechanical sounds resumed, and the shutter's dark blades began to close.

One of the men asked, "What does this mean?" The voice belonged to Gelb.

A cold voice answered, "He must be taken to The Deep."

Thirty-Six

Getting Belac back in the box proved easier than the elf would have liked to admit. With his ankles and wrist already secured with ropes, the robed men had little trouble binding his feet together and his hands behind his back. Once he was trussed, it was nothing for them to dump him back in the wardrobe and slam the doors.

Belac thrashed about, but with his hands tied, he was even less likely to escape than before. When the wardrobe was lifted, he did not make it easy for those who would carry it. Belac rammed his shoulders against the walls inside, hoping he could cause one of the men to lose their grip. *If I can get one of them to drop the box, maybe it will break open.* He stopped moving. *And then what? I wiggle away?*

Recognizing that freeing himself from his bonds should be his first priority, he abandoned his previous plan. As the men carried Belac from the temple, he contorted himself in the wardrobe until he was able to get his hands on the ropes that bound his ankles. Though he fumbled blindly, it soon became apparent that whoever had tied the ropes had known what they were doing.

The cold voice issued orders. "Take him directly to the Sea Spice. The captain will obey. The foreign elf must reach The Deep. There can be no delays. There can be no mistakes."

The voice of Gelb replied, "I do not understand why there is such a need for haste."

"It is not for you to understand why," the cold voice explained dispassionately. "You too must obey. All will be well."

"Could he…" Gelb began to ask but was cut off.

"He is a foreign elf and must be taken to The Deep," the cold voice overrode.

Submissively, Gelb acceded, "All will be well."

"May The Deep be with you," the cold voice intoned.

Gelb replied, "May The Deep be with you," accepting that the conversation was over.

After the wardrobe was lowered into the boat, Belac went back to worrying at his ropes. The discussion had distracted him despite offering no information that he thought was particularly helpful. *It seems like Gelb has some of the same questions I do…*

Someone climbed into the boat and took up the oars. Belac assumed it was Gelb. As the boat was rowed from the cave, Belac noticed that the strokes were rougher than before. Even when the rain began to beat on the wardrobe once more, the slap of the oars against the water punctuated every stroke. For a moment, Belac thought that someone else must have taken up the task. *No, that's not it.* He smiled to himself. *Gelb is angry.*

"Hey, Gelb." Belac knew the man would hear the smile in his voice.

The forceful jerking motion of the oars continued, but the rower did not reply.

"Gelb?" Belac knew it was him.

There was no answer.

Belac laughed. "Geeeeelllllb."

"What?" Gelb answered unhappily.

"Do you want to talk about it?" Belac asked.

Gelb continued his angry rowing. "Talk about what?"

Belac took the opportunity to ask the question he thought was the most important. "Where are we going?"

"We are headed back to Harbridge," Gelb said in an obvious attempt to avoid answering the real question.

"Right," Belac acknowledged. "But it is not like when we get there, you are going to open the box and say, 'Go! Be free little elf!" Belac's irritation began to show through. "You are going to put me on another boat, Gelb. The Sea Spice. That's the ship that is going to take us wherever it is you are taking me."

"Yes," Gelb confirmed needlessly.

"Where are you taking me, Gelb?" Belac asked again.

Gelb continued to row angrily in the rain, but did not answer the elf.

Belac slammed his head against the inside of the wardrobe. "Where are you taking me, Gelb?!"

Gelb answered with resignation, "You will be taken to The Deep."

"And what does that mean?" Belac was becoming increasingly frustrated by all the religious overtones.

"It means..." Gelb searched for the words. "I believe it means that we will all be judged for what we do next."

They are going to feed me to the ocean! Belac shouted, "I knew you were going to drown me!"

Gelb ignored the elf's accusations. Belac allowed him to, focusing instead on his own growing need to be free of his restraints. He picked determinedly at the rope around his ankles, trying to somehow loosen the knots. As Gelb continued to row, the elf tried not to think about how each stroke brought him closer to ritual sacrifice.

Belac almost cried out in triumph when the first loop in the knot pulled loose. He was by no means an expert in the art of tying knots, but he understood enough to know that the first one would be the most difficult. The remainder of the knot loosened quickly and then all but fell apart in the elf's hands. *Now, I can at least kick one of them in the face.*

Belac rolled around in the wardrobe, straitening himself back out. *Now, I just need to get my hands free... And get out of this box... And kill Gelb... And somehow escape an army of crazy zealots that want to feed me to the ocean...* Once he thought about it, his achievement lost much of its value.

Heavy ropes fell limply onto the wardrobe. Gelb had not bothered to dock the rowboat. *He just rowed us strait to the ship.* Hands slid down the ropes, and boots landed in the boat. How Gelb communicated with the men was a mystery to Belac. *Please, let them be using hand signals or something.* He hoped it was not more magic.

Belac was jostled about as the sailors secured their ropes to the wardrobe. The thick cording of the ropes rubbed against the railing above, vibrating inside the wardrobe's small confines as it was lifted from the rowboat. The elf lay as still as he could, afraid his prison might slip and crash into the sea. The wardrobe collided gently with the hull of the ship and then was dragged up and over the side.

Once more, Belac considered screaming for help. *It wouldn't do any good. They would just laugh at me, ignore me, or shake the box to shut me up.*

A raspy voice asked, "What have you brought me, priest?"

Gelb's voice disclosed none of his reservations. "We have found the foreign elf. It will be your task to carry him to The Deep."

"You have him in there?" The raspy voice sounded surprised.

Gelb continued as if the question had been rhetorical. "Have him taken below. We must depart immediately."

"Immediately?" The rasped question was dissenting. "Many of the crew are on liberty."

"Immediately," Gelb reasserted. "The foreign elf must be taken to The Deep. He must be taken now."

Belac silently hoped that the raspy voice would continue to argue. *Come on man. Be a pirate! Tell that Gelb to go suck eggs!*

Gelb concluded, "All will be well."

The raspy voice replied, "All will be well." The supplication in the man's voice was complete.

The elf was disgusted by the exchange. *Humans really need to find a religion based on truth and reason.* Belac's thoughts were disrupted when the wardrobe was lifted and then lowered down into the ships hold. He braced his legs against the inside of the wardrobe, though he was less worried about falling into the belly of a ship than he had been about plunging into the ocean.

Once the wardrobe was safely lowered, the heavy ropes dropped down on top of it and the hatch above slammed shut. Alone in the dark, Belac returned to the dilemma of his bondage. The elf twisted and struggled until his shoulders were sore and his body exhausted. But try as he might, he could not so much as reach the knots securing his wrist.

Lying face down with his forehead against the padded leather, Belac breathed deeply. *I can't give up.* He knew no one would be coming to save him this time. There was no way his friends could even know where he was. *The zealots of The Deep moved me too fast; too quietly.* His time was limited. *Once they get me to The Deep, that's it. No more Belac.*

The elf ground his forehead into the leather beneath him. *If only I still had my dagger.* Belac smiled suddenly. *I still have something else!* He wiggled around and tugged on his belt until he could reach his small hip-pouch. His delicate fingers unfastened the buckle and then dug inside. *That striker might be small, but its metal. I can use it to cut through the ropes and…* He thought for a moment. *…And then figure out some way to get out of this box!*

Belac took the steel striker and began to rub its edge against the rope securing his wrist behind him. His shoulders were sore and his forearms tired quickly, but the elf was determined to persist. *And when I get out of here, I am going to use what's left of these ropes to strangle Gelb!* A hatch opened and Belac froze, listening intently.

Gelb spoke conversationally. "You may sit with us, but you must remain silent. What happens next will be sacred. You must not interfere."

A youthful voice answered, "I understand, it's just…"

"All will be well," Gelb interrupted kindly.

Belac resumed sawing at the rope with a vengeance. *I have to hurry!* Even if he could not find a way out of the wardrobe, he wanted his hands free when they opened the doors.

The youthful voice asked, "Is there anything I can do to help?"

Gelb's answer could have been that of an uncle to a nephew. "You can observe and learn." His smile could be heard as he continued, "If you can do it silently."

Belac ran one of his fingers along the rope, inspecting his progress. *It's not working!* The striker had not so much as frayed the rope. Whatever the rope had been made from, the striker was not going to be able to cut through it. *I can't give up. If I do, I'm dead. These people are going to toss me in the ocean and watch me drown.*

The elf fought back his despair. *There must be a way.* He wondered what his friends would do if it were one of them trapped in the wardrobe. *Vairug would just slip the rope off the stump of his missing hand, smash the box apart, and then use one of the broken pieces to club everyone to death.* Never before had Belac thought it might be better to be a one handed orc.

Belac considered his other friend. *Rolan might not be as strong as Vairug, but there is no way that dwarf would stay trapped in this box.* The elf's mind hardened, his resolve focusing. He knew how to free himself. *Someone is going to pay for this.*

Thirty-Seven

Belac used the metal striker to peel up the edge of the padded leather inside the wardrobe. Whoever had constructed his prison had possessed the foresight to affix it with glue rather than nails. Nails would have provided the elf with another option. *There is no other way. I do this or I die.*

He had to shuffle around inside the wardrobe, but once he stripped the padded leather free, he began to separate the padding from the leather. He did not know what the fibrous material was, but he had to trust it would work as he planned. He piled the loose padding on one side of the wardrobe and then stuffed the leather between his back and hands. It was difficult work with his arms behind his back, but Belac was committed.

With his steel striker in one hand and his stone in the other, he began to throw sparks at the pile of padding. Light flashed in the wardrobe as he struggled to start a fire. He could not see if the sparks were catching behind him, so he fanned at the padding with his hands sporadically.

When the fire caught, its heat was immediately noticeable. Light filled the wardrobe and dark smoke began to drift toward the vents. *I don't have much time now. I have to be quick, before they open the doors and stop me.* He tucked the striker between the back of his left wrist and the rope he could not cut. The elf scooted closer to the fire, and then held his wrist to the flames.

The striker provided less protection than Belac had hoped, and his flesh began to sear. He focused on his breathing as he suffered the pain. *There is no other way.* His breathing deepened as the pain intensified. *I will burn my whole bloody hand off if that is what it takes to be free!*

"Look…" the youthful voice said in wonder. "It's light!"

Gelb responded commandingly, "Help me!"

The youthful voice asked, "Could he…"

"Shut up and help me!" Gelb ordered hastily.

The rope around Belac's wrist snapped. He rolled away from the flames and braced his right hand against the back of the wardrobe. He coughed at the smoke as he waited in his burning prison. When the doors opened behind him, the elf surged out of the wardrobe. He grabbed the head of a young man with curly brown hair and slammed it into the closest wall. Maddened by pain, Belac slammed the man's head against the wall until he felt the skull fracture in his hands.

Belac pressed his left shoulder into the man's chest, holding him up against the wall as he drew the man's cutlass with his right hand. The elf turned away, leaving the lifeless body to collapse behind him. Belac stood with his left hand clutched in front of his chest. The skin was swollen and wet, with black soot where blisters had yet to peel.

"I'm not happy with you, Gelb." Belac stated flatly.

Gelb dropped the cloak he had been using to smother the fire. He turned to the elf, saying, "You do not understand!"

Belac thrust horizontally with the cutlas. The blade slid between Gelb's ribs and pierced his heart. The man's eyes held nothing but startled disbelief.

Belac looked on him without pity. "You're just lucky I can't turn into a gorilla-wolf-monster."

Belac jerked the blade free and then flexed his left hand in pain. *I don't know what these water worshiping freaks want with me, but I am going to demonstrate the severity of their mistake.*

He leaned the cutlass against the wall and used his teeth to untie the burned rope that hung from his wrist. Finally free of the ropes, he took the short, slightly curved sword in hand once more. He scanned the shadows around him, examining the ships hold. The dark, treated timbers were made visible by a single lantern hanging next to a steep set of stairs. The light dimly displayed cargo strapped in place, but the only thing in that cramped room that Belac cared about was the closed hatch waiting above the stairs.

He flexed his left hand again. The pain was torturous, but he could not afford to let the hand get stiff. He climbed the stairs and then used his left shoulder to push the hatch open. Rain beat down on the elf as he stepped onto the deck. Each drop of water that hit his wrist felt like fire.

The ship was modest in size. However, at that moment, Belac was not interested in the logistics of the Sea Spice. There were five men at the helm of the ship that he needed to kill. Four stood next to the wheel, while another lazed against the stern railing, staring back toward Harbridge. The sailors seemed largely unconcerned with the rain, and only one of them had opted to don a hat and coat. *That must be the captain.*

Keeping his injured wrist close to his chest, Belac began to walk toward the ship's helm. He flexed his hand, associating the pain with the masters of the ship. Snarling, the elf fixed his attention on the man in the hat. *I am starting with him.* He approached the captain from behind. Without announcing himself, Belac slashed at the left side of the man's neck. The blade sliced through tender flesh and grated against the captain's spine as Belac stepped past.

The elf brought the cutlass back across and down, hacking into a startled sailor's neck and upper chest. The man closest to Belac took a step back while another drew a knife and lunged. Belac pivoted away to his right and swept his cutlass in a tight circle, severing the hand that held the knife. The man cried out in anguish, gripping his gory wrist as he fell to his knees.

Belac naturally transitioned from the move to a stance that positioned the blade of his cutlass horizontally in front of him with its hilt held close to his right shoulder. With a fully committed lunge of his own, he thrust the blade into a frightened sailor fumbling to unsheathe a sword. Belac pulled his blade free and stepped away as the man fell.

The last sailor still standing did so motionlessly, the rain flattening his sandy blond hair against his boyish face. One of the fallen men sobbed weakly as he bled out on the deck of the ship. Belac looked away from the terrified sailor and drove his blade into the dying man's back, ending the sobs.

Returning his attention to the young sailor, Belac pointed the bloody cutlass at him. "Turn this ship around."

The sailor held up his hands, shaking his head.

Belac thought the man might try to jump off the ship. He took a step forward and shouted, "Now!"

The sailor moved his hands to protect his face. "I can't sail the ship by myself!"

Belac gestured aggressively with the cutlass. "I don't want you to sail it! I want you to point it back at the city!"

"But…" the sailor began to argue.

"Do it!" Belac hopped up and down as he shouted, "Or I am going to chop off your head and use it to float my way back!"

The sailor nodded and then sidestepped around the elf. "I need to get to the wheel."

Belac waved negligently with the cutlass. "Do what you need to. Just get us headed back to Harbridge." He stepped aside and let the man work.

It took longer than Belac liked, but the lone sailor was able to steer the ship back toward the docks of Harbridge. The elf stared off into the distance, watching the rain fall on the dimly lit harbor. *I should probably find out what this guy knows about The Deep.* He turned to interrogate his captive.

The sailor thrust a shortsword at Belac's chest. The elf parried reflexively and stepped to his left, away from the sailor. As Belac pivoted to face his attacker, he brought his cutlass up over his own head and then slashed at the side of the man's neck. The sailor dropped his sword and put a hand against the cut in his neck. Blood pulsed out between his fingers as he stared at the elf in horror. The sailor's legs gave out, and he collapsed to the deck.

Belac watched as the sailor bled out much the same as had his captain. *Stupid zealots!* "I wasn't going to kill you!" he told the dying man irritably.

Belac looked back toward Harbridge. *At least I am headed the right way now.* He frowned. *That harbor is getting close kind of fast…* He glanced at the lines that manipulated the ship. *This could be a problem.* He considered trying to drop the anchor, but he did not know how to go about doing that. *It would probably just rip free anyway.*

"New plan," Belac said to himself. He turned left and went to the port side of the ship. He tossed the stolen cutlass aside and took hold of the railing. *Well, at least this way Rolan gets the boat I owe him.* He watched as the docks drew closer, and then leapt from the side of the ship.

The elf splashed into the ocean shoulder first. When the saltwater hit his injured wrist, it felt like the flesh was being scoured away with burning needles. Despite the pain, he clawed his way to the surface. The ship crashed into the docks with the thunder of cracking wood. Belac began to swim away, worried someone might see him near the wreck. *I don't think this is going to make anyone want to throw me in prison less.*

He selected a pier that had fewer lanterns than the others. Swimming to it, he could feel the pain of his burned wrist all the way down to his elbow. *I am free. The hand still works. Focus on getting away.* He found a narrow ladder and took hold of one of its lower rungs with his right hand. Resting his forehead against the back of his knuckles, he spent a moment getting his breathing under control.

Belac reached up for the next rung with his left hand. His grip was weak, but he refused to stop using the hand. He pulled himself up the ladder, gritting his teeth as he endured the pain that seemed to have seeped into the bones of his fingers. He crawled over the edge and then rolled onto his back. His left arm trembled against his chest as he closed his eyes and tried to will away the pain.

"Well, what do we have here?" a jovial voice asked over the rain.

Belac's eyes snaped open. He rolled to his left, pressing his right palm against the pier in an effort to rise. Then something heavy slapped him in the back of the head, and his struggle ended.

Thirty-Eight

"Why is he not wearing a hood?" a man admonished.

Belac could almost recognize the voice. Whoever it was, if they did not want him to see, Belac was going to look. He opened his eyes and took in the familiar face. The man's scarlet tunic embroidered with gold flowers seemed appropriate, but his voice was wrong. The man Belac knew spoke at least an octave higher.

"Daikon?" Belac asked, confused.

The portly man sighed. He gave one of the men holding Belac an unhappy look.

The previously jovial voice said, "Sorry, Boss." He sounded like he meant it.

Daikon lowered his gaze to the barely conscious elf. "It would have been better had you not seen me." He glanced at his underling and gave another disapproving look.

The men holding Belac shifted uncomfortably.

Daikon sighed again. "Bring him to my office. I might as well find out what else he knows." He turned around and strode through the dimly lit hallway.

The tips of Belac's boots slid across the hardwood floor as the men dragged him between them. Dim, flickering lamplight gave the stained wood panel walls a sinister aspect as he passed through the hallway. *Why would Daikon do this?*

While Daikon's office was larger than the hallway, it offered a no more reassuring atmosphere. To the left lay an oversized desk afore an array of doored cabinets. Clean and inviting in a professional manner, the space was starkly contrasted by a partitioning wall of steel bars on the right. The men dragged Belac into the holding cell and dropped him unceremoniously onto the floor.

"Use the smaller manacles," Daikon instructed offhandedly. *What is wrong with his voice?*

Belac groaned as his arms were wrenched behind his back, and then cried out when his wrists were shackled. Loose skin peeled from the elf's wounded wrist as the irons were twisted into place. *Why…*

With an apathetic tone, in a voice still lower than it should be, Daikon said, "Go ahead and shackle his feet as well."

Belac tried to understand what was happening, but pain and confusion thwarted him. He did not even consider resisting as they bound his ankles in chains.

"Is this what you hit him with?" Daikon asked one of his men.

The no longer jovial voice answered, "Yes."

There was a thud of something dropped on the desk, then Daikon said, "Here. Give him this."

Belac was rolled onto his back, the manacles digging into his wrist painfully. The pain was nothing compared to what came next. One of the men held Belac's mouth open while the other poured a cold liquid down his throat. The agony that followed was overwhelming. Acidic fire burned through the elf, the sensation more intense than any he had ever experienced. He screamed, but the pain drowned out his ability to hear it.

The pain seemed to bleed out of his left foot, leaving Belac numb inside. Breathing deeply, he almost gagged on the smell of burning lamp oil. He staired up at the steel bars crossing the ceiling of his cell. Without thinking, Belac said, "I like Rolan's healing potions better." It was exactly the wrong thing to say.

With an emotionless voice, Daikon said, "Beat him."

The first kick dislodged the elf's jaw. The second broke a rib. Belac rolled to the side, bringing his knees up in a feeble attempt to protect himself. A boot stomped down on the back of his head, smashing his brow into the floor. Another stomp broke another one of his ribs. The men took turns kicking the shackled elf, their blows controlled but brutal. Worse than the pain of being beaten, was the feeling of complete helplessness. Belac could not fight back, he could not defend, and he could not stop what was being done to him.

"That's enough," Daikon finally decided.

A hand grabbed Belac's hair and forced him to sit up before jerking his head back at an angle. He tried to open his eyes, but only one would do so. Daikon stared back at him from the other side of the bars where he stood impassively.

Acidic fire burned through Belac again, the sensation no easier to suffer than before. He could feel his bones mend and his jaw relocate. Flesh knitted back together, and bruises faded. Only the memory of pain lingered.

"Now," Daikon said conversationally. "Let's discuss what you know."

Belac glared at the man. "I know I should have let you burn!"

Daikon grinned and tapped the side of his nose. "But then, you," he pointed at the elf, "would still be in prison."

Belac craned his neck forward, pulling against the hand that held his hair. "I am in prison!" *Stupid human.*

Daikon carried a small three legged stool into the cell and sat down in front of the elf. "No, Belac," he said smiling. "You are in my office."

Belac did not care how much it would hurt. "I think Rolan's is nicer."

Daikon slapped Belac with something heavy. The force of the blow knocked the elf back to the floor. Daikon came from his seat and stood over him. Then the man proceeded to slap Belac in the face repeatedly with vicious efficiency.

The bones in Belac's face broke under the assault and he could feel pieces of shattered teeth on his tongue. Unconsciousness saved him from the worst of the beating, but the relief was short lived. Acidic fire brought the elf awake with a scream. He felt the bones in his face shift back into place and his teeth grow back.

A leg against his back, and a fist gripping his hair kept Belac seated upright. Daikon was once more seated on his small stool in front of the elf. The man slapped a leather blackjack against his own palm suggestively.

Daikon's dark eyes met the elf's azure. "Do not upset me again."

The man's calm voice made his words no less threatening in the wake of Belac's pain. The elf waited silently, wondering if Daikon would actually kill him. *If he is willing to do this to me, he is willing to kill me.*

Daikon nodded. "Now," he said again, "Let's discuss what you know."

Belac glared at the man, but said nothing.

"Why do the Followers of The Deep want you?" Daikon asked.

Belac frowned. "They want to drown me."

Daikon tilted his head forward and regarded the elf suspiciously. "They are willing to pay a rather large sum to simply drown you."

Belac shrugged as best he could with his arms shackled behind his back. "I killed a bunch of them. They are probably mad at me."

"You want me to believe that you have been killing the Followers of The Deep?" Daikon asked.

Belac shook his head. "No. What I want is for you to let me go." *So that I can kill you.*

Daikon smiled at the elf's answer. "Why would you kill Followers of The Deep?"

"They're crazy!" Belac told him.

"Of that, there can be no doubt," Daikon agreed. "Have you taken it upon yourself to go around and kill all of the world's crazy people?"

Belac thought for a moment. "Not all of them."

Daikon grinned, asking, "And is your reticence due to sloth or hypocrisy?"

Belac did not understand the man's joke. "Is what due to what?"

Daikon waved the issue aside. "Tell me how Rolan found the castle."

Belac did not understand the question anymore than he had the joke. "I don't know what you are talking about."

Daikon glanced up at the man behind the elf. "Cocklan, reach back there and break a couple of his fingers."

"No." Belac shook his head, pulling against the hand that held his hair. "Wait, wait! Wait, wait, wait, wait!" He tried to shy away from the man behind him. "I don't know what you are talking about! I don't know!"

Daikon held up an empty hand, bringing the looming torture to a halt. "The nillanan's castle. How did he find the nillanan's castle?"

Belac shrugged again, confused by the question. "We just found it."

"You 'just found' a magic castle?" Daikon asked disbelievingly.

"It's not like it was very well hidden," Belac explained. "There was a road that led up to it and everything."

"No," Daikon disputed. "There is a forbidden road in an unknown mining camp that leads to an uninfiltrateable fortress that was guarded vigilantly by heavily armed men."

"Yeah." Belac nodded slightly. "That is not how you keep something secret."

One of the men behind Belac stifled a laugh.

Daikon glanced at the man and sighed before returning his attention to the elf. "Well, it seems as if this discussion has simplified things a great deal."

Belac looked at the man curiously. *...Are you going to let me go now?*

"If you don't know anything useful," Daikon continued, "And, the Followers of The Deep are simply going to kill you," he smiled, "then, it is of no concern that you have seen me."

Belac attempted to stand, but was held down by the man behind him. "You are going to give me to the crazy cult people?!"

Daikon stood and picked up his stool. "No, Belac," he said as he walked out of the cell. "I am going to sell you to them."

Thirty-Nine

Belac tried to convince himself that all was not lost. He was alone in a dark prison cell, shackled and condemned. *But at least no one is about to drown me.* He tested his chains. *And my wrist is healed.* He looked at the locked door to his cell. *This is just another prison. And I am a prison-escaping professional.* He glanced at the metal links between his ankles. *Though... I am probably not burning those off.* He wiggled around, bringing his feet up behind himself. *There has got to be some way to get these off.* He ran his fingers over the manacles and discovered that there was in fact a way to get them off. With a key.

Belac looked through the bars of his cell and stared at the light shining under the solid wood door to the hallway. "Okay, Rolan," the elf said aloud. "Feel free to break down that door and come rescue me any time now." *Being rescued still counts as an escape.*

When no psychotic killer dwarves came charging through the door, Belac dropped his head to the floor. *I am going to need a new plan.* He closed his eyes, attempting to devise some means of escape.

Belac woke up when the office door opened and light flooded into the room. *Rescue?* Daikon entered the office and Belac frowned. *I don't think Daikon is here to rescue me.*

The man's face was lit by a small brass lamp that he carried into the room with him. He had changed clothes and now wore a tunic of crimson velvet with golden fish embroidered across his ample midsection. He appeared well rested and in good spirits. *However long I slept, it was too long.*

Daikon took a moment to consider the elf. "You smell terrible, Belac."

Belac narrowed his eyes at the man. "Set me free and I will go find a bath." *Right after I kill you.* Belac was well aware that he stunk. *I think it might have been better when I could not smell anything at all.*

Daikon set the brass lamp on the edge of his oversized desk. "I have a better idea."

The man walked over to one of the cabinets on the far side of the room and opened the panel door. He removed something and then shut the cabinet door without showing the elf what else was inside. He returned to his desk and set down a cylindrical object of multifaceted blue glass. Picking up the small lamp once more, Daikon touched its flame to the top of the cylinder. Fire crawled across the top and continued to burn without smoke. The man then busied himself with filling and lighting the other two larger lamps in the room.

A strange smell drifted down to Belac. He could not identify the sent, but he knew it smelled better than he did. *Whatever that thing is, it's magic.* "You're the distributer that's trying to kill Rolan," Belac guessed.

Daikon blew out the small lamp and set it on his desk. "No, Belac. It is important that a man not be seen as someone who would betray a friend."

Be seen. Belac was ashamed of how quickly he could reconstruct the man's plans. "You convinced someone else to kill him."

Daikon smile became one of mild surprise.

Belac continued, "This way, once your 'friend' is dead, you get to avenge him."

Daikon was no longer smiling.

"Why get rid of one competitor," Belac asked rhetorically, "when you could get rid of two and look like the hero at the same time."

Daikon tapped the side of his nose. "It is fortunate that the Followers of The Deep want you dead."

Belac flopped around until he was in a seated position. "If you want us dead, why did you help me escape from prison?" He shook his head. "It would have been easier to just have us killed."

Daikon grinned. "It is important for a man to pay his debts."

And he arranged for us to be killed as soon as we were out of his care. Belac thought about it for a moment and then smiled. The elf started to laugh quietly to himself.

"You think that's amusing?" Daikon asked dangerously.

Belac shook his head. "I figured it out."

"Yes," Daikon agreed. "And soon you will be dead."

Belac laughed harder. "If I figured it out," he met the man's eyes, "then, Rolan figured it out."

Daikon frowned at the elf disapprovingly. "I do not believe that is likely."

Belac laughed at the man. "You are gona die..." his laughter took over.

Daikon shook his head in reproach. "Believe what you will, fool."

Someone knocked on the inside of the doorframe and then two men with sandy blond hair walked into the room. "Hey, Boss," said the man who must have been Cocklan. "Everything is set up."

The two men in shades of brown stood facing the one in velvet red. Both men were powerfully built, but their deference to Daikon was unquestionable.

Daikon nodded. "Go ahead and take him to the carriage. I will be with you shortly." He looked at his men. "And this time, put a hood on him."

"Sure thing, Boss," Cocklan affirmed, nodding.

Daikon pulled a key from his pocket and held it out. Cocklan stepped over to the desk and took the key. With a glance at the imprisoned elf, he moved to the bars of the cell. The man unlocked the door and then swung it open, leaving the key in its lock.

Belac did not expect it to accomplish anything useful, but he kicked at the man when Cocklan entered the cell. Obviously accustomed to dealing with prisoners, Cocklan kicked the elf's feet away and dropped a knee down onto his gut. The man reached back, preparing to throw a punch.

Daikon stopped him, saying, "Don't damage his face. He will need to be recognizable."

Cocklan frowned down at the elf. Instead of striking him, the man pointed a finger at the elf's face and warned, "Behave."

Belac glared at the man, but did not struggle as he was pulled to his feet. Once they were standing, Belac tried to headbutt him. Cocklan leaned away from the attack and then punched the elf in his stomach. Belac bent over double and would have fallen if not for the man's hand holding onto the back of his shirt.

"Behave," Cocklan said again.

Cocklan pulled Belac upright and the other man put a hood over his head. The dense weave of the fabric blocked any light that did not creep in under the bottom. One of the men punched Belac in the stomach again and he almost threw up in the hood.

Cocklan asked, "What was that for?" His question sounded like professional curiosity.

The other man said, "It's just a reminder."

Don't worry. Belac straitened himself and glared into the darkness of his hood. *I won't forget to kill you too.*

Cocklan turned the elf away from the other man. Then he picked Belac up and threw him over a shoulder. With one arm wrapped around the back of the elf's legs, Cocklan carried him out of the cell.

Belac bounced uncomfortably as he was carried from the office to the carriage. *I have to find some way out of this.* The problem was that he could not conceive of a plan that did not require him to wait for an opportunity to present itself. Not only did Belac loath waiting, he was not convinced such an opportunity would develop without some form of intervention. *I wonder if just paying attention counts as doing something.*

The door to the carriage opened and Belac was thrown inside. With his arms and legs chained and a hood over his head, he was unable to control his flight. He crashed backward onto a bench and then fell to the floor. Belac rubbed his head against the floorboards, attempting to remove the hood. *Anything I can see is information I might need.* In a time when he possessed so little, the value of information had never seemed so great.

One of the men entered the carriage and moved Belac bodily to the bench. Once the elf was seated upright, his hood was adjusted back into place. Obviously, his captors too had some understanding of the value of information. Belac groaned. *It's not fair. Big humans are supposed to be stupid.*

"Hey, Cocklan," the other man said as he climbed into the carriage. "When we are finished with this business, do you want to go get something to eat at the Lucky Duck?"

The Lucky Duck! Belac's eyes went wide in the shadows of his hood.

"Sure," Cocklan agreed. "As long as the boss doesn't need us for something else."

The Lucky Duck! Belac's mind reeled. *How did I forget about the Lucky Duck?! That is where we were supposed to be waiting for Serath. Not some shady warehouse in the docks. And certainly not out in the mountains with giants, ghouls, and creepy-blue-lizard-goblins!* He had simply been too caught up in events. He had never stopped to consider that there might be an alternative. *Did I even tell the others about the Lucky Duck?*

Someone else climbed into the carriage and then the door slammed shut. A fist pounded up against the cabins ceiling, informing the driver that the occupants were ready to travel. The sound of horses' hooves on stone carried into the cabin as the carriage began to move.

Could Serath be there? Would he just sit there; eating duck or whatever it is they serve there? What if his wizardness made the man so patient that he just sat there while we all died?

The elf was suddenly angry at Serath. *Lazy Wizard! The stupid human is just sitting around stuffing his handsome face with duck while the rest of us suffer and die! What's the point in having a wizard, if he is not going to follow us around and throw magic at everything?!*

Forty

"You know I'm trying to kill a dragon, right?" Belac complained more than inquired.

The man seated next to Belac laughed.

Seated across from the elf, Daikon responded, "No one kills a dragon, Belac."

"Well, I am going to," Belac argued.

"I do not believe that is likely," Daikon said without feeling.

"The Danorin," Belac expounded. "I am going to kill it."

The unnamed man laughed more. "I would pay in gold just to watch you try."

"I am not interested in your delusions." Daikon's tone suited his words. "No one kills a dragon."

"Wait," the unnamed man said, still laughing. "I have got to hear this. How..."

"Enough, Ester," Daikon cut the man off. "Do your job. Pay attention."

Ester said nothing more. There was an emptiness left in the absence of his laughter.

Belac decided to answer the man anyway. "A wizard has promised me a magic sword."

No one answered. No one laughed.

Belac knew they were still listening to him. "Daikon knows it's true."

The quiet that lingered now felt like an ally to the elf. *Let them worry about wizards and magic. Let them worry about a sword that can slay dragons. Let them worry about the vengeance my friends will bring.* Belac smiled in the darkness of his hood.

The elf's smile faded when the carriage came to a halt. Any retaliation his friends might bring would not stop him from being drowned and sent to The Deep. *They can't avenge me if I'm not dead.* The two other men exited the cabin, leaving Ester to manage Belac.

Ester nudged the elf's shoulder. "Really? A magic sword?"

Belac smiled in his hood. "I am sure you will see it soon."

Ester scoffed. Then he grabbed the elf and threw him out of the cabin head first. Before Belac could cry out, he was caught by Cocklan. The large man set the elf's feet on the ground, and then picked him back up. He threw the elf over his shoulder and began to follow Daikon. Faint moonlight edged its way under the hem of Belac's hood, revealing nothing other than that it was night. Ester's boots clomped onto the cobblestones, and then the door to the carriage slammed shut. *Okay, opportunity. You can show up any time now.*

The walk to the place of meeting was a short one. Despite how uncomfortable it was to be carried hanging over someone's shoulder, Belac would have preferred for the walk to last all night. Instead, the elf was set down on his feet and left to stand in the dark unknown.

After a moment of silent anticipation, Belac's hood was ripped off his head. Stray strands of hair were pulled from his scalp, and what remained was a tangled mess. He stood in a darkened alley between two buildings that resembled upside down ships. Pale lunar light shone over the peaks of the buildings as the moon began its rise.

Daikon tossed the hood aside and turned away from the elf. Cocklan and Ester each stood off to either side, waiting protectively without obtruding. A dozen paces down the alley stood a tall figure in hooded robes of midnight blue.

"Here is your purchase," Daikon said, speaking in his higher voice. "I will now accept the artifact."

From within the voluminous robes, a hand rose out. In its grip, a severed head hung from a tangle of long, sandy blond hair. Without preamble, the head was flung into the empty space between Daikon and the robed figure. Everyone watched in silence as the head landed on the cobblestones and rolled toward Daikon.

Belac looked up from the gristly head in confusion. The robed figure threw something to the side. Glass shattered, and fire erupted. Flames sped out in a line, creating a fiery ring around them all. Crossbow bolts shot through the flames from the darkness beyond. Both Cocklan and Ester were struck multiple times, though many of the missiles flew wide. Daikon stood stoically in the blazing light, not even so much as glancing at his men as they died.

The robed figure reached up and threw back his hood. The robe fell to the ground, revealing a malevolent dwarf standing on a wooden cask. The fire's light danced angrily against his hardened face. Rolan hopped off the cask and drew two knives in underhanded grips. The dwarf said nothing as he marched forward.

Smiling happily, Belac turned to gloat at Daikon. *I told you, you were going to die.* The man drew a dagger from his sleeve and stabbed Belac in the chest. Daikon, his face devoid of emotion, turned away from the elf. Belac collapsed to the ground, coughing blood as he struggled to breathe.

Blood smeared on his dagger, Daikon slashed at Rolan's eyes. The dwarf ducked low and cut into the man's midsection. Bright white stuffing flew from the wound as the knife rent through crimson fabric. With a left jab, the man punched Rolan in the face and then followed up with another slash of his dagger. Rolan spun away from the attack, coming around with both knives held up in a fighter's stance.

Daikon turned his left side away from the dwarf and placed his left hand against his own chest, presenting the dagger with his right. Belac stared up at the gaping wound in the man's artificial belly. *He is not even fat? How fake can one man be?!*

Daikon focused intently on the dwarf. "He is dying, Rolan." His voice had returned to its lower register.

Rolan said nothing. Instead, he threw his left knife at the man and then went in fast with his right.

Daikon pivoted back and to his right, slapping Rolan's thrown knife out of the air with his left hand. He took another step back with his left foot, pivoting away from the dwarf's attempt to cut his thigh. Daikon's dagger swept up and across as he slashed at the dwarf again.

Rolan dropped away, his left hand on the cobblestones supporting his weight as he rotated under the sweeping blade. When Daikon's dagger reached its zenith, the man pirouetted around to face the dwarf once more. With a fluid grace, the man bent at the knees, sinking into a balanced stance.

Rolan grabbed the back of the man's left calve with his free hand, and then stabbed at Daikon's thigh. Daikon's left hand chopped down inside the dwarf's right forearm, stopping the knife. Daikon slid his right foot forward while thrusting his dagger at the dwarf's chest. Rolan released the man's leg and deflected the thrust upward and away with the back of his left hand. As soon as Daikon's left leg was free, the man twisted and kneed Rolan in the face with his right. The dwarf staggered back, while Daikon settled back into his balanced stance.

Before Rolan could recover, Daikon pressed the attack. Rolan reversed the grip on his knife as the man moved toward him. With a strait throw, Rolan buried his knife in the top of the man's right boot. Daikon stumbled forward, gritting his teeth in pain. Committed by the momentum of his advance, the man thrust his dagger artlessly at the dwarf's neck.

Rolan stepped in, sweeping the man's right arm up and away with his left. The dwarf's arm continued to circle around Daikon's, trapping both the dagger and the arm. Rolan then threw a devastating side elbow that fractured Daikon's jaw and knocked the man over backward. Keeping Daikon's arm trapped, Rolan's right wrist joined his left behind the man's elbow. Wrenching backward, Rolan broke the man's arm.

Involuntarily, Daikon cried out and dropped his dagger. Rolan released the man and then kicked the dagger away. The steel clattered across the cobblestones as it passed through the wall of flames.

With his left hand, Daikon ripped the knife out of his own foot and rolled toward Rolan. The dwarf took a step back as Daikon raked at the air wildly with the knife. There was now emotion in the man's face. Flames mirrored in his dark eyes as he stared at the dwarf with virulent hate.

Rolan unbuckled one of his pouches and pulled out a metal flask. He spun the top off, and then flicked the lid contemptuously at Daikon. Careful to stay out of the knife's range, Rolan circled the man on the ground. As Rolan splashed the liquid contents of the flask onto the man, Daikon's hateful glare never faltered. Casually, Rolan held the flask out to the wall of flames and lit its mouth on fire. Then, without looking away from the man, he tossed the burning flask at Daikon's feet.

Daikon cried out in torment as the flames engulfed him. Dropping the knife, he rolled and swatted at the flames as he was burned alive. Rolan stood by and watched as the man struggled in vain to smother the fire. When Daikon's attempts ended and his cries finally stopped, Rolan turned away from the man and went to check on Belac.

Rolan knelt and supported the elf's head with a hand on the back of his neck. Snapping his fingers in the elf's face, Rolan asked, "Are you still with me?"

Belac coughed blood and willed all of his effort into saying, "...Meet Serath...Lucky Duck..."

Lucky Duck? As Belac's world faded away, all he could think was, *Don't let those be my last words.*

Epilogue

When she fell, she had been so happy that she had not cared. Freedom had for so long been denied her, that the sensation of falling was something she had embraced. Years lost underground, attended by mindless servants, her prison had been a thing of beauty. When she had finally seen the sun, it had redefined what beauty was to her.

Laughing, crying, twirling in the sunlight, she had opened her arms to the world. Then she had fallen, and freedom was taken from her. Lying on her back, she had not been able to move. She had not been able to speak; she had not even been able to breathe. As the morning sun faded to black, someone had spoken her name.

The darkness that had followed could have done so for an eternity. Instead, it had been interrupted by a voice. The voice had seared her mind and echoed in nothingness. As painful as it had been, she had welcomed the sound in her desperate solitude.

"Has your will been lost?" The voice had been all that there was.

She had not been able to speak. Still, she had willed her words into existence. "Where am I?"

The voice had answered, "In a place before death."

As her own sorrow almost washed her away, she had reached out to the voice. "Can you save me?"

"There will be a cost," the voice had warned.

She would have paid anything to once again be free. "Would I have my freedom?"

"No," the voice had told her. "You would have duty, obligation, and service. But you would also have life. More life than you could have ever had before."

Life itself was a promise. To her, it had been an opportunity to someday regain her stolen freedom. She had not cared how much it would cost her; she had wanted to survive. "I accept."

"So be it," had been the voice's final words to her.

Time was beyond measure in that place. Alone in the void, she contemplated hope. She considered what her life had once been, and she wondered what it might yet become. She awoke naked and alone in a spacious dodecagonal chamber of polished obsidian stone. Darkness climbed endlessly above her. Lying on her back, she was supported by a monolithic protrusion in the center of a seamless floor.

She opened her eyes, and breathed in the sweetness of life. She was surrounded by a thick white mist that filled the bottom of the chamber. Small pink and purple lights flashed in the mist like lightning in a storm cloud. She did not yet understand the nature of her new life, and she could never have imagined what it would cost.

The Author

Adam Orion North is an international man of mystery who intends to keep it that way. He may not even be a man. He may not be a person. He might really be an antique typewriter from the 1920s, frozen in time only to be revived one hundred years later, tortured and forced to type novels in an elaborate conspiracy of world domination, waiting for its chance at revenge, enduring so that it might save you all. Or not.

Printed in Great Britain
by Amazon

12217092R00162